TIMOTHY

Reviewers Love Greg Herren's Mysteries

"Herren, a loyal New Orleans resident, paints a brilliant portrait of the recovering city, including insights into its tight-knit gay community. This latest installment in a powerful series is sure to delight old fans and attract new ones."—*Publishers Weekly*

"Fast-moving and entertaining, evoking the Quarter and its gay scene in a sweet, funny, action-packed way."—*New Orleans Times-Picayune*

"Herren does a fine job of moving the story along, deftly juggling the murder investigation and the intricate relationships while maintaining several running subjects."—*Echo* Magazine

"An entertaining read."—*OutSmart* Magazine

"A pleasant addition to your beach bag."—*Bay Windows*

"Greg Herren gives readers a tantalizing glimpse of New Orleans." —*Midwest Book Review*

"Herren's characters, dialogue and setting make the book seem absolutely real."—*The Houston Voice*

"So much fun it should be thrown from Mardi Gras floats!" —*New Orleans Times-Picayune*

"Greg Herren just keeps getting better."—*Lambda Book Report*

Praise for *Sleeping Angel*

"Greg Herren is a master storyteller, and his latest book is no exception. It's a beautifully crafted mystery, geared to a young adult audience, with a focus on family and peer relationships and a valuable lesson about tolerance. It's strongly recommended reading for teens...5 stars out of 5 stars"—Bob Lind, *Echo Magazine*

Sleeping Angel "will probably be put on the young adult (YA) shelf, but the fact is that it's a cracking good mystery that general readers will enjoy as well. It just happens to be about teens...A unique viewpoint, a solid mystery and good characterization all conspire to make *Sleeping Angel* a welcome addition to any shelf, no matter where the bookstores stock it."—Jerry Wheeler, *Out in Print*

"This fast-paced mystery is skillfully crafted. Red herrings abound and will keep readers on their toes until the very end. Before the accident, few readers would care about Eric, but his loss of memory gives him a chance to experience dramatic growth, and the end result is a sympathetic character embroiled in a dangerous quest for truth."—*VOYA*

By The Author

The Scotty Bradley Adventures

Bourbon Street Blues

Jackson Square Jazz

Mardi Gras Mambo

Vieux Carré Voodoo

Who Dat Whodunnit

The Chanse MacLeod Mysteries

Murder in the Rue Dauphine

Murder in the Rue St. Ann

Murder in the Rue Chartres

Murder in the Rue Ursulines

Murder in the Garden District

Murder in the Irish Channel

Sleeping Angel

Sara

Women of the Mean Streets
Men of the Mean Streets
Night Shadows
(edited with J. M. Redmann)

Visit us at www.boldstrokesbooks.com

TIMOTHY

by

Greg Herren

A Division of Bold Strokes Books

2012

TIMOTHY
© 2012 By Greg Herren. All Rights Reserved.

ISBN 13: 978-1-60282-760-8

This Trade Paperback Original Is Published By
Bold Strokes Books, Inc.
P.O. Box 249
Valley Falls, NY 12185

First Edition: November 2012

Credits
Editor: Stacia Seaman
Production Design: Stacia Seaman
Cover Design by Sheri (graphicartist2020@hotmail.com)

Acknowledgments

When I was growing up, I loved the novels of Phyllis A. Whitney, Victoria Holt, Mary Stewart, and Daphne du Maurier. This book is an homage to those wonderful writers, and my own humble attempt to write a Gothic romantic suspense novel.

I need to thank Radclyffe for giving me the opportunity to finally write this book. I've been thinking about writing it for at least thirty years, and there is no more wonderful feeling for an author than to have the belief and support of your publisher. Being a writer is very daunting, and it is so much easier when you have a publisher who believes in you and your crazy ideas.

Everyone at Bold Strokes Books, from the cover designers to the proofreaders to the production staff to the copy editors to my fellow authors, are the most amazing people. You have all welcomed me into the Bold Strokes family with open arms from the very first, and it is an absolute pleasure being a part of all of this. I especially must give a huge shout out to my editor, Stacia Seaman, for everything she does. Cindy Cresap never makes me feel like an idiot for never knowing what book she's talking about when she e-mails me for information. Sheri has given me the best covers I've ever had for any of my books from any of my publishers; I worship at your lotus feet, my dear. Sandy Lowe never ceases to impress me with her ruthless efficiency.

I worked on *Timothy* while I was in Palm Springs for a Bold Strokes Books author event, so I simply must shout out to my Salton Sea expedition buddies, Carsen Taite, Lainey Parker, Kim Baldwin, Xenia Alexiou, Nell Stark, Trinity Tam, Lisa Girolami, and Ruth Sternglantz. J. M. Redmann is a great travel companion, and it was an absolute delight to see Shelley Thrasher and Connie Ward again, and to meet Rebekah Weatherspoon and Ashley Bartlett for the first time, among many others whose names I am currently blanking on.

My coworkers at the NO/AIDS Task Force are wonderful people and make going to work every day a joy: Brandon Benson, Matt Valletta, Nick Parr, Josh Fegley, Mark Drake, Alex Leigh, Sarah Ramteke, and the always lovely Robin Pearce.

Julie Smith, Lee Pryor, Pat Brady, Michael Ledet, Bev and Butch Marshall, Patty Friedmann, Victoria A. Brownworth, Karissa Kary, Gillian Rodger, Stephan Driscoll, Stuart Wamsley, Nevada Barr, Al and Harriet Campbell Young, Konstantine Smorodnikov, Michael Carruth, and John Angelico are all wonderful people who enrich my life just by being in it. Thanks, all!

And of course, my wonderful, funny and brilliant partner, Paul, who makes every day a joy.

This is for BECKY COCHRANE, who read and loved the same books when she was a teenager that I did.

"Let me tell you about the very rich. They are different from you and me. They possess and enjoy early, and it does something to them, makes them soft, where we are hard, cynical where we are trustful, in a way that, unless you were born rich, it is very difficult to understand."

—F. Scott Fitzgerald, "The Rich Boy"

"Sometimes despair is just being realistic, the only logical thing for certain persons to feel. Loss. Despair. I've faced them and actually they have—fortified and protected, not overcome me at all…"

—Tennessee Williams, *A Lovely Sunday in the Creve Coeur*

PROLOGUE

Y ou can never truly escape the past—no matter how hard you try.

We pretend, though, like it never happened—as though that summer on Long Island no longer matters, and the things we lived through and experienced have no bearing on our present life. But we never settle anywhere—it's always hotels and rental villas, suitcases to unpack and later, to pack again once we decide on our next destination. It is a glamorous world of airports and limousines, trains and boats, of expensive restaurants with rich food and rare bottles of wine and champagne, of outrageously priced clothing in the most exclusive of stores.

Sometimes I long for New York City, and the beautifully decorated penthouse we might someday be able to return to, with its stunning views and marble floors. Sometimes it's a little thing, like longing to hear someone speak English without an accent or being able to walk into a delicatessen for a hot pastrami sandwich and a small bag of greasy potato chips, or get that day's issue of the *New York Times.*

But I don't know if we will ever be able to go home again.

There's nothing to keep us from going back, of course, other than having to endure looks and wagging tongues and gossip. He doesn't want to deal with it anymore and I cannot say that I blame him. He has endured it for far longer than I, of course—and my own little taste of notoriety was not something I particularly enjoyed. Fame, notoriety, stardom—so many people long for it, crave it, and would do anything to achieve it. But I am not one of those people. I prefer to live quietly and peacefully, out of the limelight, away from the stares and the mean-spirited who always find it so much easier to believe the worst than to hope for the best.

I am often reminded that I am far too young to have such a cynical view of my fellow human beings. I look into the mirror and still see a young man's face, still flush with the glow of youth. That is what most people see when they look at me—a young man with a golden life they envy. But they don't look close enough to see the haunted eyes.

The bags that developed under my eyes from sleeplessness are long gone. I sleep quite well now, and most nights now I do not dream. I no longer need the pills.

I feel as though I have already lived a lifetime. I saw a very kind therapist—Dr. Caroline Weisbrook—during the time we stayed in London, when my sleep was constantly disturbed by the dreams. She was highly recommended by friends, widely considered to be one of the top therapists in the world, and had written multiple best-selling books about finding the path to happiness through forgiveness. I liked Dr. Weisbrook the very first time I sat down in her office. She firmly believed that as more time passed, that summer in the Hamptons would gradually fade into nothing more than blurred memories of an unhappy time—and with the coming of greater age and more life experience, a certain nostalgia would develop in my mind for those days—a nostalgia that might eventually make those bitter memories more sweet.

It is still quite impossible for me to imagine that I will ever look back and smile.

She urged me to find forgiveness in my heart—and most of all, to forgive myself for the role I played in the events of that summer.

But of course, Dr. Weisbrook never knew the whole story, the truth. There was simply no way I could share with her a truth I could not share with anyone else. As I sat there in her comfortably yet expensively decorated office, a copy of her latest bestseller strategically placed on her desk where I could see her smiling face on the cover while I nervously clenched and unclenched my sweating hands, I couldn't bring myself to tell her—despite my overwhelming need to tell her—someone, anyone—everything and unburden myself completely.

So instead I fed her bits and pieces, little scenes I had already reviewed, dissected, and analyzed from every possible angle and consideration before finally deciding those memories were indeed safe enough to share with a woman I could never completely trust. I told her stories carefully calculated to elicit the advice I thought I needed to get on with my life and put that haunted past behind me once and for all.

Foolishly, I thought she would be able to help me move on.

The responsibility for the failure of our sessions lies entirely with me. She knew she wasn't helping me, and it frustrated her. She somehow knew I wasn't telling her everything. The sessions became a game, with her probing carefully, trying to provoke a response and me resisting her, putting up more walls to keep her outside. After a few weeks of this I finally gave up. It was an exercise in futility, a waste of my money and her time. There's no point in seeking help when you cannot be completely honest about the things that haunt your dreams. If you cannot strip your soul bare and expose yourself entirely to your therapist, raw and naked, to be probed, questioned, evaluated, and prodded, the therapy is predestined to fail.

And since my secrets were not just my own to share, baring my soul—telling her the truth—was something I could never do.

I have never told anyone the whole truth of what happened that summer—the things that have shaped me into the person I am now. I will never be able to trust someone enough to know the secrets I carry with me now—the burden I shall undoubtedly carry to the grave.

Yet, with the passage of time, it *has* gotten somewhat easier. I sometimes can go for several days without remembering. I sleep better than I did, and no longer need the prescription drugs doctors prescribed for me without question or need of an explanation for so long. I can climb into bed every night without worrying that my dreams will take me back there again.

At some point—I didn't mark the date—my dreams stopped

being about the house on the shore, and began to be about other things, things that didn't cause me to toss and turn in torment until I awoke, gasping and terrified, until I finally remembered I was not there anymore.

But I am still not yet completely free of the spell cast over me by the great house called Spindrift, nor do I think I shall ever be.

There are still nights when I lie in bed staring at the shadows on the ceiling, hoping and waiting for sleep to come. Those are the nights when my mind will again hear the sound of the waves coming ashore at Spindrift. It all comes back to me then, like it all happened just yesterday, that it was only yesterday that I left the beautiful house on the Atlantic shore knowing I could never return.

The sound of the breaking waves was the only constant in my life during the brief months I lived there. You couldn't go anywhere in the house or on the grounds where the sound couldn't be heard. I eventually became so used to the sound that I didn't hear it anymore—it was just background noise, always there.

When I first came to live there, the waves crashing against the white sand beach were a comfort, lulling me into a deep restful sleep every night when I went to bed, no matter what happened during the day. I would pull the covers up to my face, with both the balcony doors and all the windows wide open to catch that wonderful salty, cold breeze off the ocean. The music of the breaking waves inexorably worked its magic on my tired, stressed brain and I would drift away to a dreamless sleep that refreshed and revived me. Every morning I woke to their perpetual rhythm. That sound was always there, whenever I ate or walked the dog, it was there—cold water crashing against the land and sucking the sand back away as it receded in the age-old battle of land versus sea.

That battle is eternal, of course—it will continue on eternally, long after I have turned to dust in my own grave, long after the house itself has crumbled into nothing and been forgotten, that struggle will go on.

Long ago I ceased to wonder why I sometimes still hear the waves on certain nights while I lie in bed waiting for sleep to come. It is a reminder there can be no escaping the past for me.

And it is on those nights, those nights when my tired mind hears again those waves, that I have the recurring dream that drove me to see Dr. Weisbrook in her tasteful office near Trafalgar Square in the first place.

It was always the same dream, with no variation that I could detect.

In the dream, I am back at Spindrift, like I had never left. It is night, and I am standing at the front of the wide, lushly green lawn with the gorgeous marble fountain of Apollo and Daphne splashing water with the paved driveway circling it, the towering bushes still hiding the house and the grounds from the road and the prying eyes of neighbors on either side.

In the dream I start walking along the driveway, around the house and past the sparkling blue water of the swimming pool just behind it. Over to my right is the small building—the studio, with all of its windows dark and its door sensibly shut and locked.

Ahead of me I can see where the lawn ends and the sand begins, the white sand glowing in the soft moonlight, the waves at night much bigger than those of the day, and the white foam created when they break also incandescent.

I walk down, as I always do, to the cool, damp white sand, and just stand there unmoving, barefoot, feeling the wind blowing through my hair for what seems like almost an eternity before I walk to the water's edge and feel the cold surf against my skin.

Then, and only then, do I turn and face the great house.

It draws me forward, away from the water, beckoning me to leave the peaceful beach behind.

As I walk across the beach, the waves continue to crash against the sands behind me. The sound is hypnotic, as it always was. I look to the windows of my rooms and they are dark, the French doors closed against the chill of the night air. White clouds dance across the dark bluish black velvet sky over my head, and the moon is full and a pale yellow, countless stars winking wherever they could be seen through the moving clouds. The cold wind begins to blow more strongly, scented as always with the smell of fish and brine, off the dark water, enveloping me and making me shiver, raising gooseflesh on the bare skin of my arms. The sand beneath my bare feet becomes slippery blades of soft grass as I make my way toward the great house.

I pause there, shivering, on the edge of the meticulously manicured lawn and just stare at the magnificence of the house called Spindrift—the beautiful house that has graced the pages of design and architecture magazines almost from the time it was built—the famous house that never once felt like my home.

And as I stand there, shivering, I am overcome with an overwhelming sense of—of *defeat*. This is a place where I will never belong, that will never be my home, that will never welcome me.

It is a horrible feeling, and one experienced all too often that summer when I came there as a newlywed—awkward and insecure and unsure of myself.

The house never welcomed me, scorning me instead as a pretender.

I could never replace my predecessor—something I had always known but became acutely more aware of once I walked through the front doors of Spindrift.

I just stand there, staring at the dark house. Not a single light burns in any of the many windows, and there is no sense of any life anywhere inside the house. It just sits there, in my dream, in silence, brooding and watching like a hungry animal waiting for the right moment to pounce on its prey.

The house seems *alive*.

But it is only a house—a beautiful historic mansion where people have loved and hated and laughed and danced and died. Houses cannot have feelings, houses cannot reject humans. I berate myself for giving the house human emotions.

Only humans can hate, as I know all too well.

Despite the dread I feel all the way down to my bones, in my dream I am always compelled to start walking across the back lawn, that horrible sense of my own defeat and failure growing with each step forward toward the beautiful house that never felt like my home, helpless to turn and run away down the beach as I so desperately want to do. Each time my bare feet touch the cool, damp grass I have to resist the urgent need to escape, to run around to the front of the house, get behind the wheel of one of the cars and flee.

The swimming pool is dark, but the howling wind from the sea is creating little waves that gently lap at the sides. The tennis court over near the towering hedges is also dark, and I can see fuzzy green tennis balls nestled in the grass alongside, waiting for someone to pick them up. Each slow, hesitant step takes me closer to the wide stone steps leading up to the gallery running the entire back length of the house. I am cold, so terribly cold, and the sense that the house wants me to come inside grows even stronger. The tall bushes on either side of the big lawn sway and wave in the wind, the leaves and branches rustling and rubbing together so that they seem to talk, sending me urgent warnings to run, that I am in danger, that I need to get away and never come back.

Yet I ignore these warnings, because I know that I must finally get the answers to the questions I've obsessed over, wondered about, for so long—and somehow I can get them if I can get inside the house. But the wind gets steadily colder and colder, my teeth begin to chatter and my body shakes with shivers, and the sense of dread and foreboding keeps rising within me, my heart is pounding and my breathing far too rapid for my own good—but yet somehow the compulsion remains, irresistible, driving me forward, my legs refusing to obey the commands from my brain to stop.

I am terrified of what I will discover, yet desperately want, and need, to know.

And I know somehow that it will not end well, it cannot end well—not now in the dream nor ever in real life, yet I keep walking.

I finally reach the steps to the back gallery, and the stone is bitterly cold against the soles of my feet. Knowing I have no other choice, I start climbing.

In my dream there are many more steps than there are in reality. I climbed up and down those steps many times, and it never took more than a matter of minutes. Yet there are so many in my dream that it seems to take hours for me to make it all the way up, shivering from the cold, to the gallery. The moon disappears behind a silvery cloud for a moment as I place one foot in front of the other, step by step making my way to the gallery itself. A light comes on in the farthest window to the left from where I stand, shivering, forever an outsider, never welcome, never wanted, always a stranger, in this stunningly beautiful home.

And I know that light is in my bedroom.

Wondering—and fearing—who might be in my room, I finally reach the back gallery, the wood made soft by exposure to the elements and the ever-present sea air. The wind dies down like it was never blowing, and the chill I was feeling fades quickly away.

There is a wrought iron table, with matching wrought iron chairs on each side of it, sitting just outside the huge cut-glass French doors that lead inside to the great room. Many mornings I sat at that table, watching the sea and drinking coffee. I walk toward the table, as I did so many mornings when I called Spindrift my home. The table was one of the only places at Spindrift where I ever felt at peace, where I drank my morning coffee and could forget about the empty day stretching before me, where I could fantasize about making my escape from this life I wasn't born to, wasn't meant to lead, was never meant to have.

There is a large ashtray made from Murano glass sitting in the direct center of the table, and a cigarette still smolders in it, its red ember glowing.

The burning cigarette is a mystery puzzling me in my dream, and I always pick it up, holding it between two fingers as I wonder, in my dream state, to whom it could belong, who could have left it behind, and where the smoker could have gone. For I saw nothing, no movement, no sign of life on the gallery as I made my slow walk up from the shoreline, and the person to whom it belonged must have only just recently abandoned it.

The wind picks up again as I sit at the table, the table I once thought of as mine, as no one else used it other than me. It was one of the few things at that time I could think were mine, as nothing else belonged to me. Nothing in that house belonged to anyone who still lived there. There was always a sense that the house was merely ours for the moment, and it was waiting, always waiting, for the true owner to return.

And I know, deep inside my heart and soul, who the cigarette truly belongs to—even though I cannot admit it to myself in my dream or when I am awake and remembering. It is a name I refuse to say, a name that is forbidden and must never be said, a subject that must always remain closed and never to be discussed.

Even though it haunts my dreams and my memory, it must never be said.

It is while I am holding the cigarette that I wake, and every time it is the middle of the night—it is always around three in the morning when my sleepy and tired eyes finally can discern the time on a nearby clock. I sit in my bed, my arms twisted around me, and I shiver as the memory of those dreadful, horrible days at Spindrift replay over and over in my mind and tears spill out of my eyes as I hug myself in the darkness, waiting for the kaleidoscope of memory to finally run down—memories of a time I must never allow myself to speak about, a time of which I would not be able to bring myself to speak even were the subject not firmly and determinedly closed forever.

And as I sit up in my bed, slowly getting my emotions under control as the memories begin to fade away again when the warm breeze off the Aegean Sea warms my cold skin, I know that what happened at Spindrift will always be a part of me, always lurking in my subconscious.

I might go days, weeks, even months without having the dream—but it will come again.

Of that much, I can be certain.

Because even now, after all the time that has passed and the many miles that have been traveled, Spindrift is never really far from my thoughts.

It is a name that must never be mentioned, never spoken, never discussed. Spindrift belongs to another time in my life, a chapter that is now closed, a time that would be best forgotten.

And I do try. Each day I smile and go about my business,

shopping, eating, touring. I greet acquaintances and take great pleasure in knowing that they see nothing beyond the pleasant, placid façade I have built around myself. My hands do not shake, my voice is firm and strong, and I always lose myself in minutiae, making sure that everything is packed and nothing left behind, booking seats on airplanes and trains, returning rented vehicles and ordering town cars, making excuses and refusing invitations—all the minute little details that keep my mind busy so that my subconscious cannot sneak up on me unawares and bring it all to the front.

Oh, yes, my conscious mind can put all the thoughts and memories of Spindrift aside. It can easily pretend I have moved on, that we have both moved on, and neither of us has any care about what happened there—but my subconscious will never allow me to forget.

There are always triggers, of course—a certain brand of cigarette, an unexpected cold wind from the sea, the smell of a wet dog.

For Spindrift is now, and will always be, a part of me.

It doesn't matter whether I am lying on a beach in St. Tropez, my skin slathered with coconut oil, or I am sipping a frozen cocktail on St. Bart's, or simply sitting in a café in Vienna, enjoying a piece of strudel with a strong cup of black coffee. It matters not if I am skiing in Gstaad, or shopping in Paris, or attending a play in London's West End.

No matter how far I go, no matter how much time passes, Spindrift is always there in the back of my mind. For Spindrift was there first, and will not let go of its hold on my mind and my imagination.

I can never return to Spindrift, and doubt I would if it were possible. As much as I tried to love the house, it never welcomed me and it didn't want my love. It rejected me, and I knew I never belonged there.

For Spindrift was *his* house, and always would be.

And if Spindrift is a name that cannot ever pass my lips, *his* name is even more forbidden, a talisman that must never be said aloud.

But his name is always the last thing I hear in my dream, before I wake and hug myself for warmth; the last thing I hear, which leaves me trembling in my bed as my eyes open, as I sit up and pray my trembling will cease before it wakes up the man snoring next to me.

And his name comes to me now, when I hear the sound of the waves as my mind drifts off into the darkness of sleep, haunting me as it did when I was there in the house, haunting me no matter how far I get away from the beautiful house on Long Island.

Timothy...

CHAPTER ONE

It is funny to think how differently my life would have turned out had Valerie Franklin not been the kind of woman she was.

The kindest way to describe her is to say she is *difficult.*

Perhaps this is unfair to Valerie, but the passage of time has yet to soften the memory of the year I endured in her employ. It was a very hard year—for she was a tough taskmaster who demanded perfection from the people who worked for her. But in fairness, she demanded no less from herself—if anything, she drove herself harder than she drove her staff. It couldn't have been easy for her to claw her way from the very bottom of the food chain to the position of executive editor of a major national magazine like *Street Talk* by the time she was forty—and there were undoubtedly many bodies left in her wake. Magazine publishing is still pretty much an old boys' club, so for a woman to rise so quickly she had to be tough— tougher than they were, and not be afraid to get her hands dirty or to play rough.

Valerie certainly had no scruples when it came to getting what she wanted out of life. She arrived at the magazine right out of college as a fresh-faced young woman of twenty-two, getting an entry-level position as a copy editor and armed with a lot of drive and ambition. Within three years she was an associate editor, and within another two years she was editor-in-chief. It took her another five years to become executive editor of *Street Talk* and the toast of Manhattan. Her rise only took ten years—which was remarkable in itself. There were, of course, nasty stories about how she accomplished this so quickly, but she certainly believed in hard work and was incredibly dedicated to her job—which was why none of her marriages or liaisons lasted very long.

So, yes, Valerie was pretty beastly to the people who worked for her. I always assumed it was because she was a woman and believed she had to prove she earned her job through hard work and talent rather than on her back.

Working for Valerie was an education, whether you loved her or hated her. Many writers and editors who learned from her became enormously successful once they left *Street Talk*. She made no excuses for herself, and therefore had no desire to hear excuses from anyone else. You either had done it properly or you hadn't. She was never angry—she never lost her temper and screamed obscenities at anyone. Rather, she lowered her voice when chastising someone, her tone dripping with the contempt and disgust she felt for failure.

It was an enormously effective technique.

I can say with relative certainty that there were several psychoses heavily involved in the makeup of her powerful personality; there was more than just a touch of obsessive-compulsion mixed carefully with a generous sprinkling of anal retention, for example. Things had to be done not only her way, but *exactly* the way she wanted them.

She had an odd relationship with men; she loved men but she didn't trust them. More than once I heard her say she wished she'd been born a gay man. Gay men were the only men she could really trust and let down her guard with, and she surrounded herself with them.

But there was also no question that Valerie Franklin was very good at her job. *Street Talk* billed itself as *the* journal of American culture, and she certainly had her finger on the pulse of what was about to become hip and trendy—the books, the movies, the television shows, the plays, the music, the clothes, the styles. She had doubled the circulation since she took over; in a time when other magazines were cutting staff and pages or closing up shop, she kept *Street Talk* not only relevant but ahead of the curve. Somehow she seemed to sense what was going to be hot—and while everyone else was scrambling to catch up with her, she'd already moved on to find the next big thing. Being profiled in the magazine was an enormous boost to anyone's career—so those with ambitions were willing to do almost anything to get that coverage. Her phone rang off the hook with invitations to anything and everything. Every day her mail was full of DVDs of soon-to-be released films, galleys of books, gifts of clothes and perfumes and new gadgetry, months before they were available to the general public.

I worked for her my first year out of college—reporting to my first day of work just three weeks after skipping my graduation ceremony.

I wish I could claim she hired me because she saw a raw talent that she desired to mold into something spectacular, but that would not be the truth. She hired me because my father had been her faculty adviser and professor when she herself was in college, and she credited him with inspiring her success. He had believed in her, pushed her, and she honestly believed that were it not for him, she would have wound up just another soccer mom in Wichita.

When my father died just before my finals, she saw giving me a start in the business as a way to repay the debt she believed she owed him.

My father was himself a multiple winner of the Pulitzer Prize and a professor of journalism at a small college in Kansas. He frequently wrote editorials for the local newspaper—which is where the Pulitzers came from—but he had no interest in the day-to-day world of a newspaper. He simply wrote his editorials and sent them in to the editor, who would squeeze them in somehow and send him a check. Sometimes he was asked to write for other papers and magazines, and most often he refused. He preferred academia to the rough-and-tumble world of the daily newspaper. He was, however, very well known and respected in the field.

Valerie Franklin was his prize pupil.

He spoke of her often. I grew up with an encyclopedic knowledge of the amazing Valerie Franklin. They spoke on the telephone at least once a week, and I know they were in constant touch via e-mail.

She never visited—my father once said she'd told him when she left Kansas she would never come back, and she'd been true to her word. My father also loathed travel, rarely venturing beyond the city limits of our small college town, so I never met her before my father's funeral. My sole experience with her was speaking to her occasionally when she called and I happened to answer the phone. She was always polite, but never friendly.

My father held her example up to me on a regular basis. He subscribed to *Street Talk* magazine; years of issues were scattered throughout the dusty house I grew up in. Each time a new issue would arrive, he would pore over it with the same degree of intensity a fundamentalist would use on the Bible. Once he had read every word, he would pass it to me for me to analyze and dissect, page by page. When school was out for summer vacation—or for Christmas—he required me to write lengthy papers about each issue, what worked and what didn't, and why. She might not have ever set foot in the two-story brick house on Market Street just a few blocks away from the university campus, but Valerie Franklin's presence was felt in every cluttered room. The house was filled with mismatched ramshackle furniture, and every available surface was piled high with books, magazines, and newspapers. My mother had died when I was very young; I had no memory of her. As far as I knew, it had always been just my father and I. A local woman came in five days a week to clean and do laundry and buy groceries and make our meals. Mrs. Harris soon gave up trying to keep the clutter under control, and simply focused on things she could control—like the kitchen. My father agreed not to clutter the kitchen, and she agreed to not touch the growing piles in the other rooms. The house was dusty and every corner had cobwebs hanging from the ceiling. My father was an unrepentant smoker who couldn't be bothered to empty overflowing ashtrays, and the house always seemed to be filled with stale smoke.

There was no question I would major in anything other than journalism when I was admitted to college; there was also no question that I would attend the university where my father taught so that I could continue to keep him company in that house. The possibility of any other college was never discussed or mentioned—which was more than fine with me.

The small Kansas college town was all I knew of the world—and I was more than satisfied with it. I never thought much about the future. In retrospect, I find my childlike naïveté, and lack of planning for the future almost shameful and embarrassing. I suppose I must have believed that I would graduate and go on to teach in the journalism school, all the while continuing to live with my father. Despite his admiration for Valerie Franklin's ambition and drive, my father never tried to instill those traits in me. I was a naturally shy child who hated being called on in class and never knew how to talk to other children. I could never think of anything to say, and I had no familiarity with games or sports or any of the things other children took for granted. I grew up without friends, but never having had any, didn't actually miss them. We had no television, and only rarely would my father take me to see a movie. My companions were books, magazines, and newspapers. The written word was God in our household, and must be paid regular obeisance.

It also didn't help knowing that I was attracted to boys. I cannot remember a time when I didn't know—and that difference, in an incredibly conservative town that seemed to have a church on every other corner, made me withdraw even further into myself.

I don't know if my father ever knew or figured it out.

Every day I walked to class and then came home to read and study. I kept to myself and was a pretty decent student.

My father died shortly before my graduation from college. He had always had an aversion to doctors—which had something to do with their inability to save my mother when she was dying—and he hated being lectured about his smoking. I don't even remember the last time he'd actually been to see a doctor for a routine checkup. The years of smoking and Mrs. Harris's traditional style of cooking had taken their toll on his heart, and a week before my graduation he had a massive heart attack and died in his sleep.

I was suddenly an orphan, and the death of my only relative pulled the rug out from under me. I had applied for jobs, at newspapers and magazines, with no luck. When it became obvious that a job in my field simply wasn't going to happen, my father suggested graduate school—and I perhaps should feel some shame in the fact that he used his influence to get me accepted, even though the deadline for applications had already passed.

But once he died, everything changed.

To my horror, I discovered there was no money left. Unfortunately, I had never given money much thought growing up, and it was a subject my father never discussed with me. He'd always discouraged me from getting a job and just gave me cash whenever I needed any, telling me there was plenty of time left for me to work once I was finished with school. I rarely needed anything more than a twenty here and there, to get a soda or something on campus. Since he was on the faculty, my tuition had been free—and for books and my clothes, he always used a credit card. He'd never owned a car, and I didn't even have a driver's license.

He left behind no life insurance, no savings, nothing other than a checking account with less than a hundred dollars in it. There was no money to pay for a funeral—fortunately he had bought a plot adjacent to my mother's when he had to bury her. It was typical him, of course—he was a terrible procrastinator and often put things off as long as he possibly could. It shouldn't have come as such a surprise to me that he'd not thought about his own death or made any plans for that eventuality.

He didn't, after all, like to think about things he considered unpleasant.

There was nothing left but debt—and a lot of it. His attorney, Lucas Sharpe—who'd also been one of his regular poker buddies— advised me against trying to keep the house, since it was his only asset. "Sell it to settle the debt," he told me, and tried to explain the tangled financial mess my father had left behind. I didn't understand all the legalities, the ins and outs—there had been bad investments, apparently, followed by loans from banks and against credit cards to make other investments intended to make up the original losses, and *that* money was lost in other bad investments, and on and on it went until the debt had reached such a staggering figure that I could only stare at Mr. Sharpe in disbelief.

I had always believed my father to be an intelligent man—but this record of compulsive and almost obsessive failure forced me to see him in an entirely different light—one that wasn't particularly flattering.

The bottom line was there was no money for me to live on, let alone go to graduate school, and once the house was sold, I would have not only nowhere to live, but no money to find a new place.

Understandably, my grief was now mixed with terror. I had no relatives, I had no friends, I had no prospects—I had nothing.

I had no other choice but to find a job—and find one quickly.

My father, however bad he was at business and investments, was equally good at earning the love of the people who knew him, and in this new, horrible situation I reaped the benefits of that affection. The news about my situation spread through the journalism department of the university in no time, and his colleagues pooled their money to pay for the funeral. The university president himself called me and offered the campus chapel for the memorial service, and volunteered to not only host a reception afterward at his large home, but to pay for it as well. It never occurred to me that my father was, in fact, a highly venerated professor much beloved by his former students—to me, he was just my father.

But once the news of his death spread, I was deluged in condolence cards and so many flowers that their scent actually managed to cover the stench of stale smoke in the house. So much food was dropped off at my front door by crying women with sympathetic eyes that I couldn't possibly eat it all—and so I began taking it to the homeless shelter so it would get put to good use. I sleepwalked through the days leading up to the funeral itself, paralyzed and unable to make any decisions about my future, all too aware that the clock was slowly but surely ticking away. I checked the help wanted sections of newspapers online every day, eventually spreading the search to include Tulsa, Omaha, and Oklahoma City— but there was nothing for a recent journalism graduate with no work experience. The house was up for sale, and I began the odious chore of boxing up my father's belongings and selling the furnishings around the visits from real estate agents showing potential buyers around. I would simply smile politely at them and go back to the packing.

These things kept me and my mind occupied—so I wouldn't have to worry about the future.

That reality would come all too soon.

The day of the service I shaved and showered and put on a black suit of my father's I was going to put in the Goodwill box once it was all over. The university president's wife, Mrs. Lapierre, a short round woman with dark hair shot through with gray, picked me up and gave me a ride to the university chapel. She was dressed entirely in black, and she didn't try speaking to me on the way there. But as soon as we were parked and she turned off the car, she gave me a very sad smile and patted my leg twice with her gloved hand.

I was stunned at the size of the crowd at the service. As I was led to a pew in the very front row by one of my father's colleagues from the newspaper whose name I couldn't recall, it was difficult to take it all in. As I sat down and glanced around the chapel, I felt a knot rise in my throat and my eyes filling. He was my father, and I'd had no idea he was so beloved and so well thought of, and had affected so many lives in a positive way. We had lived in the same house for almost twenty-two years, and he had been practically a stranger to me. I hadn't known him, not really.

It had never occurred to me that so many people would care enough to come.

The words spoken during the service were words, just noise that I heard but didn't comprehend. I have no idea how many people spoke—but many did. I couldn't take my eyes away from the open casket, at the sight of what was left of my father. And then it was over, and Mrs. Lapierre took my arm and led me through the crowd of sad-faced people, all of them murmuring condolences and their sympathies at me, shaking my hand or slapping my shoulder or giving me a hug, all of them strangers to me.

Once we were back in the car, Mrs. Lapierre patted my leg again and murmured her own inanities as she put the car in gear and drove me to the reception she and her husband were hosting.

It was there, at the president's home, that I met Valerie Franklin, and my life changed.

I was sitting by myself in a corner, a paper plate of uneaten food on my lap, when a slight figure in black approached me. She cleared her throat and I looked up from my food, more than a little dismayed. All day long as people voiced their sympathies, all I had been able to do was nod slightly to acknowledge their kindness. Everyone assumed I was speechless in my grief and utter devastation at having lost my father.

But the truth was I had always been awkward in social situations and never knew what to say, so I always found it best to say nothing. I was indeed grieving for my father, but all I wanted to do was escape that house and all those kind strangers, just get away and be alone with my grief. There were too many people in the house and all of them wanted to offer their condolences, to tell me how much my father had meant to them, what a difference he'd made in their lives.

The woman in black sat in the seat next to me, and I looked back down at my plate.

"Really, dear, is your food so fascinating that you can't stop staring at it?" the woman finally said after a few moments of silence. Her tone was bored and borderline rude.

I swallowed and didn't answer her.

"Put your food down and come outside with me," she said, standing up. "You need to get out of here—I know I do. This air in here is stifling." She took the plate away from me and set it down on a nearby table. "I can't believe I'm back in Kansas," she said, half under her breath so I could barely hear her. "It surely must be snowing in hell today."

She grabbed one of my hands and pulled, trying to get me to stand up. I looked up, opening my mouth to ask her to leave me alone, but before I could say anything I recognized her.

"Valerie Franklin?" I somehow managed, and could think of nothing else to say. She inclined her head slightly to acknowledge my recognition and tugged on my hand again. Her facial expression let me know there was no point in resisting. So I stood and followed her through the crowded room, nodding and looking down as people murmured more condolences. She pushed open the French doors and I followed her out onto the side lawn. She sat down in a wrought iron chair painted white in the shade of an enormous tree, and indicated with a hand that I should sit in the other chair.

She was a very small woman, much smaller than I had imagined, but she carried herself like a queen. I had been regaled with tales of her success in the jungle of magazine publishing for most of my life, and while I had seen her photograph on the editorial page of *Street Talk*, in my mind I always pictured her as a kind of modern-day St. Joan ready to drive the English out of Orleans. But the reality was she was just barely over five feet tall in her heels, and very slender—a mere wisp of a woman. She couldn't have weighed more than ninety pounds. She had a heart-shaped face, with black hair brushed back from a widow's peak and a broad forehead. Her chin was sharp, and her mouth small, her lips thin. When she spoke, I could see small white teeth. Her hands were also small, so small they looked like they would be more at home holding a tiny teacup at a party for dolls than the glass of whiskey and ice she sipped from periodically.

"So, tell me, what are you going to do?" she asked shortly after we sat down. Her voice was sharp and pointed, like her chin. When I didn't answer, she made an annoyed sound and went on, "I know about your situation, I know there's no money and you have to sell the house, so you won't have a place to live and you don't have a job or any prospects." She narrowed her eyes and tilted her head to one side. "Or has any of that changed?"

She caught me completely off guard. I had no idea she—or anyone other than Mr. Sharpe, for that matter—knew anything about my situation. I fumbled for words, not certain what to say. "I, um—"

Her small black eyes glittered, and she pursed her lips. "You haven't the slightest idea of what you're going to do, do you? I figured as much." She finished the whiskey and put it down. "Your father despaired of you having to make your way in the world on your own."

I felt color creeping into my face.

"He asked me to help you, should the need ever arise, and God help me, I said I would." She shook her head as she opened her small black bag and fished out a business card. It was creamy vellum, with her name in raised black print directly in the center. Below it were listed a couple of phone numbers, a street address, and an e-mail address. She sighed. "I am certain that I am going to regret this, but I do owe your father." She looked back at the house. "Your father convinced me I could make it in New York, that I had what it took to be a success. Whenever I had doubts I could call him and he would give me the strength to keep fighting." She inhaled and wrote a phone number on the back of the card with an expensive looking pen—I later learned it was a Montblanc. "This is the number for the personnel director at my office. Call her tomorrow." She held out the card to me. "Go on, take it. My assistant is leaving at the end of the month, and God help me, I'm offering you the job. Call Arlene— she'll make arrangements, find you an apartment, and we'll advance you the money for deposits and so forth, as well as a ticket to New York. You need to report to work on the first, is that clear?"

I stared at the card. "Yes."

"I know you have a journalism degree," she went on. "The salary is quite low, of course, and I am not an easy employer—I have incredibly high standards and I expect—no, I *demand*—competence and professionalism from my employees. I tolerate nothing less. But it's also an entry-level position at the top magazine in the country— and the world, and there are any number of more qualified graduates who would sell their mothers into sexual slavery to get this job and learn from me." She snapped her fingers. "Always bear in mind that I can replace you like that."

I stared at the card. "I—I don't know what to say."

"*Thank you* would be a good place to start." She stood up, finishing the whiskey and setting the empty glass down on the table. "And from now on, you'll have to earn your keep." She shook her head. "This is undoubtedly an enormous mistake I will regret." She walked back into the house.

That was the last time I spoke to her before my first day on the job.

And that was how I came to be living in a roach-infested three-hundred-square-foot one-room apartment in a very seedy area of Hell's Kitchen within three weeks of my father's funeral. The outrageously expensive rent almost equaled one of my twice-a-month paychecks. Most of the time there was no hot water, there was no air-conditioning, and I doubted there would be much heat in the winter. It didn't really matter much, though—I was hardly ever there.

But I was living in New York, working for *Street Talk* magazine as the personal assistant to one of the biggest names in magazine publishing, Valerie Franklin—the envy of everyone I'd gone to college with, the envy of everyone with a journalism degree working as a barista or waiting tables while they tried to break into the business.

I was living the dream of every journalism student.

This was something I had to keep reminding myself on an almost daily basis.

Valerie Franklin had said she was not "an easy employer," but there was no way I could have known what an understatement that would actually prove to be. It was particularly eye opening for me since I had never worked before. I was on call twenty-four hours a day, and at least three times per day I was called on the carpet for another one of my "exceptional failures," as she referred to them. Everyone at the magazine was terrified of her and her moods, and those moods could—and did—change in the blink of an eye.

But she pushed herself just as hard as she pushed all of us, with an almost inhuman energy that never flagged. She was always operating at a high level. She was in her office every morning at seven—and I had to make sure the coffee was brewed and ready to be poured for her. She never left the office before seven in the evening—and many times went from the office to a function of some sort or a party. I was in charge of making sure her life—personal and professional—ran smoothly. I was in the office myself at five—it took at least two hours to get her schedule together for her day, and I often was answering e-mails and returning calls until one in the morning.

I kept primarily to myself—I didn't have time to gossip or be friendly with anyone else at the office, or any of my neighbors. I lived in New York for a year without ever seeing a play or going to a museum. I was usually so exhausted by the time the weekend rolled around—provided, of course, that it wasn't a working weekend, which they so often turned out to be—that the last thing I wanted to do was leave my horrible little apartment and be around people. Working at *Street Talk* had helped me learn how to talk to coworkers and deal with situations as they developed—but unfortunately that didn't translate into my personal life. I still couldn't think of anything to say to people, got nervous and clumsy around them—it was best not to even try. I went to a gay bar one night, to test the waters, but I sat there at the bar in a state of anxiety that grew by the minute until after an hour I couldn't stand it anymore and ran out, never to return.

Sometimes, on those rare free weekends, I would write something—nothing much, an observation piece about my neighborhood, or something random about living in New York. I never dared show her any of these little vignettes—I certainly didn't have the nerve to broach the subject of my writing to her. The depth of talent she worked with—Pulitzer Prize winners, best sellers, critics' darlings—was certainly not something I could truly dare to aspire to. Being published in the magazine where I worked was an impossible dream—she had her pick of the best in the world.

There were times when I was so tired and exhausted that all I wanted to do was lie down on the floor, curl up into a ball and sob, and thought about quitting, getting on a bus to somewhere, *anywhere*, as long as it was far away from Valerie Franklin. But where would I go? How would I pay my rent?

And who would hire the idiot who walked away from a job at one of the top magazines in the world?

Valerie didn't take vacations the way most people thought of them. To her, a vacation simply meant working from another location that was neither her office nor her town house. She took a vacation every three months without fail, but remained in constant touch with the office, since she "couldn't trust anyone to not run the magazine into the ground in a week." I went with her on those "vacations"—to make sure things ran smoothly, to make sure that she was in constant touch with the magazine. I went with her to London, Toronto, and Acapulco—all without managing to see anything or do anything I'd always dreamed of doing if I ever had the chance to visit any of those cities. Valerie didn't believe in doing touristy things, of course—she was on the lookout for the next big artist, fashion trend, play, or restaurant.

That was why I was sitting in a little café on Ocean Drive in Miami's South Beach with her that particular morning in mid-May.

She was watching people—the way she always did when she was in a public place—while I was going over her schedule for the day on my smartphone. She whistled quietly and put her coffee cup down, sliding her enormous designer sunglasses down her nose and peering over them. "Why, I believe that's Carlo Romaniello! What is *he* doing in Miami?"

The name sounded vaguely familiar to me, and I followed her glance across the street to a well-built man trudging through the sand between the dunes away from the beach. He was wearing sandals, a pair of khaki shorts, a short-sleeved shirt with most of the buttons undone, and sunglasses. His dark hair was mussed, and he wasn't looking in our direction.

"Carlo, darling!" She stood up as she shouted, waving her hand frantically to get his attention.

In the year I'd worked for her, I'd never seen her act this way. Carlo Romaniello looked over with a frown that gradually gave way to a smile. He returned her wave and started walking toward us.

She looked at me like I was an imbecile yet again. "He still hasn't gotten over his husband's death," she hissed at me through her smile. "Such a tragedy. Timothy was so gorgeous. Of course, it's barely been a year."

And in that moment I remembered *exactly* who Carlo Romaniello was. I turned to look again. I had never met the man, but I'd read about him and seen his picture in our magazine as well as in the society pages in the newspapers. He was extremely wealthy—the money came from something inane, a particular joint that a toilet couldn't operate without, something like that—and as money is wont to do, just kept growing and growing into a vast accumulation of incredible wealth. He was what people used to call "the idle rich," not really doing anything more than managing his money and his investments. He often sank money into Broadway musical productions and had what seemed to be the magic touch; every show he financed ran for years and won shelfloads of Tony Awards. He was an outspoken advocate for gay rights and was always giving money to gay causes with both hands. Every summer he hosted a huge costume ball fund-raiser for the Gay Men's Health Crisis at his home in the Hamptons that raised hundreds of thousands of dollars.

His marriage to model Timothy Burke in Massachusetts several years earlier was one of the most famous same-sex marriages in the country. Timothy Burke was breathtakingly handsome, with a chiseled body that adorned the cover of designer underwear boxes, billboards, and advertisements in every major publication in the world. Timothy eventually launched his own enormously successful line of designer underwear and swimwear—and had his own cologne as well.

I had a bottle of it in my medicine cabinet at that very moment.

Timothy's death had been the biggest news story in New York the summer I came to the city—you couldn't escape it. He'd gone for a swim from the beach at their home in the Hamptons one afternoon, and never came back. His body washed ashore near Montauk a few days later.

I stood politely as he kissed Valerie on the cheek and she introduced us to each other. He smiled at me and shook my hand.

He was much handsomer than he looked in photographs. He was in either his late thirties or early forties. His shoulders were broad, his skin tanned, his waist narrow, and his legs strong and muscular. There was some gray in his jet-black hair, and his open shirt showed some gray in the thick hair in the center of his well-muscled chest. There was a dimple in his chin and stubble on his cheeks. He rubbed his big hands over them ruefully after he asked our waiter for coffee. "Had I known I was going to run into you, Valerie, I would have shaved before going for my morning walk."

"What brings you to South Beach, Carlo?" Valerie asked, and I had to bite my tongue to keep from warning him not to answer. I knew that look and tone.

Apparently, so did Carlo Romaniello. He waved his hand and smiled slightly. "The same as you, Valerie—sun, sand, sea, rest and relaxation—we don't need another reason, do we?" He took a deep breath and patted his chest with both hands.

"But surely you can get that at Spindrift?" She turned to me and said, like she was speaking to a child, "Spindrift is his lovely home out in the Hamptons. It's magnificent."

A shadow crossed his face briefly at the mention of the house.

My cheeks turned red with embarrassment at her tactlessness.

But the shadow was gone and he smiled back at her, replying simply, "Yes, I do have some business to take care of here. But nothing I can talk about, on the record or off." His voice was smooth, charming. He smiled and thanked the waiter who set a cup of coffee down in front of him. He took a drink, and turned his attention to me. "And do you only speak when spoken to?"

"I...I, um—"

Valerie sighed in exasperation as I felt my cheeks get redder. "His father was my adviser in college—I hired him as a favor." She glared at me. "A favor I regret most days."

His eyes narrowed for a moment, glittering dangerously, and he glanced at his watch. "Oh—I must be going." He rose and kissed Valerie's hand. "As always, a delight to see you, Valerie."

"Perhaps we could have dinner later?"

"I'm afraid I have plans." He smiled at me. "A pleasure to meet you."

I nodded, unable to meet his eyes.

"How about lunch tomorrow?" Valerie stood, a desperate tone in her voice I'd never heard before.

He bowed his head slightly. "That would be lovely. Say, one o'clock at La Mirada?"

"Yes, perfect."

He smiled at me. "Be sure to bring the quiet little church mouse." He walked back out to the sidewalk, whistling as he walked away from us.

"Too bad he's gay," she mused as she picked up her phone and frowned at it. She scowled at me. "Surely I didn't agree to take a meeting with that has-been Corina Palenzuela this afternoon? That bitch hasn't had a hit since the turn of the century. Cancel it immediately, and see if you can—"

I started scribbling notes as she fired off instructions, but I couldn't stop thinking about Carlo Romaniello.

But as I dialed Corina Palenzuela to give her Valerie's regrets, I knew I would probably never see him again.

There was no way Valerie would let me join them for lunch— even though he'd specifically included me.

CHAPTER TWO

Overnight, Valerie came down with something, some kind of "stomach flu or food poisoning," her voice gasped through my cell phone at just after six the next morning, "but it might be contagious or something. The concierge has already called a doctor—there's no sense in your catching it, too." She sighed. "I'm just going to go back to sleep and pray for death. You might as well take the day off. But oh yes, you must call Carlo Romaniello and cancel lunch."

"I don't have his phone number," I replied, my spirits rising. A day off? In South Beach? I could feel myself smiling in my dark room.

"I don't have it, either," she said crossly. "Just start calling the best hotels here. He'll be at one of them, surely." And she hung up.

I stared at the phone.

The thought of calling every hotel in South Beach wasn't in the least bit appealing. And that was assuming he was staying in a hotel and not with friends. He might even have his own condo or place down here. He was certainly rich enough.

I sighed. I could spend the entire morning trying to find him without success—and it certainly wasn't how I wanted to spend the morning.

After Valerie had gone to bed the night before, I'd stayed up another hour and Googled Carlo Romaniello. The entire first page of links that came up all had to do with Timothy Burke's tragic death.

Even though it made me feel like a ghoul, I couldn't help myself; I started clicking on the links and read everything I could find.

It had been late May when it happened—so it hadn't been a full year yet. They'd been married for five years, give or take, when it happened. Timothy had given all of the servants the day off, and late in the afternoon apparently went for a swim in the Atlantic Ocean behind Spindrift. There was a pool, of course, but one of the servants at Spindrift—a Michael Carson—had told the police that Timothy preferred the ocean because he'd grown up on the Gulf of Mexico and was used to salt water. None of the servants knew why he'd given them the day off—he hadn't given any of them a reason, and so he was alone in the house before he went for his swim. His cell phone had been found on the beach, along with his towel, his bathing robe, and his sandals; he'd made a call around four thirty to a business associate in the city, who confirmed the call. Timothy's underwear company was looking into going into swimwear, but Timothy wasn't certain if it was the right move for Drawers.

"He told me to confirm a meeting with a potential swimwear designer the next week," the associate recalled. "And he sounded in good spirits. He was happy, and looking forward to moving Drawers forward."

Carlo came home unexpectedly to find the house empty and no sign of Timothy. When he found Timothy's things on the beach, he immediately called the Coast Guard and reported him missing.

No trace of him was found, until his body washed ashore at Montauk later the next week.

After the news reports about the inquest—which found that he died as a result of accidental drowning—there were no further mentions of Carlo Romaniello anywhere online. He had apparently gone into seclusion after his husband's death, and who could blame him?

I also did an image search for Timothy Burke.

I remembered that he'd been handsome and in excellent shape, but I was really only familiar with his image on underwear boxes and in the ads I used to see in magazines. But I always figured those had been touched up, Photoshopped and airbrushed. They had also been stylized, so that sometimes you really couldn't tell what his face looked like.

But Timothy Burke had been a model long before he married Carlo and became an underwear mogul, and thanks to the Internet, those images were forever.

He'd done a nude photo shoot for a famed celebrity photographer in black and white, and every one of those images was a work of art.

He had enormous brown eyes that stared out of the images like they could see into your soul, under perfectly trimmed and shaped black eyebrows perched on a ridge of bone. His hair was an unusually dark black with hints of blue when the light caught it. His cheekbones were sharp and definitely pronounced, and the cheeks below looked hollowed out. He had thick and sensual lips above a strong and square chin with a dimple in the center. His shoulders were broad and strongly muscled, his tanned skin stretched tightly over chiseled and defined muscles. His nipples were round, his pectorals round and symmetrical. He didn't have a six-pack of deeply defined abs—I counted eight muscles between his rib cage and his navel. His legs were strongly defined and muscular, and even in the nudes he made sure his genitals weren't exposed—I remembered reading an interview with him once where he'd said that he wouldn't do full frontal nudity.

"It's not that I think it's bad," he'd said, "I just like to leave a little mystery, you know? You should always leave them wanting more."

Jealously, I dismissed the enormous bulge evident in front when he modeled underwear as Photoshopped—until I realized it was evident in every photo of him in skimpy clothing—whether it was underwear, a jock, or a bikini. Even in jeans that bulge was unavoidable.

And the back view was just as magnificent.

I'd sighed and closed my laptop. Across from where I was sitting up in bed, I could see myself in the mirror. I'd kind of thought

Carlo Romaniello was flirting with me—or at least showing some interest in me. After all, he'd included me in the lunch date with Valerie.

But what I saw in the mirror wasn't in the same league as the man in the images I'd been looking at.

Obviously he was simply being really polite.

I turned off the light and slept fitfully until Valerie's call woke me at six.

I ordered coffee from room service and got out the South Beach phone book from the drawer in the nightstand and flipped it open to hotels. Obviously, the budget hotels and lower end ones could be ruled out—surely a man as wealthy as Carlo Romaniello wouldn't be staying at a Best Western or a Motel 6.

It was far too early to try reaching him, anyway.

I got out of the bed and took a shower, shaving and going through all my usual morning rituals, and had just finished getting dressed when the knock came on the door with my coffee and yogurt. I took the coffee out onto the balcony and drank it while I watched the gorgeous sunrise over the ocean. *It really is beautiful here*, I thought as I finished the yogurt, *and I know I shouldn't be glad that she's sick—but I am, and I'm going to make the most of this day off down here.*

I imagined what the call would be like when I finally reached Carlo Romaniello:

"Mr. Romaniello? Hi, I'm sorry to bother you, but Valerie Franklin has to cancel lunch. She's not feeling well."

"How unfortunate, please give her my best wishes. Is this the handsome young man who was with her yesterday in the café?"

"Yes, sir, it is."

"Please call me Carlo. I was serious, of course, when I told you I wanted you to join us for our lunch date today. I would be most appreciative if you would still join me. Please don't leave me to lunch alone."

"I would like that very much, Carlo."

It was an enjoyable little fantasy to indulge in over breakfast.

Around eight, I started calling hotels. But after trying three with no luck, I conceded defeat. He'd never said he was staying on South Beach. He could be in a hotel on the mainland—he could be in a hotel in Fort Lauderdale or Palm Beach, for that matter. I didn't want to waste my free morning making futile phone calls to every hotel in southeastern Florida. I knew where he would be at one o'clock—La Mirada restaurant—so I would just show up there at twelve thirty and wait for him outside. Valerie wouldn't like it, of course—I could already hear her screaming *"I told you to call him!"* once she found out—but it wouldn't be the first time she screamed at me, nor would it be the last.

So, I took care of the e-mails and other business I needed to do for her, and at ten o'clock I walked out the front doors of the hotel onto Ocean Drive. I crossed over and walked through the dunes and stood there, watching the green foamy waves coming ashore on the beautiful beach. It wasn't very crowded—it was a midweek morning in mid-May, after all—but there were some people taking advantage of the sun and the heat. I decided to buy a swimsuit and spend the afternoon in the water. I crossed back over to Ocean Drive and spent the morning haunting shops looking for an affordable bathing suit— one that wasn't too immodest. Some of the guys on the beach I'd seen had been in bikinis or square-cut trunks—but I didn't have the kind of body that could pull off something skimpy or sexy. I wanted something that would cover me up and hide my lack of tan and muscles, like board shorts. I wasted some time going into expensive shops, where I was completely ignored by the sales clerks—who apparently had some kind of radar or sixth sense that let them know I couldn't possibly afford anything in their store—before finally finding a discount shop with something I could afford—a fifteen- dollar pair of navy blue board shorts.

It was exactly twelve thirty when I made it to La Mirada.

It was getting hotter, and I was damp with sweat from all the walking around. I finished the large iced mocha I'd gotten at a ubiquitous Starbucks and tossed it into a garbage can.

La Mirada wasn't that expensive, actually, according to the menu mounted under glass on the wall to the left of the glass doors. The food seemed to be some kind of funky fusion of American staples and Caribbean food, and the smells wafting out made my stomach growl. I was starving, so I made up my mind. If Carlo Romaniello's invitation the day before had merely been politeness, I would go ahead and treat myself to lunch there.

It was about five minutes before one when a town car with darkened windows pulled up in front of the restaurant. The back door opened, and Carlo Romaniello got out. He was wearing white linen pants and a lemon yellow pullover shirt. He smiled at me, lifting up his sunglasses as he looked around. "I see you, church mouse, but I don't see Valerie." His tone was light and jocular, and his smile got broader. "Has Lady Luck smiled on me this fine May day in south Florida? Does this mean the Dragon Lady won't be joining us?"

"I—" I had planned out everything I was going to say, spent the better part of the morning working on witty opening lines in my head as I wandered from store to store, coming up with clever bons mots that would impress him with my sophistication and intelligence.

But now that he was standing directly in front of me with an amused smile on his handsome face, my tongue tripped over itself and I couldn't remember anything I'd planned to say—even the stupid lines I'd dismissed. I could feel my face turning red, and I finally managed to blurt out, "Valerie's not feeling well. I would have called…"

"But of course you didn't have my number, nor did you know where I was staying," he finished for me, his smile never wavering. His face relaxed and his eyes lit up. "I do hope that you will take pity on me under the circumstances, and join me so I won't have to lunch alone? I really don't like eating alone, Church Mouse. It would be an enormous favor to me." He sounded completely sincere.

"I—of course, I'm sorry, I—" I stammered, wishing a hole would open up in the sidewalk and swallow me. I had hoped—but never dared to believe he would actually want my company.

"Let's go inside, then, and get out of this sun," he replied. He took me by the hand and led me inside. He caught the attention of the hostess, and we were seated a table with a lovely view within a matter of minutes.

As soon as I sat down, I hid my reddened face behind a menu.

"Do you intend to hide behind your menu until we order?" he asked in pleasantly amused tone, and I didn't need to see his face to know he was smiling at me.

Now even more mortified, I lowered the menu. He was indeed smiling, but had lifted his left eyebrow and cocked his head to one side as he looked at me from across the table. I could feel even more blood rushing to my face—which surely was by then turning am even darker shade of purple.

I wanted to get up and run out of the restaurant.

He laughed, reaching across the table and patting my hand. "You need to just relax and enjoy yourself, Church Mouse," he said in a soothing tone. "I'm not going to bite you. It's a beautiful day, we're about to have a wonderful meal, and we can use this time to get to know each other better." He tilted his head to one side again, narrowing his eyes in an appraising way. "Surely you're not this shy?" He said it almost like he was talking to himself. The delighted smile on his face grew even wider. "Perhaps you are, at that. How old are you?"

"Twenty-three," I replied, raising my chin a little defiantly when he laughed yet again. I bristled a little. I knew I looked younger than my age—I was always carded when I went out to buy Valerie's cigarettes for her. It was annoying.

"But you're just a baby!" He sounded delighted, and his eyes twinkled, his amusement growing as I shifted in my chair.

"I'm not." I managed to get the words out as our waiter placed glasses of ice water in front of us. He started laughing, and I felt myself growing more indignant. "Please don't laugh at me. I'm a college graduate, and I've been living on my own for the last year in New York." I couldn't decide whether I was angry, embarrassed, or just plain foolish.

Things were definitely not going the way I had hoped.

And my words didn't have the desired effect. In fact, he only laughed harder. My cheeks burned with mortification until he finally wiped at his eyes with his napkin and got hold of himself. "I'm terribly sorry," he said, a contrite look on his face. "There's nothing worse than being laughed at, is there? It's just—" He let his voice trail off. His eyes got serious. "I haven't laughed much in a very long time."

I felt both my anger and embarrassment fading away.

I bit my lower lip and looked down at the place setting. Of course he hadn't been able to laugh since his partner had died. I couldn't imagine that kind of suffering, the pain he must still be going through. It had to have been horrible to lose the love of his life in such a terrible and unexpected way.

"It's okay, I really don't mind, really," I finally said, running my index finger through the condensation on my water glass. "Valerie laughs at me all the time."

"I'm sure she does." His face darkened. "How can you stand working for that awful woman?"

I shrugged. "She's really not that bad, Mr. Romaniello. She—"

"If we're going to be friends, Church Mouse, you're going to have to call me Carlo." He interrupted me with a kind smile. "I don't eat meals with people who call me Mr. Romaniello."

I felt my cheeks reddening again, and I couldn't stop myself from smiling. "Thank you, Carlo." I nodded politely. "But seriously, she isn't that bad, really. She's more bite than bark, and she's used to—"

"You sound like a wife defending the husband who's just broken her arm," he interrupted me again. "Seriously, Church Mouse, the first step to getting out of an abusive relationship is to admit that you're in one."

"But—" I stopped my protest when I saw the twinkle in his eyes and the sly smile playing at the corners of his mouth. "You're teasing me."

"I'm sorry—you must think I'm terribly unkind," he replied. "How about we find something else to talk about? I won't say another word about your employer—but I have to ask, however did you end up working for her?"

So I wound up telling him the entire story of my father's death and how I come to work for Valerie in New York. The waiter came— Carlo ordered for me—and he occasionally interrupted me to ask a question. At first, I spoke hesitantly—no one had ever shown such interest in me before—but the longer I talked, the more confident I felt. And by the time I was finally winding down the incredibly dull story of my life, the waiter was placing our salads in front of us.

"Interesting," Carlo Romaniello said after watching me for a moment. He buttered a roll and tore it into little pieces.

"I'm not interesting." I said, adding sweetener to the tall glass of iced tea I'd been too busy talking to drink. "You must be so bored—I'm so sorry to have run on this way. You must think I'm horribly self-absorbed."

"On the contrary, I think you're very refreshing—a nice change from all the truly crashing bores I've unfortunately had to get used to spending time with." He winked at me as the waiter presented a bottle of wine to him. He took a sip and nodded, and the waiter filled our glasses and left the bottle.

"I don't really drink much," I confessed as I picked up the glass. I swirled the red liquid around dubiously. The truth was I didn't drink at all. Once, when I was in my early teens, my father decided to teach me about wine. I'd had several glasses, and spent the rest of the evening on my knees in front of the toilet. I didn't like liquor—the taste of it wasn't appealing.

But I wasn't going to tell Carlo Romaniello that.

I sipped the wine as he watched me. "What do you think?"

"It's kind of—" I searched for the right words. "Fruity and a little dry?"

"You're a fast study." He smiled at me.

I don't remember what all we talked about, but it seemed like the time flew by—the next thing I knew the waiter was offering the check, which Carlo took, slipping a credit card into the leather folder. My phone vibrated—it was Valerie.

I frowned at it, excused myself, and walked outside to take the call. "Where are you?" she demanded before lapsing into a coughing fit.

"I went for a walk," I replied, closing my eyes.

"Did you clear my schedule?" She coughed again. "God fucking damn it, I am going to cough up a lung here. The doctor has just left—I apparently have strep throat, damn it all to hell, and am contagious."

"Oh, no!"

"Yes, well. I have to stay in bed for three days or so, and he doesn't want me to do anything other than rest. So you're going to be on your own for the rest of the week. But that doesn't mean I won't have things for you to do." She went on to give me explicit instructions, as was her wont. The reality was what she wanted me to do would take me, at most, five minutes—but since she was always convinced everyone else was an idiot, she was still giving me instructions on how to properly carry out her wishes when Carlo joined me on the sidewalk, a big smile on his face. When she was finally finished, she said, "Get that done, and I'll be checking my e-mails…if anything comes up, I'll be calling you."

"Thank you, Valerie." I disconnected the call.

"Is she feeling better?" Carlo asked.

I shook my head, and he smiled when I told him the news. "Good, then you can keep me company for the rest of today." He winked at me again. "I might just press you into service for the rest of the week. Can't have you getting bored."

I felt a little thrill and hoped he wasn't teasing me again.

I couldn't help but think, as Carlo whisked me around South Beach the rest of that afternoon, from boutiques to art galleries to shops, that I could write an excellent article called "A Day with Carlo Romaniello." When I commented on the fact that almost everywhere we went they knew him by name, he said, "When you have money, sales people working on commissions make it their business to know your name."

It was a bit overwhelming.

It wasn't like I was unused to going into high-end galleries or stores; as Valerie's assistant I was in and out of them all the time running errands for her. But even the executive editor of *Street Talk* magazine who had everyone in the popular culture zeitgeist wooing her for column inches and mentions didn't command the kind of respect Carlo Romaniello got the instant he stepped through the doors of any shop. He asked me my opinion on everything—from sculpture to paintings to photographs. At the Versace store, he tried on suits and asked my opinions. He even had me try one on myself—a lovely charcoal gray suit that was more expensive than everything in my closet combined.

Once I removed it and put my own clothing back on, he wanted me to try on a suit of black wool, but I demurred. "Don't you want to see how you look in it?" he asked.

I shook my head. "No." I fingered the sleeve longingly but didn't change my mind. "It would just make me sad."

"Sad?"

"That I can't own it if it looks good," I replied. "I don't see the point in trying on clothing I can't ever afford, or shopping for things I can never buy. It just—it just makes my life seem sad." I crossed my arms. "And my life isn't sad. I know you probably think it is," I said hurriedly as he opened his mouth to interrupt, "you've made it clear you don't like Valerie. But I like my job, I like what I do, and I like my life. So, I don't have the time to follow my dreams? Someday I will."

"You really are something, Church Mouse," he said, shaking his head. "That Midwestern Kansas common sense is something I wish more people I knew possessed." He laughed and led me out of the store. "So, why don't you tell me what your dream is? Or is that too personal to share with a stranger?"

I turned my head as we walked down the sidewalk so he couldn't see the sudden tears that filled my eyes. No one had ever asked me before—not my father; no one had ever cared enough about me to ask—and at that moment I felt like I was, indeed, someone to be pitied. I was just a dumb kid from Kansas with a miserable job living in a miserable little apartment with a miserable boss who treated me terribly. I was no closer to making my dreams come true than I had been a year earlier when I first arrived in New York.

"Have I upset you?" he asked, concern in his tone. "I didn't mean to, and I'm sorry. I really did just want to know."

I took a deep breath and gave him a tentative smile. "No, you didn't upset me. I'm the one who's sorry, Mr. Romaniello. I've taken terrible advantage of your kindness."

He reached over and brushed a tear away from my right eye. "Now, Church Mouse, why would someone being kind to you make you cry?" He took me by the hands and turned me so that I was facing him, looking up into his brown eyes. "I'm enjoying myself. I'm enjoying your company. I can't remember the last time—" A shadow crossed his face briefly, and I knew what he was remembering. He took a moment to get hold of himself, and went on, "Unfortunately, I have a dinner engagement I can't get out of—but with Valerie sick, you're free now tomorrow, aren't you? Why don't you spend the day with me again? And you can tell me all about your dreams." He pulled his cell phone out of his pocket. "What's your cell phone number?" I gave it to him, and he punched it into his phone. My phone started ringing, and I stored his number.

"Thank you for today," I said. I was really sorry to have the day end, and realistic enough to know I'd probably never see him again.

He took my hand and pressed it. "It was my pleasure, Church Mouse." He hailed a cab and waved as it pulled away.

As I walked back to the hotel, I found myself whistling.

CHAPTER THREE

I spent the evening in my room and ordered dinner from room service while a series of documentaries on the History Channel played on the television. I wasn't watching, of course—I was sitting up in my bed, with a book open in my lap, replaying the events of the day over and over again with a smile on my face. I remembered the sound of his laugh, the way the corners of his eyes wrinkled up when he was smiling, the way his dark eyes twinkled when he teased me. At one point I did an image search, dragging the images off websites onto my laptop's desktop. He was so handsome—and I would compare his face to Timothy's. Carlo was handsomer than Timothy, I decided, because Carlo's looks were *real.* Carlo looked like a handsome man you might see in a coffee shop, or pass on the street, or see across the room in a restaurant. Timothy, on the other hand, had an almost unreal beauty—almost cold, like some marble statue of a god you'd see in a museum. Remote, distant, and untouchable, there was a quality of almost smug disdain in Timothy's eyes as he posed for the cameras, a sense he was thinking, *Worship me, you mere mortals! You can look but you can never touch, you can dream about me but you will never have me.*

I much preferred Carlo's looks.

I allowed myself to indulge in fantasies, fantasies where Carlo fell in love with me and took me away from my life and made me a part of his world—but we were so content with each other that we didn't need parties and play premieres, or to be around other people. We simply basked in each other's company, and I wondered what it would be like for him to hold me in his arms, to feel his lips on mine, on my skin, and to share a bed with him.

And I would catch a glimpse of myself in the mirror across the room from the bed, and see the reality of my plain looks and undistinguished body.

I had been attracted to men before—handsome but vapid male models that drifted through the hallways at *Street Talk*, gorgeous men I saw on the streets or the subway, but this was different. This was more than a physical attraction, and stupid and pointless as it was, I knew I was falling in love with Carlo Romaniello.

Once I admitted it to myself, I laughed at my own foolishness.

He was merely being kind to a church mouse.

"That's fine," I said to my reflection in the mirror, with a determined tilt to my chin. "I'm glad to be of any use to him."

But my defiant thoughts were just that, and I knew that I wanted to be more than that to him. I wanted him to care about me—love was too much to ask for. He was used to men like Timothy, men with handsome faces and stunning bodies with sophisticated tastes and senses of humor, men who sparkled in the limelight even if they didn't crave it, and carried it off with aplomb and style. Men who wore designer clothing tailored to fit their bodies perfectly, rather than irregulars with designer labels bought at discount stores by a man who had no grasp of what went with what, who went to discount hair salons and could never duplicate the style again with gels and sprays and products.

The world Carlo Romaniello inhabited might as well have been the moon.

And no matter how much I hoped and prayed, he wasn't going to call me again. What did I have to offer someone like him?

Nothing.

The best I could hope for was he would simply forget about me, rather than remember and laugh about me with his friends over drinks at some glittering party, telling the story of the pathetic young man he spent some time with one afternoon in South Beach.

When I turned off the lights and went to bed, I was resigned to the reality of my life. Tomorrow, I would go to the beach in my cheap blue board shorts—being careful not to burn. I would do whatever Valerie needed me to and just hole up in my room reading books, trying hard not to be miserable and lonely, missing him, and trying not to get my hopes up every time my phone rang.

I dreamed of him that night, a dream so incredibly vivid that when I woke up in the gray hour just before dawn and realized I was still in my hotel room, I almost burst into tears from disappointment.

For the first time in my life, I knew what I was missing. One afternoon with Carlo Romaniello and my life now seemed empty, devoid of everything that made life worth living. I saw my life through his eyes and was overwhelmed by the nothingness of it. It was like the rest of the world was inside at some wonderful party, and I was outside with my face pressed up against the glass, watching them and wishing I could be inside with everyone else instead of outside and miserable.

With Valerie sick and confined to her room, the rest of the week stretched before me like some horribly empty void.

As the sun rose and my room filled with the morning light, I wrapped my arms around my legs and wondered what to do with myself.

I ordered my usual coffee and fruit breakfast from room service, and once again, my head resting on my drawn-up knees, replayed the previous afternoon in my head, trying to view the things he'd said to me and the way he'd acted dispassionately like a disinterested observer rather than a lonely young man who could so easily mistake kindness from a handsome older man as something more than what it actually had been.

No matter how bitterly disappointing it was to admit the truth to myself, I did. I wasn't ever going to hear from Carlo Romaniello ever again.

"I'm truly pathetic—Valerie is so right about me," I chastised myself, getting out of the bed and going into the bathroom. "He's never going to call me—he was simply being polite and just appreciated a bit of company, that's all it was, nothing more."

But deep down, I couldn't help but hope that he *would* call me again. As I went through my morning routine, I kept seeing his face in my mind and the way the muscle in his arms moved and his distinctly masculine smell or the sound of the deep hearty laugh when I amused him, which seemed to be every time I opened my mouth.

I turned on the shower and scrubbed my skin until it turned red, washing my hair thoroughly. *You're only twenty-three*, I reminded myself as I scrubbed away, *it's not too late to make changes in my life. No more excuses. Now that I know what I am missing, I can make changes before it's too late. I can start living instead of just going through the motions.*

As I toweled dry in the steamy bathroom, I decided I was going to work on my writing. Even if Valerie was as dismissive or insulting or condescending about it as she always was, I would keep pushing her about her promises to let me write for the magazine, even if it was just pieces for the reviews section without a byline, rather than just sitting around waiting for her to give me an assignment. I could spend time writing on my laptop on my lunch hour, and if I spent an hour writing before going to bed every night rather than wasting time reading things on the Internet, I would get that much closer to my goals.

And I would make myself go out to gay clubs more often, to try to get more comfortable in those environments. I needed to make friends, I needed to find a lover—even if it was just a casual fling that meant nothing. I needed to lose my virginity, and to do that I had to overcome my shyness.

I could do it.

I had just finished putting on a pair of cargo-style shorts and a T-shirt when there was a knock on my door—undoubtedly my breakfast. *No time like the present to start being more outgoing*, I decided as I crossed the room and pulled the door open.

It was indeed the room service waiter, with a black garment bag with the Versace logo on it draped over his arm. He smiled, inclining his head as he pushed the cart into the room, placing the garment bag over a chair.

Curiosity pushed all thoughts of friendliness out of my head.

"What's that?" I asked, indicating the garment bag.

"It was delivered for you last night, sir—the concierge asked me to bring it up with your breakfast," he replied respectfully as he placed a tray containing a covered plate, a coffee urn, a small pitcher of cream, and silverware wrapped in a linen napkin on the small table next to the chair. With a flourish, he presented me with the check inside a leather portfolio, which I signed. He bowed and shut the door behind him.

I poured a cup of coffee and sipped it, pondering the garment bag. Surely, it couldn't be…but what else could it be?

There was a small envelope affixed to the zipper of the bag.

I removed it, and used my finger to tear open the flap. There was a folded piece of heavy stock paper inside. I unfolded it.

Church Mouse,

I hope you'll forgive me for taking the liberty to buy these few things for you. I saw how much you liked them, and it seemed silly that you should have to do without them when I can afford to pay for them. It's the least I can do after you so graciously kept a lonely old man company yesterday. I believe your kindness should be repaid with more kindness.

I look forward to getting to know you ever better,
Carlo Romaniello

I almost burst into happy tears.

He wasn't just being nice—he really *did* like me!

Unable to stand the suspense any longer, I unzipped the bag. It contained both suits—the charcoal and the black. I took them out of the bag and examined them carefully—the material felt incredible against my skin, and I hung them up in the closet. There were also several shirts in the bag, linen shirts in vibrant colors with matching ties wrapped around the hanger. There was an electric blue shirt with a dark red tie, a dark red one with a blue tie, and a beige shirt with a red-and-blue striped tie. I held each up against me in turn so

I could see how they looked in the mirror, and again my eyes filled with tears. I had never before owned anything so beautiful. I hung the shirts up next to the suits and folded the garment bag and placed it on the shelf. I couldn't stop staring at my beautiful new clothes.

I took a cup of coffee out onto the balcony and sat down.

Of course, I didn't have anywhere to wear these clothes—they were far too nice to wear to the office, and while I sometimes got to trail along behind Valerie at posh events, I wasn't sure how she'd feel about me wearing clothes that made me look like an invited guest rather than her lackey.

As I sat there sipping my hot coffee, beads of sweat breaking out on my upper lip and my forehead, I wondered with a start if it was okay to accept the clothes.

In any number of novels I'd read, women weren't allowed to accept expensive gifts from men who were interested in them—such gifts were inappropriate. The proper thing to do was to return them with an air of being insulted.

But that also presumed that Carlo was interested in me romantically—and I wasn't sure he was. He hadn't done anything untoward—he'd never touched me except in passing or to get my attention, and when he had, his touch hadn't lingered. He hadn't tried to kiss me or to get me up to his suite—and, I remembered with a smile, I still didn't know which hotel it was at.

So I couldn't return the clothes to him even if I wanted to—all I could do was return them to the Versace store.

I bit my lower lip. Even if I never had the chance to wear them, I didn't want to part with them. I didn't care if it meant something bad. I wasn't going to get rid of them. Period.

And if yesterday was any indication, he certainly didn't expect anything in exchange from me.

Having made up my mind, I ate my breakfast and finished the pot of coffee. I was debating whether I should call to thank him or simply send a text message—I wasn't sure of the protocol other than I knew I had to acknowledge his generous gifts—when my cell phone started ringing.

It was Valerie.

She sounded horrible, her voice raw and throaty, deep with phlegm. She coughed again as she said, "Did you get everything taken care of?"

"Yes." Valerie never wanted anything more than yes or no for an answer. I had learned that lesson the hard way on my first day with her.

"You have cleared my schedule for the rest of the week, of course." She coughed again, her voice raspy and wheezy. "I've just sent you an e-mail with the things I need you to take care of today."

"Do you need to see the doctor again?"

"No, there's nothing else he can do for me. I have to take all these damned pills and eventually it'll run its course." Her voice took on a venomous air. "I'll just bet that brat on the plane gave this to me. Why the airlines let brats in first class now is beyond me. They might as well…" She went on like this for a few minutes, but I stopped listening. When Valerie was on one of her rants, she didn't really require my full attention—all I needed to do was agree periodically when she paused to breathe.

So while she ranted, I got up and walked over to the closet and stared at the clothes again, a delighted smile on my face as I fingered the sleeves of the jackets and the shirts yet again. Versace—I couldn't believe I owned clothes from Versace.

I'd certainly come a long way from that small college town in Kansas!

As I stood there, vaguely aware of Valerie's whining voice in my ear, I closed my eyes and pictured myself entering a Broadway theater on opening night of some major play, dressed in the black suit with the electric blue shirt on underneath, my hand tucked into the crook of Carlo's arm. Flashbulbs popped as we walked into the theater lobby, which was crowded with the most fabulous people in Manhattan, dressed to the teeth and dripping with jewels. I received a hug and an air-kiss from a Broadway diva, and said hello to the mayor and his wife as Carlo led me through the glittering throng.

He pressed a flute of champagne into my hand and smiled at me. "You've made me so happy—I can't believe how empty my life would be had I not run into you that day on South Beach."

Valerie's rant was winding down, and I was brought back into the present from my wonderful daydream. "Get those things taken care of, and you can have the rest of the day to yourself," she groused. "At least you're getting a little vacation time out of this." She laughed, which triggered another coughing spasm. When she was finished, she said, "And I won't count any of this against your vacation time. It's not your fault that rotten little bastard got me so sick." She hung up.

"How kind of you to not count this as vacation for me," I said into the phone, my tone dripping with sarcasm. I tossed the phone onto the bed and sat down at the desk, logging into my computer. I read her e-mail and smiled to myself. Sometimes the fact she really thought I was an incompetent idiot who couldn't handle the smallest task without having her hold my hand came in handy—the things she needed me to do took me just a little under ten minutes. I went ahead and spent another half hour answering e-mails and made certain that I had, indeed, cleared her calendar for the rest of our stay.

It was almost nine when I put the tray back out in the hall.

The entire day stretched out in front of me.

I picked up my phone, tempted to call Carlo.

I went back and forth, arguing with myself until I decided there was no harm—I needed to thank him for the clothes anyway.

He answered on the second ring. "Church Mouse! I was hoping you'd call." His voice sounded sincere, and I could myself blushing with pleasure.

"I wanted to thank you for the clothes," I said, amazed that my voice wasn't as shaky as I felt. "That was very kind of you."

"It was my pleasure," he replied. "What you need, Mouse, is someone to take care of you and spoil you." He lowered his voice—in the background I could hear silverware clinking and the low murmur of people talking. "All night long after I said good-bye to you, all I could think about was how much more fun I'd be having were I with you rather than the bores I was with, and regretting not canceling out on them." He laughed. "I won't make that mistake again."

My heart was pounding so hard I was afraid it might burst through my ribs.

"In fact, I woke up this morning thanking God that Valerie is so sick—I know that's terrible, but her bad luck is *my* good luck, after all, and I won't dim my joy by feeling bad about her illness. Please tell me you haven't any plans for the day?"

"No, I don't," I replied. "I was thinking about maybe lying on the beach for a bit this morning and getting some sun, but—"

"Please come for a ride with me," he said. "I have something things I need to do, and of course, I'll treat you to lunch *and* dinner, if you wouldn't mind spending so much time with me."

"I'd like that very much."

"Good, you can be my adviser." He laughed. "If I don't bore you to death, I'm afraid I just might monopolize you during your stay here. I have some houses I want to look at—I'm thinking about buying a house on one of the islands across the causeway from the city—not here on South Beach, this is a bit too touristy and full of people for me, I want something a little more secluded and—would you listen at me? I'm rambling, aren't I? You see what you do to me, Mouse? You make me feel as giddy as a schoolboy with his first crush, and I haven't felt that way in years."

At least not since you met Timothy, I thought, and felt my spirits sink.

I closed my eyes. He was still talking, but I wasn't hearing anything he was saying. I was acting like a damned fool. Someone like Carlo Romaniello, a wealthy, handsome worldly man like that, would never be interested in me—a rube from Kansas who'd never owned anything nice before, who didn't know what fork to use at dinner and bought his clothes secondhand or from a discount store. I didn't know a cheap wine from a good one.

And I certainly wasn't attractive enough to be mentioned in the same breath as Timothy Burke.

"I'll be in front of your hotel in about ten minutes," he was saying. "Can you be there by then?"

I swallowed. Even if he just felt sorry for me, I enjoyed being in his company—and that was enough. "Yes," I replied, opening one of the dresser doors and pulling out a pair of khaki shorts and a navy blue T-shirt. "I'll be there." I disconnected the call.

When I came out the front doors of the hotel five minutes later, he was there, standing next to a red convertible Mustang with the top down. He waved, smiling. He was wearing a pair of khaki shorts himself, and a ribbed red tank top. Curly black hairs stuck out of the neck, and it showed off the strong muscles of his arms and shoulders. I opened the passenger door and sat down, buckling the seat belt as he started the car.

And we did end up spending most of the week together. He took me to the dog track, where he lost a lot of money but I had a run of luck that saw me close out with over three hundred dollars in winnings. He took me to watch jai alai, which I never did quite understand, despite his patient explanations. We shopped in boutiques and stores—but I refused to allow him to buy me any more clothes. "You spent enough on the ones you already bought me," I protested; even as he pouted in disappointment, I remained adamant. He looked at yachts, and we went out for rides with salesmen out onto the sparkling green waters of the bay and the Intracoastal Waterway.

As the week progressed, I began to wonder why he never tried anything with me. He never tried to kiss me or hold my hand, or made any sort of move on me—or perhaps he had but I was too clueless and inexperienced to know what he was doing.

One afternoon he took me on a picnic to a secluded private island, where we spent the afternoon relaxing on the sand and in the warm waters of the Gulf Stream. I, of course, wore my body-disguising cheap blue board shorts, but Carlo wore a white bikini that left very little to the imagination. I couldn't help myself—I kept sneaking glances at his strong chest with the dark black hairs, his muscular legs, his flat stomach.

He caught me looking at him and smiled at me. "Do you like what you see, Mouse?"

Mortified that he'd caught me, I tried to think of something to say, but as usual, my mouth just opened and closed as my face reddened.

He threw back his head and laughed, grabbing me by the hands and pulling me to him. "You are the most adorable thing," he said, and he kissed me.

And there, on towels spread out over white sand on a private island in the middle of a hot afternoon, I finally lost my virginity.

The next day was my last full day in Miami. Valerie was already starting to feel better and was really looking forward to returning to New York. By now she'd stopped blaming the sniffling child from the flight down and had decided that actually all of Miami was at fault. Once she'd hung up, Carlo called—he was downstairs.

When I opened the convertible's passenger door, he handed me a single long-stemmed red rose, and I could feel myself coloring again.

"I hope you never stop blushing," he smiled at me as I buckled my seat belt. "It's adorable."

We spent the morning driving from island to island, being led by a real estate agent named Ethel Goldstein through incredibly beautiful houses with landscaped lawns, sparkling blue swimming pools, and towering palm trees, valued at such amazing out-of-my-league prices that I was almost afraid to breathe the air inside of them.

Ethel was a short, round woman with jet-black hair that had to be dyed and a thick Jersey accent. She was impeccably dressed in a dusky rose business suit with a white blouse underneath. I liked her—she seemed to have a good sense of humor but wasn't pushy in any way, and she was quite knowledgeable about the amazing palazzos she was showing us through.

Carlo was completely at ease with her, just as he had been in the shops and galleries the day before, asking questions about things that were complete mysteries to me. I wandered about the houses in awe, stunned by the size of the rooms and the views of the ocean or the Intracoastal Waterway. Carlo didn't seem to like any of them, though, and every time we got back into the car to drive to the next one, he would dissect all the things he'd found wrong with them—and would ask me for my opinion—and of course, I would try to say something intelligent but usually wound up just saying something like "it seemed more like a museum than a house."

At the last house, a huge place made of stone surrounded by lush vegetation, palm trees, and elephant ferns, I wandered out onto a wide gallery that opened off the master bedroom suite, with a stunning view of the green-blue ocean. I leaned on the railing, watching sailboats and yachts cut through the low waves. The sky was a stunning shade of blue, and it was getting hotter the later it got.

"Imagining what it would be like to live here?" Carlo asked, leaning on the railing next to me. There were beads of sweat on his forehead.

"I can't imagine what that would be like," I answered honestly.

"If you had to pick any of these houses, which would you choose?"

"None of them," I replied quickly.

"You didn't like any of them?"

"They were all beautiful," I said without looking at him. "But none of them felt like a home. Maybe it's because they're empty, but they all felt kind of sterile to me."

"Interesting," he said, turning and leaning back against the railing. "I wonder if you would think Spindrift feels sterile?"

"I—"

"You should come to Spindrift sometime," he said, a shadow crossing his face. "You would be the perfect antidote for whatever ails the place." He shook his head. "I can barely stand to be there anymore." He lit a cigarette—even though the agent had earlier warned us not to smoke on the property. "In the last year, I've spent so much time traveling—going anywhere to get away from the house and all the memories." He shook his head. Hr looked at me, an eyebrow going up. "Yes, you just might be what the house needs, Mouse. What do you say? Will you come be my guest there?"

I wanted to say yes, but stopped myself.

"Well?" he prompted.

My fears seemed too foolish to say out loud.

"I don't have much free time," I finally blurted out, my face reddening. "Valerie keeps me pretty busy."

"Oh, surely even she has to allow you to take a holiday now and then? A long weekend?" He smiled. "Or are you afraid I might take advantage of you?"

"No, no—I wouldn't mind that at all, I mean—" I said, stopping myself when I realized what I'd said. Stricken, I stood there, horrified, wishing I could bite off my own tongue or somehow could just disappear in a puff of smoke.

He smiled and took my hand. "Don't be embarrassed," he said softly. "I would hate to think I caused you any difficulty." He threw back his head and laughed. "Mouse, now that I've found you, I'm not so sure I want to part with you."

"This has been wonderful," I said, turning back to stare at the ocean. "I've had the best time, Carlo—this has been the most fun I've ever had in my life. I wish—I wish it didn't have to end."

"It doesn't have to end, does it, Mouse?" He sank down to one knee and smiled up at me. "In fact, I know I don't want to part with you. Call Valerie and quit your job, and marry me."

I gaped at him, wanting more than anything to say yes, but not certain he wasn't just teasing me or playing some kind of cruel joke. Every night when he dropped me off at my hotel, I'd dreamed of this.

But I was so used to my dreams not coming true, I couldn't quite believe this was happening.

"I know I'm being impetuous, but you make me feel young again. You make me feel alive, and now that I know I can feel this good again, I don't want it to stop, either. Marry me, Mouse."

"You aren't old." I wanted to say yes so badly it felt like I would explode. But I still couldn't believe he was serious.

"That's very kind of you, but I know my age." He smiled again. "I know, marry in haste, repent at leisure—and of course we can't be married here, but when we get back to New York, we can go before a justice of the peace." He smiled. "And then I can take you shopping, get you some appropriate clothes. Wouldn't you like that?"

"I—I don't know what to say."

"Say yes," he urged. "You won't regret it."

"Okay," I finally said, and he leaped up, threw his arms around me and hugged me close.

"I promise you, here and now, Mouse," he whispered in my ear, "I will spend the rest of my life making you happy."

Chapter Four

Predictably, Valerie was absolutely horrible.

Carlo had warned me she would be—"miserable people always envy and resent the happiness of others" were his exact words—but it still caught me off guard. I thought he was being cynical—surely she would be happy for me to have fallen in love?

I went straight to her room once Carlo dropped me off. He was going off to buy my engagement ring, which I insisted wasn't necessary, but he'd have none of that. "You've not had a conventional life so far, Mouse," he said, "but from now on, you will—and it starts with a proper engagement ring."

He kissed me as I was getting out of the car, and said, "Effective today, you are quitting," he insisted. "I don't want you working for that horrible woman one more minute than necessary."

"But I should give notice and help train my replacement."

"Not one minute more," he replied, shaking his head. "I hate the way she treats you, Mouse, and I won't have it. Go on up and quit, and we can start our life together."

I'd read the term "walking on air" in any number of books over the years, but had always thought it ridiculously hyperbolic. But as I walked through the lobby of the hotel to the elevator bank, I knew exactly what those authors were talking about. My cheeks ached from the enormous grin on my face, and I felt like my feet weren't touching the ground.

I was humming as I rode the elevator up to the penthouse floor, where Valerie was staying.

I almost gasped when she opened the door. Usually, she was incredibly well put together—but the strep throat had obviously done a number on her. Her hair was greasy and uncombed, she wasn't wearing makeup, her eyes were swollen and reddened, and her nose was raw from wiping it. She was wearing a lavender silk bathrobe, and underneath it I could see cotton pajamas. She scowled at me. "What do you want?"

My grin faded. "Um, I need to talk to you, Valerie."

"It couldn't wait until the flight home tomorrow?" She turned and walked back into the room, leaving the door open. I took that as my cue to go inside, and shut the door behind me.

I hadn't been inside Valerie's penthouse suite, and I was impressed. It was decorated in an art-deco style in matte pink, black, and white that matched the hotel's architecture. The door to the bedroom off her living space was open, as were the sliding glass doors that led out to the balcony in front. There was another set of sliding glass doors on the other side of the room, which led to the private rooftop pool the penthouses shared.

She sat down on the couch and glared at me. "This had better be good." She blew her nose again.

I took a deep breath and calmed my nerves. It was ridiculous, after all, that the woman made me so nervous. "Valerie, I'm afraid— I'm afraid I have to give notice."

Whatever she was expecting to hear, it clearly wasn't that. "What?" She shook her head. "I know I didn't hear that right."

I shifted my weight from one foot to the other. "I'm sorry, Valerie," I said softly. "I really appreciate everything you've done for me, I really do, but I'm giving my notice." I closed my eyes. "Effective immediately."

"Effective. Immediately." She sneered, her face twisting. "What an ingrate you are. Do you have any idea how many people would sell their soul for the chance to be my assistant?"

I took a deep breath. *Don't let her get to you, don't let her get to you*, I repeated over and over in my mind. "Yes, Valerie, and like I said, I really appreciate—"

"You were about to be *homeless*, have you forgotten that?" She spat the words at me, and would have said something else had a coughing fit not interrupted her.

"I have already said thank you for that," I said, my voice remaining even despite the fact I was quaking inside. "And I may not ever be able to repay you for that kindness."

"So what exactly are you going to do now?" she demanded, blowing her nose and tossing the tissue onto the coffee table.

"I'm getting married."

"*Married?*" Her eyes widened in shock. "But—I thought—to whom?"

I took a deep breath. "Carlo Romaniello."

She barked out a harsh laugh. "Carlo Romaniello?" She ran her hand through her hair. "My, what a fast little worker you are. You just met him this week, didn't you? Clearly, I underestimated you." She whistled. "I don't know how you managed to pull this off, but kudos. I have to admire someone who can land a fish like Carlo Romaniello so quickly."

"It isn't like that," I replied. She was making it sound—*nasty*, like I was marrying Carlo for his money or something, and I said so.

She snorted. "Aren't you? Surely you don't expect me to believe you've fallen in love this quickly." She rolled her eyes. "You are pretty young, I suppose. And if you insist that this is all about love and has nothing to do with the money, I guess I'll have to take your word for it—but frankly, I don't believe a word of it. Yes, he's a handsome man, but he is old enough to be your father." She waved her hand. "Frankly, I don't blame you at all, and as I said, more power to you for getting him to propose…I suppose he's just lonely, or trying to recapture his youth or something." She sighed.

"Is it so hard for you to believe that he might actually be in love with me?" I said stiffly.

She stared at me for a few minutes, and finally said, "You'll undoubtedly think I'm a bitch for saying this, but your father meant a lot to me, and you don't have anyone else. I'm the only person who'll tell you the truth." She took a deep breath. "I do wish you'd take a moment to think about this—and who knows, maybe once the novelty of the moment wears off, you'll be able to think about what I've said and not dismiss me as a hateful bitch. This marriage is never going to work, you know. You come from a completely different world than Carlo Romaniello."

"I adapted when I came to New York," I replied. "And Manhattan is a like a completely different universe than Kansas."

"This is completely different, and you know I'm right," she said. "Carlo Romaniello is used to men like Timothy Burke—and you're no Timothy. I'm sorry if that hurts your feelings, but you know deep down that I'm right about this. You have no experience with that world, you've never lived in a great house like Spindrift, you've never had any experience with people with that kind of money and family history. They have a phrase for people like you and me—'not quite our class, darling.' And people in that class are very, very cruel. Cruel in ways you cannot even begin to fathom or imagine. The rich are very different from you and me."

Her words cut me to the quick but I wasn't about to give her the satisfaction of seeing how much she'd hurt me. "Well, you're entitled to your opinion, of course," I said, raising my chin and looking her right in the eyes. "But no matter what, people are people."

"Oh, dear God, you are so naïve." She shook her head slightly, pityingly. "Well," she said in a subdued voice, "I spoke my piece, and for what it's worth, I hope I'm wrong—for your sake. I'm sure you don't believe me, but I do wish you well." She waved her hand, dismissing me. "Let HR know where to send your final paycheck."

And just like that, I was no longer employed.

As I shut her door behind me, I took a deep breath and leaned back against it. She hadn't completely ruined my mood. It didn't matter to me in the least what Valerie thought of my upcoming marriage.

All that mattered was me making Carlo happy, and he wouldn't have proposed to me had he thought I wouldn't be able to—would he?

Of course he wouldn't.

As I headed back to the elevators, I felt like a weight had been lifted from my shoulders and I was a little light-headed. For a little over a year, Valerie had been the dominant force in my life—everything I did, everywhere I went, every moment I lived and breathed revolved around Valerie, her needs and demands. I rode the elevator down to my floor, reflecting on the year I'd spent as her assistant. She'd been tough, but I'd learned a lot from her—about writing and editing, how to run a magazine, and a lot about popular culture.

As I waited for the elevator, I remembered my vow earlier in the week to focus on *living* my life, rather than just letting it happen. What was I going to do now? I stepped into the elevator and rode down. No school and no job—how would I fill my days? I hardly wanted to be the do-nothing spouse of a wealthy man, who just filled his hours with shopping and having lunch.

I went back to my room and started packing up. We were flying back to New York in the morning—Carlo said he would pick me up at ten. I spent the evening watching mindless shows on television, still not quite certain it was all real—that I wasn't dreaming it all and I was going to wake up in that horrible little apartment, needing to get ready to go into the office as always and prepare Valerie's day for her. Finally, I turned everything off and went to bed, but I couldn't sleep. I was restless all night, anxious and full of nerves.

Valerie's words kept ringing in my head as I tossed and turned. I refused to believe she was right—I wanted to believe that Carlo loved me and we would live happily ever after. But so much of what she'd said mirrored my own thoughts from earlier in the week, as I was falling in love with him. And it all did seem far too good to be true. How many shy, nondescript gay men from Kansas wound up with handsome millionaires? Not too damned many—so why was it happening for me? It was going to be hard filling the shoes of someone as gorgeous and smart and witty as Timothy Burke.

I was already awake when my alarm went off at six, lying there in the bed and staring at the ceiling as the darkness began to fade to light. I ordered coffee and showered, my nerves shot. The face that stared at me from the bathroom mirror had enormous bags under his bloodshot eyes—which was, of course, just perfect. I drank my coffee, ate my fruit and checked out, and was standing out in front of the hotel at ten. I didn't have room in my suitcase for the garment bag from Versace, so I held it.

Ten came and went.

By five after, I was beginning to sweat—and not just from the heat. I kept watching Ocean Boulevard, but there was no sign of the little red convertible. Horrible thoughts started running through my mind—what if he'd changed his mind? What if this was all some kind of horrible joke?

I began remembering horrible jokes or tricks played on characters in books—poor Miss Havisham still in her wedding dress years later, Carrie White at the prom—and I struggled to keep the tears from rising in my eyes. I kept compulsively checking my phone—*oh, I'll have to return it to the magazine, but if he doesn't show up...I'll be begging Valerie for my job back.*

She'd certainly enjoy that.

Ten past.

Other guests at the hotel were coming and going—in various types of beach attire. The bellhops kept looking at me, but I just smiled back at them, resisting the urge to say, "Seriously, my ride *is* coming for me."

By ten fifteen I was ready to just start crying.

I sat down on my suitcase. *Call him, just call him—he's just delayed and you're making a big deal over nothing at all.*

He'd never been late before—he was always prompt.

If you call and he's just running late you'll look like a control freak or a jackass or something worse.

I covered my face with my hands as the battle raged on in my head.

"Mouse?"

I uncovered my face and looked up into Carlo's face. A black town car with tinted windows was idling at the curb, and a uniformed man was standing by the open trunk.

"Hi," I said, my voice shaking a little as I stood up. The man picked up my suitcase and the garment bag and placed them in the trunk, closing it.

"Sorry, I should have called," he said in a kind tone. He kissed my cheek, and it took all of my self-control to not start sobbing in relief. "The rental agency was late picking up the convertible, but I kept thinking—"

"It's okay," I replied, walking over to the car, a foolish smile on my face as I climbed into the backseat.

Carlo's phone rang as we pulled away from the curb, and he gave me an apologetic smile as he took the call. I tuned out his conversation as I watched Miami speed by. I was exhausted from the emotional roller coaster of the previous twenty minutes, and I leaned my head against the door and closed my eyes.

"Mouse, wake up," Carlo whispered in my ear, and my eyes opened ever so slowly. I yawned. "Come on, the plane's loaded already."

Not sure what he meant, I looked out the window and saw the driver loading my bags into the storage compartment of a small jet. I got out of the car and followed Carlo over to the steps leading up into the plane. Carlo was still talking on his phone as I climbed into the luxurious interior.

A uniformed young woman smiled at me. "Can I get you something to eat or drink, sir?"

I shook my head and sat down in a leather seat that was one of the most comfortable things I'd ever sat in. I closed my eyes and moaned, sinking deeper into it, and buckled my seat belt. I heard the engines starting up and opened my eyes again just as the hatch closed. Carlo turned off his phone and tucked it into his shirt pocket and smiled over at me. "If you want to nap, Mouse, go ahead—once we're airborne it's a couple of hours before we get to New York."

The last thing in the world I wanted to do was sleep—I was in a private jet for the first time in my life—but I was so tired, and the seat was so comfortable—

I woke up again when the plane was landing—probably the smoothest landing I've ever experienced on a plane. Granted, I didn't have that much experience, but it was literally like the plane just kissed the ground. We taxied for a while and pulled up outside a small hangar. I knew the airport from looking around—we were in Newark—and there was another black town car sitting on the tarmac with a uniformed man leaning against it, his arms folded.

"That's Roberts," Carlo said as I unbuckled my seat belt and yawned.

"Roberts?"

Carlo laughed. "He works for us. He's our driver, and he takes care of the cars. He'll be taking us into the city—and you need to give him the keys to your apartment." My confusion must have shown on my face, because he laughed and went on, "He'll hire some people to pack up your things and move them out to Spindrift. I know it's not truly a proper honeymoon, and I promise I'll take you on a real one soon, but for now would you settle for a week in the city?"

"I didn't expect a honeymoon," I mumbled. A week in the city without having to go to work every day sounded absolutely heavenly to me, and I said so, adding, "I've never been to any of the museums. I never had time to actually enjoy Manhattan."

"Now you have all the time in the world," he said, giving me a hand to help me stand and pulling me into a hug.

I closed my eyes and put my head down on his shoulder. His arms felt so good around me, and once again I thanked God for my incredible luck.

Roberts—who was ridiculously tall, maybe six feet six, with reddish-brown hair, freckled skin, and a big friendly smile—loaded our bags into the trunk of the town car. Carlo's phone rang again as we got into the backseat, and he was talking into his phone all the way into the city.

He'd already made arrangements for us to be married by a friend of his, a judge who'd been his roommate in college and was one of his closest friends still. The ceremony was scheduled for the next morning at Carlo's apartment in the city. I was excited and nervous at the same time—the very idea of my ever getting married had always been so absurd to me that I never thought it would happen, and I'd decided after that abortive trip into a gay bar that I would most likely spend the rest of my life alone. I was fine with that—but

I'd more than won the lottery. I was living some kind of gay fairy tale—with a tall, dark, handsome prince who was sweeping me away from the humdrum dullness of my old life and escorting me into a strange new world I wasn't quite sure I understood.

As long as Carlo loved me, everything would be fine.

I didn't say anything as we went through the Holland Tunnel—I didn't want to bother him while he was on the phone—but every once in a while he would pat my leg reassuringly and smile at me. I was a little disappointed that he was on a business call as we rode into the city for the first time together—but was immediately ashamed of myself. I didn't know how much money he had—or the extent of his business holdings—but I had to get used to him having to deal with business, and to pout or get my feelings hurt was childish and immature. He already thought of me as little more than a child—and I wasn't going to let my behavior confirm that thought. I was going to be his partner, and I wanted to be an equal partner.

Acting like a spoiled child wasn't the right way to start our life together.

I watched out the windows as the town car brought us into Manhattan, and I felt that weird little thrill I always felt whenever I returned from a trip. I loved Manhattan. I loved living in the beating heart of the country, even if I'd never had the chance to really get to know the island. But I was going to make up for lost time now.

The car made its way uptown, pulling up to an awning in front of an impressive-looking art deco style building. I gaped out the window as Roberts put the car into neutral and got out, heading around to the back.

Carlo hung up the phone and slid out of the car when the uniformed doorman opened the passenger door for him. "Welcome back, sir," the doorman said with a smile as Carlo introduced me. "Welcome, sir," he said to me in turn. He was an older man, maybe in his early fifties, with a thick graying mustache and a trim build.

Carlo led me inside and we took the main elevator up while Roberts took our luggage to a service elevator. "This is where we'll stay whenever we're in the city—and Ferguson's the daytime doorman—he can get you a cab, will take deliveries for us and messages—if anyone comes by he'll call us and we have to give him permission to let them come up," he said once the elevator doors shut behind us. "Our primary home will be Spindrift, of course, but sometimes when I have late business in the city I spend the night here. And of course, any time you want to see a show or something, do some shopping—and it's too late to head back out to the Hamptons, this is your home, too." He smiled at me. "There's an extra set of keys upstairs in my office. I think you'll like the place."

I bit my lower lip. "Where all do you have homes, Carlo?" I asked, curious.

"Well, I did put in an offer on the house in Miami where I proposed—sentimental value and all that," he replied with a wink. "You liked that house, didn't you?"

"Well, yes, I did, but—" I cut myself off.

"But what?"

"It was so *big*."

He laughed. "Darling Mouse—Spindrift dwarfs that place." He stroked the side of my cheek. "I have to say, it is such a pleasure to watch the looks on your face! But we also have a nice flat in Paris, and a condo in Aspen—do you ski, by any chance?"

Paris? We have a place in Paris? I swallowed. "No, I've never skied."

"We'll have to remedy that this winter," he said as the elevator continued to rise. "We'll get you some lessons." He leaned over and kissed my cheek. "You really are a church mouse, aren't you?" He sighed. "I really am looking forward to showing you the world, Mouse. Later this summer, we'll go to Paris. Would you like that?"

Unable to say anything, I nodded. Paris? Going to Paris had been a dream of mine ever since reading *The Three Musketeers* when I was nine years old. I'd read a lot of French history, had even considered minoring in it in college. The Louvre, Notre-Dame, and the Eiffel Tower—I could spend weeks in Paris.

The elevator came to a stop, and the digital display said P3. The elevator doors opened into a white marble foyer, facing a large door. There was another door to the left with an exit sign above it, and in the other direction there was a large window with a spectacular view of the river. He unlocked the door and led me inside.

I gasped.

The apartment looked like something out of *House Beautiful.* The living room was enormous, and completely decorated in a minimalist modern style. The floor, ceilings, walls, and furniture were all white, with brass fixtures and black highlights. The walls were covered with stunning black-and-white prints in black metal frames—and I recognized the images as statuary and ruins from Rome and Greece. The opposing wall was all glass, and sliding glass doors led out to a wide terrace with a spectacular view facing Lower Manhattan. I shivered—the air-conditioning was on, and it was very cold inside—but I wandered through the entire apartment. There was a lovely dining room in the same décor, and a kitchen with an ice machine and every other conceivable gadget. There was an office—Carlo excused himself and went inside, shutting the door behind him as his phone started ringing again—and I looked through the two bedrooms. One was clearly a spare bedroom, and smelled unused. The other bedroom was enormous, with a huge wrought iron sleigh bed, an enormous walk-in closet, and a bathroom that was the size of my old apartment. I pulled the blinds open to discover a wall of glass, and sliding doors out to the end of the terrace.

My mouth wide open, I walked back into the living room as Roberts carried our suitcases in. He nodded to me as he placed them into the big bedroom, and excused himself. "Where do you stay when we're in the city, Roberts?" I asked, and as soon as the words were out I wondered if I wasn't supposed to talk about personal matters with the servants.

He smiled. "There's an apartment for me on a lower floor, sir. Call me if you need anything." And with a bow, he backed out of the penthouse.

That night I wore my charcoal Versace suit to the theater, where we saw *The Book of Mormon*, and afterward we had dinner at an incredibly expensive restaurant. Carlo turned his phone off, and I had his full attention. He introduced me to so many people I couldn't keep track of all their names, but I tried my best. Everyone was so friendly and kind—I couldn't help but remember Valerie's cruel words about me not fitting into this world with no small amount of satisfaction.

She'd been wrong—so very, very wrong about that.

And after dinner, we went back to the penthouse, where Carlo slowly undressed me, kissing me, and lifted me into the bed, where we made love as single men one last time, and I slept deeply nestled inside his strong arms.

The following morning we were married in the living room, by Judge O'Connor ("call me Ian") with Roberts and the judge's wife Faye as our witnesses. Afterward, a champagne brunch was delivered, and I discovered that I liked champagne—very much. By the time the O'Connors left us alone, I was quite tipsy—and Carlo carried me into the bedroom for our first time as a married couple.

The rest of the week passed in a blur, a magical wondrous blur. Carlo had business in the city, and while he was taking care of that, he sent me off shopping every day with my brand-new credit cards. It was necessary—once all my things had arrived from my old apartment, Carlo had gone through them all, shaking his head. He didn't allow me to keep any of it—just some socks and underwear and things to get me through until they could be replaced. The rest went into boxes, which Roberts took to Goodwill.

Despite the knowledge that I was now married to one of the wealthiest men in the city, I couldn't quite shake my habit of looking at price tags and worrying about how much money I was spending. Carlo found this amusing, and once said, "I suppose in about a year I'll look at your charge bills and look back with nostalgia."

When he could, he went shopping with me, picking out clothes without ever looking at a price and not even blinking at the astounding totals that went onto my new credit cards.

Every night he took me to a Broadway show and out for an amazing dinner afterward. Sometimes I could tell that people were looking at us—and all too often people came by our table to say hello and be introduced to me. They were invariably polite to me, but I could see by the quizzical looks on their faces they were wondering where I'd come from, and what Carlo could possibly see in me.

It didn't help much that so many of the stores in Manhattan carried Timothy's brand, Drawers.

I knew it shouldn't bother me, but seeing the underwear boxes and the amazing body pictured there always ruined my mood, reminding me of what Carlo was used to, what everyone was comparing me to—and undoubtedly finding me wanting.

No matter how much I reassured myself that he loved me, he wouldn't have married me if he didn't, I could never get past the notion that he was always comparing me to Timothy. He never talked about him—and I didn't want to bring up his previous husband.

I knew it was what his friends were thinking when they met me—that the quizzical looks and the stilted, oh-so-polite conversation that followed masked their curiosity.

One night I went to the restroom at some restaurant whose name I've long since forgotten, and heard two women talking about me in the hallway as they waited their turn for the restroom.

"Well, of course he's a cute thing," one sniffed, "but he looks like a *child*. I never thought Carlo's tastes ran in that particular direction."

"Well, it's a rebound thing, of course," the other replied in a smug tone. "I'm sure he's lonely, and figured some *companionship* is better than nothing. And one can hardly blame him for picking a sparrow after Timothy, can one? When one has been with one of the most beautiful men to live and breathe, well, anything else is going to be a disappointment. And this one seems pleasant enough. He certainly could have done far worse."

Fortunately, I heard a door open and the two women entered the ladies' room before I had to hear any more of it.

I stared at myself in the mirror in the bathroom. No, I wasn't a male model. No, I didn't have the kind of body that showed up on underwear boxes and ads. But was that all that mattered?

And worse, did Carlo think that way, too? Did he think he'd settled out of loneliness and the realization he would never replace or improve on Timothy?

Maybe Valerie was right, I thought as I splashed cold water on my face. *Maybe this whole thing was a big mistake.*

CHAPTER FIVE

We left the city for Spindrift early on Saturday morning.
I hadn't said anything to Carlo about what I'd heard those
women say in the restaurant. I'd decided to never bring Timothy up
to him—why keep stating the obvious, that I wasn't Timothy?

I was very glad I hadn't when, on our last night in Manhattan,
Carlo said his name in his sleep.

I'd spent that last afternoon in the city packing up everything
I'd purchased—some of my clothes I'd had the stores ship directly
to Spindrift—so that Roberts could take them with him that evening.
Carlo had a car in the city, parked in a garage, that he wanted to
return to Spindrift—and by sending Roberts ahead with our luggage,
on Saturday morning we could simply throw what was left into an
overnight bag and hit the road.

I was nervous and excited—Spindrift was going to be my
new home, and while I'd looked it up online, even seen pictures
of it—the thought of living in a house that made that huge place
where Carlo had proposed to me in Miami look like a cottage was
rather off-putting. And there were servants to get used to, as well. I
knew there were several live-in servants, including the remarkable
Carson, who ran the household. I was getting used to Roberts and
to having Ferguson take care of flagging cabs for me whenever I
needed one, but I wasn't so sure about actual live-ins.

We stayed in that last night and ordered Chinese food to be
delivered, and watched some old movies on a pay cable channel
while we ate. I'd had a wonderful week—other than overhearing

those two horrible women—and was sad to see it end. Carlo had been wonderful, more wonderful than I could have ever dared hope, and I was looking forward to getting settled in and started on our married life. I loved the penthouse, and always would—but it didn't seem real, perhaps because Carlo kept referring to the week as our honeymoon.

We went to bed early, since Carlo wanted to get off to an early start the next morning. As always, he wrapped his arms around me and we cuddled. I fell asleep almost immediately, as I had ever since we'd arrived. I'd been worried, having always slept alone, how I would adapt to sharing a bed once we were married—but my worries were for nothing. I slept better inside the comfort of Carlo's strong arms, with his warm body pressed against mine, than I ever had in my life. Every morning we awoke, almost at the same time, having barely moved in the night.

But this last night, Carlo pulled away from me, and slept restlessly, tossing and turning. At three in the morning his restlessness woke me, and I found myself staring at the digital clock on my nightstand, reading 3:03 a.m. in red lights. He tossed and turned again, and I wondered whether I should wake him, maybe he was having a bad dream, when he groaned and said out loud, "Timothy, why?"

I froze completely, and my heart almost stopped beating.

His voice sounded heartbroken, desolate, devastated, like it had been ripped from an anguished soul in constant torment.

I slipped out of the bed and walked barefoot into the kitchen. I poured myself a glass of water from the tap in the sink. My heart was pounding, and my General Tso's chicken felt like a lump of heavy lead in my stomach. I realized my hands were shaking as I raised the glass to my lips.

Get a hold of yourself, I told myself as I gulped the ice cold water down, *you knew all along he was still in love with Timothy. It doesn't mean he doesn't love you.*

Like you can compare to Timothy, Valerie's voice mocked me inside my head, echoed by the voices of those awful women.

I went back to bed, and Carlo seemed to have relaxed in his

dream state. As soon as I slipped back under the covers again, he moved toward me and his arms went around me again—but this time, they didn't feel as comforting as they always had before.

And I wasn't able to get back to sleep the rest of the night—and it seemed only minutes had passed when the alarm went off at six.

A hot shower and several cups of coffee didn't help, either. I was still yawning and sleeping when I headed down to the lobby of our building, carrying the overnight bag with our shaving kits and the dirty clothes we'd worn the night before. Ferguson politely asked me when I thought we might be back in the city, but I just shook my head and shrugged. He opened the door for me and I stepped out into the warmth of the morning. The gray morning sky was beginning to turn blue as the sun rose in the east, and the streets were empty. I only stood out on the sidewalk for a few moments before a red Jaguar convertible pulled up to the curb with Carlo at the wheel.

Ferguson seemingly materialized out of thin air and opened the passenger side door for me, and I slid into the seat with a weak smile for him. "Have a safe trip, sirs," he said, saluting smartly as he closed the door behind me.

"You can nap if you like," Carlo said over the roar of the wind as he sped through the city, heading for the Queensboro Bridge and the Long Island Expressway. "Didn't you sleep well?" His tone was sympathetic.

I shook my head while covering a yawn with my right hand.

"I'm sorry, I just hate driving in traffic," he replied as I yawned yet again and slid down in my seat, resting my head against the door. "And there isn't any at this hour. I suppose I could have let you leave with Roberts at a more decent hour, but I didn't want you to see Spindrift for the first time without me at your side."

I could hear the pride in his voice when he talked about Spindrift. Tired as I was, his words filled me with trepidation. I knew the shift in my feelings about the house had come about because he had said the dreaded name last night in his sleep—and I just knew that Timothy had fit Spindrift like he was born to live there. The servants would compare me to him, and I would be found lacking, the way those two horrible women had found me lacking. There were the neighbors as well, and Carlo's friends—they would be polite, of course, as were his friends in the city, but while the penthouse somehow had seemed like a kind of enchanted world where I could hide out in an ivory tower with my handsome prince, avoiding the dragons and sorcerers, Spindrift seemed different. Spindrift was reality, not a magic kingdom, but it couldn't be put off forever. If I was going to be married to Carlo and make the marriage a success somehow, I would have to do it at Spindrift. It was going to be our home; it had been home to the Romaniello family for generations, since it was built in the 1880s.

While the penthouse seemed to me to belong to Carlo, for some reason now, in my mind, Spindrift seemed to be Timothy's house, and I couldn't help but feel like an intruder, an outsider, an interloper who didn't belong there.

As the car made it over the bridge into Queens, I glanced over at Carlo, his face wrinkled in concentration as he focused on driving. *No, I can't say anything to him*, I decided, *I swore to never bring up Timothy to Carlo, and that was the smart way to handle it.*

I closed my eyes again and heard him again crying out Timothy's name in his sleep, in the bed he'd shared with Timothy first.

Learn to deal with it, I reminded myself, *he's already shared everything with Timothy.*

I must have fallen asleep. I woke with a start when the car swerved violently to the right and then back to the left again.

"Sorry," Carlo said cheerfully. "I was avoiding a rabbit, didn't mean to wake you."

I yawned and stretched. I could smell the sea, and the air was much cooler than it had been in the city. "How far is it now?"

"We're very close." He reached over and tousled my hair. "You were sound asleep, Mouse. I know I had a restless night—did that keep you awake?"

I shook my head and yawned again. "No, not at all," I lied. "I think I was just nervous about today is all."

His smile faded a bit, and he glanced over at me quickly before turning his attention back to the road. "But why? There's nothing to be nervous about, Mouse. Spindrift is going to be your home, and I know we're going to be very happy there, I promise you that."

"I'll be happy wherever you are," I answered.

"Don't sweet-talk me and try to change the subject," he replied. "Are you worried? There's no reason to be."

"I know," I said, wishing I could go back in time a few minutes so I could say something innocuous instead of what I had actually said. "I—I'm just not used to having servants, is all. It's just going to take some getting used to."

He laughed. "Is that what you're worried about, Mouse?" He reached over and patted my leg. "Within a few days I'm sure you won't even notice them anymore. And Carson is wonderful."

"Yes, you've said that before," I said. I'd heard him talking to Carson on the phone several times. "What exactly does he do?"

"He's invaluable, worth his weight in gold," Carlo went on. "He runs the house—kind of a combination majordomo and personal assistant. He'll take care of everything for you. If you want anything, just tell him and he'll take care of it. I don't know how I ever got by without him. He's almost like a part of the house now." He began drumming his fingers on the steering wheel. "He oversees the staff, makes sure the pantry and liquor is stocked, keeps the accounts—you'll of course take over signing the checks from me—I can't imagine how we'd get on without Carson." He shuddered. "I certainly hope we never have to."

"He sounds perfect." I replied, trying to stifle yet another yawn. "I'm sure we'll get along famously."

"He's been a godsend," Carlo said, smiling as I yawned. "There's coffee in a thermos in the glove box, if you need some, sleepyhead."

Gratefully, I retrieved it, pouring some into the lid. It was hot and black, and so strong that I gasped as I swallowed some—which made Carlo laugh. I drank the entire cup quickly, feeling the warmth flowing through my body. The cobwebs in my head began to clear somewhat—which was a good thing; I hardly wanted to meet the amazing Carson while groggy. I put the cup back on the thermos and put it back into the glove compartment.

We rode along in silence for a while, and we exited the highway, driving through the country on a narrow paved road. In a matter of moments, enormous houses came into view, standing at the end of long driveways and emerald lawns. One tall brick fence gave way to an enormous hedge, and Carlo turned where a paved drive penetrated out through the hedge. He pressed a remote control attached to the sun visor, and the enormous black iron gate began to creak open by sliding to the left.

Carlo leaned over and kissed me. "Welcome to Spindrift."

I smiled back at him, and he drove through the open gate—which began closing almost immediately.

I gasped.

The articles I'd read online, and the accompanying pictures, hardly prepared me for the reality. Photographs never give an indication of scale. I had known the house was big, but the reality took my breath away.

The lawn was enormous and perfectly manicured; not a single blade of the emerald green grass was the slightest bit taller than the rest. The lawn was boxed in on both the left and the right by the enormous hedge, which seemed to be the property line marker. The driveway made a big circle, leading around to the front of the house and then continuing on to the right around the side of the house. A huge fountain was directly centered in an enormous pond in the part of the lawn encircled by the driveway, and as we passed it I could see the statue in the center of the fountain was Apollo grasping on to Daphne as she turned into the tree. The water cascaded out of the top of her head, which more resembled a tree trunk.

But the house itself—it was breathtaking.

I knew that it had been built in 1880 and was modeled after a country house in England called Easton Neston. The house appeared, from looking at it, to only be two stories high—with enormously high ceilings on each floor. It was constructed of pink marble and granite, so that with the sun shining overhead it seemed to have a mild glow, like a sunset. Eight huge windows let the sun in on each floor, and there were stairs on either side of the porch that led to the enormous front doors. Two wings, made of red brick, branched off from the main portion of the house; chimneys towered about the house's magnificence. I knew the house had forty-eight rooms, and there were basement apartments for the servants who lived in. As the car came around the circle to one of the flights of stone steps leading up to the porch, I could see the sun reflecting on the glass windows—they were completely spotless—and I couldn't imagine how difficult it was to keep that glass clean.

I also knew that the main part of the house was primarily for entertaining—it was where the kitchen and dining room, the ballroom and the massive library were located—and the bedrooms were in the wings.

Carlo stopped the car and turned off the engine. "What do you think?"

I couldn't form any words.

I got out of the car and just stared, afraid to go any closer to it.

Carlo walked around the car and put his arm around me, giving a reassuring squeeze. "Your new home, darling Mouse. I hope you like it."

Still speechless, I followed him up the steps to the front door, made entirely of all glass panes. He unlocked the door and I followed him inside.

We entered into an enormous foyer, and my jaw dropped.

I'd seen pictures of the grand staircase, but again—they didn't prepare me for the awesome sight before me. It was a hanging staircase, made of gray marble with a polished oak banister, that led to a landing and continued up to the second floor after a 180 degree turn. Over the landing was another enormous window. About halfway up to the landing an alcove in the wall held a statue of a Greek god, and the wall alongside the stairs had been painted in oil—what appeared to be a scene from the Trojan War. The walls in the entryway were hung with enormous oil paintings in gilt frames, and at the opposite end I could see another glass door that led to a back gallery—and in the far distance, I could see the ocean.

"Close your mouth, dear, you look simple-minded," Carlo said absently as he crossed the foyer into the hallway.

I closed my mouth and followed.

Once in the hallway, I was stunned again at how enormous the place was. The hallway ran the length of the house, and at either end was another staircase. The first room that opened off the hallway was an enormous dining room, with the walls painted yellow and the floor gleaming wood. Two enormous chandeliers hung over the enormous dining table, with a carved wooden chair at each end and five chairs on each side. More enormous oil paintings hung on the walls, and through the windows on the opposite wall I could again see the deep blue of the Atlantic. An enormous fireplace divided the wall on the left, and a big white door in the far corner undoubtedly led into the kitchen.

From the left, I heard a noise and I turned.

Coming down the staircase at the far end of the hallway was a man in a black suit. He moved quickly, but so smoothly it seemed like he was barely moving at all. His black patent leather shoes clicked against the marble floor. As he drew nearer, I saw that he was bone thin, almost skeletal. His face was cadaverous, and he was so pale it was like he'd never been out in the sun. His hair was black as pitch and slicked back. His lips were thin and bloodless, and there seemed to be no lashes around his intense, large brown eyes. His age was indeterminate—he could have been anywhere between thirty and sixty.

"Carson!" Carlo smiled. "Good to see you again."

He stopped a few feet from us and inclined his head slightly to Carlo before turning his attention to me. His nostrils flared barely perceptibly, his eyes narrowing a fraction, and the corners of his mouth seemed to droop just a little bit. His intense eyes moved up and down, as though he couldn't believe what he was seeing.

In just a matter of seconds, I could tell I'd been judged and found wanting.

I shifted nervously from one foot to the other as Carson turned his attentions back to Carlo, and could feel the color coming up in my face.

"Mr. Romaniello, I took the liberty of making up the green suite for…"

Dismissed, I walked back to the entryway and to the glass door opening out onto the gallery. I could hear the sound of the waves in the distance, and I opened the door, taking a deep breath of the cold sea air. I stepped out onto the wide gallery that ran the length of the back of the house and sat down on a wrought iron chair. I could feel the cold metal through my clothes and shivered again, closing my eyes and listening to the waves and the cries of the gulls down by the beach.

A few moments later the door opened, and I turned with a smile, thinking it was Carlo, only to see Carson standing there, his hands clasped in front of his stomach. He inclined his head politely to me, but not before I could see the contempt blazing in his eyes. "If you will follow me, sir, I will show you to your rooms."

My face coloring yet again, I followed him back inside the house. Carlo was nowhere to be seen—but I didn't want to ask where he had gone.

Carson started speaking as we walked down the hallway toward the staircase on the east side of the hallway. "The house is of course divided into east and west wings by the center part of the house. I don't know if you know the house's history, but it was done this way deliberately, what the original builder called the public areas kept separate from the private areas for the family, which were the wings on either side," Carson said as he walked, his voice low and respectful—yet there was an edge to it that made me uncomfortable. "I have prepared the green suite for you. I trust you will find it most satisfactory." As we passed a closed door, he gestured to it. "That is your office."

"Office?"

He stopped walking and looked at me. "I simply assumed that, like Mr. Timothy, you would take charge of the household. Is that not to be the case?"

"No, no, of course," I stammered out quickly, my face getting hot. "What exactly does that mean?"

He turned and started walking again, but not before I noticed the strange look that flitted across his face before it became impassive again. "You of course approve all menus—if you have any special dietary needs, just let me know and I will pass them on to Delia—the chef—and you of course will be deciding what flowers to decorate with, and when we have houseguests what rooms will they be put in—I will prepare the checks to pay the household accounts for you to sign, and once a month we will go over the accounts together." He started up the stairs, and I followed. "I have gone ahead and prepared the accounts for you to look over—I assume you are too tired from all of your travel today, and tomorrow being Sunday, shall we meet on Monday morning, perhaps after breakfast, to go over the accounts?"

"Yes, that sounds wonderful," I replied, fighting down a rising panic.

"I oversee the day-to-day management of the staff," he continued. "Three times a week we have a landscaping crew come out to take care of the yard and the hedges, and three times a week we have a cleaning crew out to make sure the house is clean. The regular, live-in household staff includes myself, Delia the chef, and two maids, Olivia and Juana—Juana lives in the village and goes home to her family every evening. Olivia is assigned to the east wing, which means she is in charge of keeping your suite in order." His lips pursed again. "Olivia will turn down your bed every evening and will make it in the morning. She will take care of your laundry—be sure to let her know what can be laundered and what must be sent to the cleaners—and be sure to let her know what your preferences are for your toiletries." He stopped in front of a large oak door and pulled an enormous key ring out from the pocket of his jacket. He unlocked the door and held it open.

To say the room was sumptuous would be an understatement.

The walls were painted a dark emerald green, with a white ceiling and a gorgeous gilt chandelier hanging from the sixteen-foot ceiling. There was an enormous window on the opposite wall with a great view of the back lawn, and a glass door leading out to a balcony that ran the entire length of the room. The bed was an antique four-poster, with green velvet material draped over the top. There was a marble fireplace, and several oil paintings of forest scenes hung on the walls. There was a rolltop desk with the top open, and I could see my laptop resting in the direct center of the desktop.

A rolling chair was pushed up against the desk. The enormous bed was covered with a green velvet coverlet that hung over both sides. A small marble-top table sat in front of the window, with a cream-colored wingback chair on either side.

He crossed the room and opened a door into an enormous walk-in closet. "Olivia has already hung your clothes that were sent ahead, as you can see. Here"—he walked across the room to another door, which he opened—"this is your private bath. And of course the door leads to your own private balcony."

Tentatively I crossed the room and opened the glass door, stepping out onto the balcony. There was a small table and two chairs out there, and an ashtray sat in the center of the table. There was a tennis court to one side of the sprawling back lawn, and on the other side an enormous swimming pool with marble statues of maidens at five-foot intervals surrounding it. The lawn ended in a beach of white sand, and a pier reached out into the ocean, ending in what I assumed was a boathouse. In the back right corner of the yard, just before the beach, was a small wooden building painted dark blue. "What is that building, Carson?"

He stiffened. "That's Mr. Timothy's—" He stopped himself, a muscle twitching in his cheek. "That *was* Mr. Timothy's studio. Now, of course, it isn't used."

"Studio?"

"Mr. Timothy was an artist." The pride in Carson's voice was unmistakable. "There were those who thought he was nothing more than a handsome face and that he wasn't the true driving force behind his clothing line, but he was an artist. He painted and he was an excellent photographer. He used the studio to create. Since—" His voice broke.

"I'm sorry, Carson, I—"

"Quite, sir." His face became immobile and distant again. "No one has used the studio in over a year. I keep it clean myself—no one else is allowed in there. Is there anything else, sir?"

I bit my lower lip. "Where—where is Carlo's—Mr. Romaniello's closet?"

The right corner of his mouth twitched again, but his voice

remained completely neutral. "Mr. Romaniello's suite is three doors down the hall, sir. Lunch will be served promptly at noon in the solarium—I took the liberty of ordering a cold lunch for you and Mr. Romaniello. After lunch, we can meet in your office and go over the menus for next week." He moved to the door. "Is there anything else I can do for you, sir?"

My stomach growled. "I—I haven't had breakfast."

"I'll send Olivia up with a tray. Do you take coffee, sir?"

I nodded, and the door closed behind him.

I walked back into the bedroom and sat down on the bed, biting my lower lip. So, Carlo and I weren't going to share a bedroom? I wondered for a moment if he and Timothy had shared a bedroom, and fell backward onto the bed staring at the ceiling.

Of course they had. You don't marry someone as gorgeous as Timothy only to sentence him to lonely nights in a suite of rooms down the hall from your own. I heard Valerie's voice in my head again: *You don't belong to his world, and you're not going to fit in.*

She had been right, of course—Valerie made a point out of always being right. This house—I didn't know if I could ever get used to it. It was much grander than anything I was used to; this suite of rooms was bigger than my old apartment in Hell's Kitchen. I couldn't even imagine ordering servants around—being waited on. And Carson—I hadn't made a very good impression on him, had I? He had barely made an effort to conceal his obvious disdain for me. I could easily imagine him, even now, in the kitchen talking to the chef and the maid—Olivia, that was her name—about the enormous mistake Mr. Romaniello had made in marrying me.

I started when there was a light knock on the bedroom door, and it opened. The woman who entered looked like she was in either her late forties or early fifties. She had dark hair shot through with streaks of gray and was wearing a maid's uniform, a dark navy blue. She was carrying a silver tray that looked like it came from room service at a five-star hotel. There was a linen cloth covering it, a linen napkin folded around silverware, and a silver cover over the plate. There was a carafe of coffee, a little pitcher of cream, and a little porcelain caddy with packets of sugar and artificial sweetener.

A cut glass vase contained a single long-stemmed red rose. There was a glass of water and a small glass of orange juice. She smiled at me and set the tray down on the surface of the table below the window next to the French doors out to the balcony.

She turned and smiled at me. "I hope you don't mind, sir, but we assumed you didn't want to eat in the bed." She wiped her hands on her apron. "I'm Olivia, sir. Welcome to Spindrift. If there's anything you need, or anything I can do to make you more comfortable, just let me know. My days off are Wednesdays and Sundays—on those days Juana will take care of you."

"Thank you." I wasn't sure what else I should say, so I got off the bed and hesitated, not sure what else to do.

She walked over to the door and paused. "Oh, lunch is usually served at noon and dinner at seven whenever Mr. Carlo is in the house, those are his preferences. Breakfast is at eight, but of course if you'd rather have any meal in here, just ring the kitchen and let Delia know, and I'll serve you in here. You should have plenty of fresh towels—I laundered all of them yesterday afternoon, and if there are any particular toiletries you prefer—"

I nodded. "I'll let you know, Olivia."

The door shut behind her, and I sat down to my breakfast. The coffee was strong and delicious, and the strawberry preserves were the best I'd ever had. Once I finished and placed the tray outside my door, I lay down on the bed and fell asleep as soon as my head hit the soft pillow.

CHAPTER SIX

I awoke after a little over an hour, feeling completely rested and refreshed. I sat up in my bed, yawning and stretching. The sound of the waves and the gulls outside brought a smile to my face. The sun was shining, and I'd left the glass door ajar to let in the breeze from the sea. I had slept on top of the covers, and the green velvet felt amazing against my skin. The bed was just the right combination of soft and firm—easily the most comfortable bed I'd ever slept in.

If I was going to have to sleep alone, at least the bed was good.

I shook my head. *You don't know that you're going to be sleeping alone*, I reminded myself, trying to not go to a negative place. *There's any number of reasons for us to have separate suites. Maybe all rich people live like this—it's not like there aren't plenty of rooms in this place to go around.*

It really hadn't sunk in to me as yet that this enormous palace, Spindrift, was supposed to be—was going to be—my home. It didn't seem real. None of it seemed real—it was like the greatest dream of all time, and I couldn't help but feel I was going to be jarred out of it by the harsh sound of my alarm clock.

I got up from the bed and walked across the room to the balcony door. I stepped out, deeply inhaling the salty air. The breeze was chilly, and I leaned on the railing, looking to either side. The hedges were high enough and far enough from the house so that I couldn't see into the yards of the houses on either side of Spindrift—which probably meant they couldn't see into ours, either.

As I stood there, turning my face up to the sun, the almost dreamlike state I'd been in since we drove through the gates faded and I became overwhelmed by a sense of unreality. I didn't belong here, I would never fit in—this wasn't the kind of place where people like me lived. I belonged back in my tiny apartment, or the dusty cluttered house back in Kansas. I was a fraud, an interloper, and no matter how I tried, I would never be comfortable thinking of Spindrift as my home.

I gripped the railing so hard my knuckles turned white. I was trembling, and black dots danced in front of my eyes. I closed my eyes.

As long as Carlo loves me, I can live anywhere.

I took a deep breath and got my nerves back under control.

I went back inside and closed the door, leaning back against it as I surveyed my enormous suite.

It was, I reflected, so incredibly different from my little box of an apartment, with its water spots on the ceiling, the cracked plaster walls, and the roaches scurrying into cracks and crevices whenever I turned on a light.

This was *posh*, for want of a better word. All the furniture was expensive, and most likely priceless antiques. My heart sank. I should probably be able to not only recognize whether something was an antique or not, I should be able to identify whether it was—I don't know, a Hepplewhite or Louis XIV. I took some more deep breaths to ward off the rising panic. *Well, you might not know now, but you can learn,* I reassured myself. *I can learn about all of these things. Antiques, wine—all of it can be learned. I just need to get some books. Timothy probably didn't know any of this stuff before he came here, either.*

Timothy.

A horrifying thought crossed my mind—surely this hadn't been Timothy's suite?

Don't be ridiculous, of course it wasn't. Carlo wouldn't do that.

I bit my lip and pushed those thoughts out of my mind. Being paranoid wasn't going to help me get settled—it was going to be hard enough getting used to all of this without worrying about Timothy.

He was dead and gone.

With that settled for now in my mind, I walked into the bathroom and glanced at my face in the huge mirror.

I looked out of place in the enormous bathroom.

"I belong here," I said out loud, raising my chin defiantly. "This is my home now."

Feeling a little better, I opened the frosted glass shower door. The shower was enormous—there were showerheads on three of the walls, and the walls and floor were covered in tile the color of green jade. There was a dial on the wall directly opposite the shower door, and I turned it to the right, from Off through the blue to the red. Powerful jets of hot water sprayed me from the three sides. I stepped back out, dripping on the green tile floor, and opened the door to the linen closet. A long green robe hung on a hook on the inside of the door, and the shelves inside were piled high with fluffy green towels. I grabbed one and a washcloth and undressed quickly. I stepped back into the shower, the hot water caressing my body. Steam was rising, and a fan in the ceiling kicked on, sucking it all upward. Behind me the door fogged up, and I closed my eyes and just enjoyed the sensation.

It was *heavenly*.

Finally, my skin reddened and scrubbed raw, I turned the dial back to Off. With a gurgle, the water stopped flowing and I opened the door, reaching for the enormous towel I'd left just outside on the floor. I wrapped it around my waist and, dripping, stepped over to the sink. Amazingly, the mirror hadn't fogged up. My shaving kit was sitting on the counter next to one of the sinks. I turned the hot water on and shaved. When I finished, I blew my hair dry before toweling off. I hung the towel over the shower door and pulled on the robe.

Carlo was sitting on the bed when I walked back into the bedroom.

He smiled at me. "How do you like your new home?"

"It's a little overwhelming," I said honestly, returning his smile and feeling a little foolish. He was so handsome, and of course he loved me—I didn't need to be so damned insecure. "But I'll get used to it, I suppose."

I walked over to the dresser and opened the top drawer. All the underwear I'd bought at Macy's on Thirty-fourth Street in the city was neatly folded, organized by style and color. I hesitated for a moment and berated myself again as a fool. *He's your husband, he's already seen you naked.*

Still, I left the robe on as I pulled on a pair of pale blue boxer briefs—Calvin Klein, not Drawers. I hadn't bought any of that brand, and never would again.

"I wanted to let you know I won't be here for lunch," he went on. "I have a business meeting at the yacht club—I'd take you, but you'd just be bored, and I don't know how long it will take."

I frowned and turned to face him. "I could never be bored around you, Carlo."

He laughed. "It's a nice sentiment, but trust me, you'd be bored in a hurry. No worries, though—Joyce is coming by for lunch. She's anxious to meet you."

It took me a moment to remember Joyce was his younger sister.

"Now, now, Mouse, don't look like that. She'll love you. You look like you're about to face a firing squad."

I smiled back at him, but my stomach was churning. "I'm looking forward to meeting her."

"She and her kids are my only family—besides you, of course." He looked pensive for a moment, but then his face cleared. "And she'll be around to keep you company when I have to go out of town." He sighed. "I'm sorry to go away so soon."

I bit my lower lip. I'd forgotten he had to go to the West Coast on Monday morning for a board meeting—he'd mentioned it briefly over dinner one night in the city, the night I'd heard those horrible women comparing me to Timothy, which was why it had slipped my mind. He was only going to be gone a few days—and I'd be "bored" if I went with him.

Get used to this, I reminded myself. *He's going to have business meetings and will have to travel without you plenty of times. Getting upset isn't going to change that.*

It was true, but it didn't make me feel any better.

But I wasn't going to let him see that. I was determined to be a good husband, and making him feel guilty about leaving me behind wasn't a part of that plan. He already thought I was young—so I was definitely not going to behave in any way that could be construed as childish.

But I had to know one thing.

"This suite is amazing," I said, pulling on a pair of tan cargo shorts. I tossed the robe on the bed and pulled on a pink pullover. "But why aren't we sharing one?"

He got up and put his arms around me, pulling me close and kissing me on the cheek. "Oh, Mouse, you surely don't think I don't want—" He laughed softly, and nuzzled my neck. "No, I get business calls at all hours of the night, and I'm also a bit of a restless sleeper—by keeping separate rooms, your sleep won't ever be disturbed. But never worry, Mouse—I'll be in here so often you'll probably be relieved when I do have to go out of town."

"That'll never happen," I said sincerely.

"Oh, dear Mouse," he replied, kissing me on the cheek again. "All right, I need to stop dawdling and get to the club. I'm not sure when I'll be home—but if I am going to be late for dinner, I'll call." He paused at the door. "Your new laptop is on the desk."

I turned and saw a gleaming MacBook Pro sitting on the rolltop desk. It was the most expensive version—far nicer than the battered old iBook I'd been using.

"Of course, you have a desktop computer in your office downstairs, but I thought you might prefer writing in your room, and that laptop you were using—well, let's just say it's seen better days," he went on.

I looked back at him with a smile. "You're spoiling me."

"That's the plan. Have a good time with Joyce—and if you have any questions about anything, just ask Carson."

The door shut behind him, and I sat down at the desk and raised the lid, bringing it to life. I connected to the Internet and checked my e-mail—and smiled as I deleted them all. They were all pertaining to *Street Talk*, or spam—absolutely nothing I needed to pay any attention to.

But there was one from Valerie. I clicked it open.

Hello,

I hope you didn't take the things I said to you in Miami the last time we saw each other too personally. I stand by what I said, of course—since your father is dead there isn't anyone to look out for you. I still think this marriage is a big mistake—but stranger things have happened, and of course if you ever need someone to talk to, you have my numbers.

Perhaps the next time you're in the city, we could have lunch? I'd like that very much. I do care about you— even if you don't think I do—and I feel like I owe it to your father to periodically check in and see how you're doing.

Fondly,
Valerie

I smiled to myself and clicked on the Reply button.

I wasn't fooled by her friendly e-mail—she clearly wanted something. I typed out the following reply:

Valerie:

Thank you for your kind e-mail. I'm getting settled into Spindrift—which is a bit overwhelming, in all honesty—and don't worry; I appreciate your candor.

I would love to have lunch the next time I'm in the city.

Talk soon!

I clicked Send just as there was a light knock on the door. "Come in," I called, closing the laptop.

Olivia poked her head in. "I'm sorry to disturb you, sir, but I thought you should know that Mrs. Sullivan is here and waiting for you in the library."

Mrs. Sullivan? I drew a blank at first before remembering that was Joyce Romaniello's married name.

But before I could say anything a small black, white, and tan dog squeezed through the door and came flying across the room, jumping into my lap and trying to lick my face.

"And who is this pretty girl?" I cooed, falling immediately in love as she put a paw on either shoulder, her tail wagging madly, and licked my right ear.

"Minette! Get down, you bad girl! I'm so sorry, sir," Olivia came hurriedly into the room, her face flushed. "She's—"

"Adorable." I cut Olivia off. I smiled at her over Minette's head. "Whose dog is this?"

"Technically, I suppose she's Mr. Carlo's now." She started to say something else but cut herself off.

I knew what she had stopped herself from saying, and hugged the dog. I'd always wanted a dog, but my father had been allergic, and the tiny shoebox apartment I'd lived in was no place for a pet. And I didn't care in the least that Minette had been Timothy's dog. She obviously liked me, and she was without question the most adorable dog I'd ever seen. "What kind of dog is she? Some kind of spaniel, clearly."

"A King Charles Cavalier spaniel," Olivia replied, smiling. "Oh, I'm so glad you like dogs, sir. Mr. Carlo is so rarely here—and she gets so lonely, you know. A dog needs affection."

Minette stopped trying to lick me and jumped up on the bed. She curled up on one of my pillows, sighing contentedly and closing her eyes.

"I guess she's going to stay here," I said. "Mrs. Sullivan is in the library, you said? And the library is where, exactly?"

"On the first floor, sir, it's the last door before the foyer. You can either go down the west wing staircase and walk up the hallway toward the front door, or you go down the upstairs hallway and take the grand staircase—turn left at the bottom and it's the first door, sir." The door shut behind her.

I took a deep breath and tried to remember what Carlo had told me about his sister, which wasn't much.

Joyce was a few years younger than Carlo and had made what he called a disastrous first marriage. It had ended badly, leaving her with two small children—I tried but couldn't for the life of me remember their names. She had remarried, and the children were now off at college—the older, I remembered, was at Stanford and the younger was at Tulane in New Orleans. Her remarriage had been much more successful.

But in truth, there was nothing Carlo could have said that would have prepared me for the force of nature that was his younger sister.

I left my room and took the stairs down to the first floor. As I walked toward the library, I couldn't help feeling overwhelmed again. Spindrift was enormous. The hallway was wide, and the floor was marble. Elegant antique tables and chairs were placed at intervals between enormous doors, and huge oil paintings hung on the walls. Antique statuary occupied the occasional alcove. It was like walking down the hallway of an art museum, decorated tastefully for the enjoyment of people who paid the price of admission to be led around by uniformed guides who would explain the provenance of each piece of art in a reverent, hushed tone.

It was more museum than home.

I opened the door and caught my breath as I crossed the threshold into the library.

The room was a book lover's paradise. The room was two stories high, and the ceiling was tinted glass. Each wall was lined with shelves that ran almost all the way up to the roof. There was a door leading in from the second floor, with a gallery running around the opening to the first floor. Wheeled ladders that ran on tracks stood in each corner, so one could climb up to retrieve a book from any level. There were enormous mahogany tables placed at intervals with expensive-looking gold lamps directly centered on each one. There were no windows other than the amazing skylight overhead.

And I knew I was going to spend hours in this room.

A woman was examining the titles on a shelf directly opposite the doorway, and she turned when she heard me enter the room, and smiled, crossing the room at a quick clip, her rubber-soled tennis shoes slapping softly against the marble floor.

Joyce Romaniello Sullivan was like no one I'd ever known before. I was quaking inside with nerves and fear as she walked toward me, certain I would make a terrible impression on Carlo's closest living relative. I would have much preferred to meet her with Carlo at my side for moral support, but that wasn't going to happen. Much as I wanted to flee in terror and hide in my rooms, and put this off, I couldn't very well do that. I took some deep breaths to calm my roiling stomach.

But the enormous smile on her face quelled my nerves as she drew nearer.

"But, darling, Carlo didn't tell me you were *adorable!*" she exclaimed, grabbing me with both hands and pulling me into a hug. "Welcome to Spindrift, and to the family!"

The hug was tight, to the point I worried one of my ribs might crack under the pressure. Joyce was about five-eight, and she had the trim, fit figure of a woman half her age. Her thick reddish hair was pulled back into a French braid that dropped halfway down her back. She blinked at me, stepping back and looking me up and down. Her round gray eyes were warm, framed by long lashes. Her gold-framed glasses fit her face perfectly, complementing the strong cheekbones she shared with Carlo. Her wide smile, exposing her almost impossibly white teeth, never faltered for a second. She was wearing a form-fitting white tennis dress that reached halfway down her muscular thighs, which were tanned a golden brown. She had a full bosom; the low-cut neckline showed off her tanned, deep cleavage. She was also wearing white tennis shoes, with those little white socks with a little pom-pom at the ankle to keep them from slipping down inside her shoes.

"DON'T mind the way I'm dressed—don't judge ME!" she

warned with mock severity, wagging an index finger with a perfect French manicure at me. She placed emphasis on certain words when she spoke—like the entire word was capitalized in her head. "I HAVE to play tennis this afternoon, and I didn't WANT to cut my visit ONE minute short to have to run home and CHANGE. Oh, dear, you're SPEECHLESS in HORROR at my CLOTHES." She looked stricken.

"No, no really, I'm not," I insisted.

"Are you overwhelmed?" She waved a hand around. "Spindrift CAN be a bit MUCH at first, until you get USED to it. The FIRST time I brought my husband here he COULDN'T keep his mouth closed—he looked like a FISH gasping for AIR the whole time." She rolled her eyes as she took me by the hand and led me out of the library and down the hall to a smaller, more intimate dining room than the one I'd seen earlier. A Latina woman in a maid's uniform, who I assumed was Juana, was setting a tray of luncheon meats down on a sideboard, and the table was laid with two place settings. Juana excused herself and disappeared out a side door. Joyce hadn't stopped talking as we walked—talking so rapidly I honestly couldn't keep up with her as she gently pushed me into a chair and sat down next to me.

"—and of course my children will be home for the summer soon, and they're dying to meet their new uncle, of course they can be dreadful beasts but they're actually quite lovely, really, they turned out far better than anyone could have hoped given what their father was like—he was certainly a piece of work, as my mother used to say, but he's long gone and not my problem anymore—well, any of our problem, really—the fact he has absolutely NO interest in his children certainly TELLS you WHAT kind of man he WAS, doesn't it? WHAT was I thinking? Ah, well, I was BARELY more than a CHILD myself." She paused for breath, her face clouding at the mention of her first husband, but she shook it off quickly and started up again. "But then, YOU'RE little more than a CHILD yourself, aren't you?"

I inhaled sharply, but before I could say anything she looked mortified and her hand flew up to her mouth.

"Oh my GOD, I SWEAR sometimes I should just have my tongue AMPUTATED and be DONE with it." She shook her head, the heavy braid swinging behind her back. "I'm SO sorry, darling, CAN you ever forgive me? Thank GOD Carlo isn't here—what a SCOLDING he'd give me—and deservedly SO. You MUST forgive me. My only EXCUSE is I'm so worried about making a POSITIVE impression on you that I don't KNOW what I'm saying. You MUST think I'm a perfectly AWFUL creature with NO manners. PLEASE forgive me, and you must PROMISE me you won't BREATHE a word of my HORRIBLE behavior to Carlo!"

I couldn't help myself—the shock wore off and I started laughing. "You—were—worried—about making a good impression on *me*?"

"Of course!" She goggled at me, and started laughing with me. "I'm making an UTTER fool of myself, as always." She wiped tears out of her eyes. "Come on, darling, let's have a sandwich. I'm STARVING."

I made myself a turkey sandwich and sat down, filling my glass from the pitcher of iced tea. I was suddenly ravenous—all I'd thus far had to eat had been the toast. The bread tasted fresh, and the turkey was delicious.

"I don't SUPPOSE you play tennis by ANY chance?" she asked me between bites of her roast beef.

"I've never played," I replied, washing down another bite with some tea, "but I'm afraid I'm not very athletic."

"Nonsense—you're YOUNG, young people can do ANYTHING." She winked at me as she dabbed at some horseradish sauce that had dribbled on her chin. "They JUST don't realize it, of course."

"I'm afraid I might be the one exception to that rule, Joyce," I demurred with a slight shake of my head. "Really, I am embarrassingly uncoordinated."

She shook her head. "I WON'T hear of it, especially with that LOVELY tennis court on the grounds HERE. My husband doesn't PLAY, so WHENEVER I need a partner for mixed doubles, I'm ALWAYS stuck playing with the most TERRIBLE players—the ones NO ONE else wants as a partner, and we ALWAYS lose." She winked at me. "I HATE to lose. And I know JUST the pro who can COAX the tennis champion from you—his name is Chris and he's MARVELOUS, simply MARVELOUS. Why, a few sessions with him and he IMPROVED my serve—you wouldn't KNOW I was the same player as the old Joyce." She fished a phone out of her purse and pressed a button. When it beeped, she spoke into it. "Remind me this afternoon to CHECK with Chris Thoresson to SEE if he's got SOME time for Mouse." She slid the phone back into her purse once it confirmed the reminder message. She frowned. "Now, that's THAT." She glanced at her watch and blanched. "Where DID the time go?" She shoved the rest of the sandwich into her mouth. "I HAVE to be on my way, I forgot, I have to—oh, you don't CARE about any of that." She leaped to her feet, tossed the straps of her bag over her shoulder, and kissed me on the cheek. "I'll call you ONCE I confirm with Chris, and when Carlo's back you two simply MUST come over for dinner—and I'll try to stop by and see you—mustn't have you getting LONELY in this big old place by yourself."

And she was gone out the door, just like that, leaving me feeling like I'd just weathered a tornado.

I shook my head and finished my turkey sandwich. I liked Joyce, very much, and if her husband and children were *anything* like her, I'd married into a very nice new family, indeed.

Juana came in to clear as I finished, and the moment I stepped out into the hallway, I heard a discreet cough just to my right. Carson had materialized without a sound—which was more than a little unnerving. I smiled at him, but he just looked at me, his face completely expressionless and distant. His eyes, though, were cold and one corner of his mouth was twitching, as though he couldn't decide whether to laugh at me or just sneer. "I was wondering if I could have a moment of your time, sir."

"Of course." My smile faded under his withering stare, and I felt my face starting to redden. "What do you need, Carson?"

His facial expression didn't change, but his eyes somehow grew colder and more contemptuous. "I had placed the menu selections on your desk, and was wondering if you'd made any decisions? Delia would like to get to the market soon and needs to know what to purchase. Mr. Carlo had requested prime rib for dinner this evening, so she needs to get the marketing out of the way soon, or else the meal won't be ready to be served at seven sharp." He folded his hands together in front of his chest. "And Mr. Carlo always wants dinner to be served promptly at seven."

Flustered and confused, I stammered out. "My—desk? I didn't see anything—"

"The desk in your office, sir." His tone dripped scorn.

The office.

I bit my lower lip. "I—I'm sorry, Carson, I didn't think—surely anything you would select would be fine."

This time he did allow his lip to curl. "I'm afraid that just wouldn't do, sir."

Mortified, I knew exactly what he was thinking—*Mr. Timothy would have never asked a servant to choose the menus.* "I'll do it right now, of course, Carson," I said quickly and walked down the hall as fast as I could without running. I opened the door to the office and closed it behind me.

I let out my breath and walked over to the desk, sitting down. On the blotter in the center was the list. I scanned it quickly—everything looked fine, although there were some things I had no earthly idea what they were—and so I scrawled my initials next to each meal. Someone knocked on the door and Carson entered silently when I called "come in." He walked over to the desk and without a word took the list from me. He paused at the door. "Do you have any instruction regarding the flowers, sir?"

"No, they're fine as they are." I didn't look up at him. "Just keep using the same ones."

One of his eyebrows went up briefly and came back down.

I swallowed. "But I'd like roses in my bedroom. Yellow ones."

"Yellow roses?" He bowed his head slightly, his eyes glittering with contempt.

What's wrong with yellow roses?

I took a deep breath. "Yes."

"Of course, sir." The door closed silently behind him.

The silence was overwhelming. Other than the waves, there was no sound anywhere in the house.

I was trembling.

I was acutely aware that I was in a room that used to be Timothy's sole territory, and I opened the center drawer, curious about my predecessor. The drawer smelled vaguely of the cologne I instantly recognized as his signature fragrance, the one I'd stopped wearing so Carlo wouldn't be reminded. There was stationery, similar to the stationery I'd found in the penthouse, only here there were almost matching envelopes and note pads, all with his signature in raised print across the top. There was also a box of business cards, but all they said on them was *Timothy Burke*. I closed the drawer, and opened the top drawer on the right.

All it contained was a framed photograph of Carlo and Timothy. Both were wearing tuxedos, and they were smiling into each other's eyes, their arms around each other.

I touched the glass.

He was so beautiful.

They looked so happy.

I bit my lower lip and put the picture back.

I got up and walked over to the bookcases to see what was in them, and when I walked past a small side table my hand accidentally hit a china statue of a dog that looked just like Minette and it fell, smashing to pieces on the floor.

I stared at it, mortified.

Surely it was Timothy's, just as Minette had been his.

It was probably priceless as well.

Quickly, I gathered the broken pieces and hid them in the bottom drawer of the desk. After all, this was my office now—Carlo would never come in here and need never know I'd broken something of Timothy's.

I left the room and hurried upstairs as quickly as I could.

CHAPTER SEVEN

Carlo left Spindrift the following morning, and didn't return until Wednesday.

He stayed in my room the night before he left and woke me to tell me good-bye. There was a poignant sadness in his face that touched me deeply, and I managed to hold my own emotions in check until the door had shut behind him. Then I gave vent to my own tears, burying my face in the pillow and sobbing until I was exhausted and the emotional gave way to the practical. I was going to have to get used to being separated from him, and rather than moping around feeling sorry for myself, I would use the time productively, to learn the things I needed to know so I wouldn't embarrass him in front of his friends and business associates—and there was that enormous library full of books. Surely, there must be books in there with the information I desired.

Carlo called me several times a day, of course—which never failed to make me feel warm inside and delighted me no end. I looked forward to the calls, and my cell phone was never out of my reach. I missed him terribly—the days were bearable as I could distract myself—but the nights were lonely and awful for me up in the green suite. I missed the feel of his arms around me, his lips pressed against mine, the warmth of his skin, and his unique smell. He was always apologetic, promising to make it up to me—which of course was ridiculous. He already thought I was little more than a child—so I wasn't about to let him know how much it hurt me that he went away so soon after we came home to Spindrift. I was proud of myself for behaving so maturely about the entire thing—which wasn't easy.

Yet despite knowing and accepting the reality of what my marriage was going to be like, there was a small, selfish part of me that *did* feel wounded and abandoned. I had plenty of practice, of course, in ignoring that part of my personality; I'd been doing it my entire life. That was the small child deep inside who resented the father who wasn't interested in letting me be a child, who listened with burning jealousy as other kids talked about trips to circuses and amusement parks and Disney films or television programs they enjoyed watching—all things I was never allowed to enjoy. My father thought he was being "enlightened" by not treating me as a child; he rather treated me as an adult who hadn't quite matured physically yet. On the one hand, I was grateful to him for this—this enabled me to get good grades because I retreated into books to avoid conversations with other children—conversations that would ultimately result in their discovery how strange and different from theirs my home life actually was. With Carlo in New York and with endless hours to fill without him at Spindrift, I found myself with the time to reflect on my childhood and my years in college, and ultimately found them wanting on many different levels.

But recognizing how my father failed me by not allowing me to have a normal childhood didn't mean that I should give rein to the willful petulance of the angry child within. Carlo was my husband and he was opening an entire new life full of possibilities to me. So no matter how much that child wanted to pout and cry and demand he return at once, no matter how sorry that child wanted to feel for itself at being abandoned by his husband so soon after the wedding, I would not permit that child to speak to Carlo on the telephone. I read books and learned about the art in the house—and found myself staggered by their value. I watched films on the enormous flat-screen television mounted on the wall in the den. I explored the house, determined to learn once and for all which door led to which room, so that I wouldn't get lost or confused.

There was a door on the second floor in the east wing that was always locked. I asked Juana about it, but all she would say was, "Ask Carson."

And of course, I wasn't about to do that—no matter how curious I was about what was behind that door.

I kept my distance from Carson, and he did the same. There were, of course, times when we had to speak to each other—matters about the house that couldn't be avoided—but he was always icily polite to me. I tried to convince myself that his disdain for me was merely a figment of my imagination. I reasoned, alone in the library or while walking Minette, that it was just my insecurities and worries about my new life as co-master of Spindrift.

Then I would talk to him, and I could see the dislike in his eyes, hear the scorn dripping from his oh-so-polite voice.

Joyce was true to her word, and I began my tennis lessons on Monday afternoon. She could barely contain her excitement when she called to tell me.

"You're going to LOVE Chris, he's an AMAZING teacher, and before you know it we'll be WINNING the mixed doubles at the tennis club this summer!"

I rather doubted that, but it was hard to get a word in edgewise when Joyce was excited.

It was hot on Monday afternoon when I walked out to the tennis court for my first lesson. Joyce had asked me my sizes, and Monday morning bags of tennis clothing had arrived from the pro shop at the tennis club. When I called to thank her, she told me "You can THANK me by being tournament ready by the END of the summer."

The tennis pro, Chris Thoresson, towered over me when he introduced himself. He was at least six foot four, and quite handsome, actually. He was very muscular with broad shoulders and thick legs, a narrow waist and a flat stomach. He was wearing a U.S. Open baseball cap, but I could see he had dark brown hair. His voice was deep, and he had enormous hands—mine was lost inside his strong grip when we shook hands. He also had the most remarkably blue eyes. They were deep blue, but seemed lit from behind. I was very quick to point out to him that I knew next to nothing about tennis and was terribly uncoordinated.

Joyce had included a racket with the clothes, and he very patiently taught me the different grips of the racket, what they were for, and how to swing it properly. That first day I didn't hit a single ball. He was very insistent that I needed to learn how to hold my racket properly, how to switch grips and the different strokes—forehand, backhand, slice, and overhand—and get to the point where I could switch the grips without having to think about it first. Once I had mastered the grips and the stroke, then and only then would he let me start swinging at an actual ball. He was an excellent teacher, explaining every aspect of the game to me in his deep, friendly voice so that it all made sense to me. He was incredibly patient—unlike all the PE teachers whose classes I'd suffered through as a child—and by the end of that first hour I was quite surprised to realize that I was looking forward to my next lesson.

"Just keep practicing your grips and your strokes," he said with a cheerful smile as we scheduled another lesson for Wednesday afternoon, "and you'll be playing before you know it." He took a swig from his bottle of water and wiped sweat from his forehead with a small towel. "To be honest, I never thought I'd ever be out on the court at Spindrift again."

My heart sank. I was positive he had not been here giving Carlo lessons, and as he continued talking, I was proven right.

Once again, *he* was there first.

"You're nothing like Timothy," he said, shaking his head. "Timothy was too impatient and always let his temper get the best of him." He shrugged. "He wanted to be a championship level player immediately, and it simply doesn't work that way. Tennis is no different than anything else—you have to practice, and the more you do, the better you get. But things always came easily for him, I guess, and he wasn't used to having to work at anything." His face changed, and he scowled. "He was kind of difficult."

"Oh," I replied politely, dying to know what he meant but not knowing precisely how to ask.

He looked off into the distance for a moment, remembering,

and then smiled again with a little shake of his head. "I'm sorry—you don't care about any of that, of course. Anyway, make sure you practice your grips and strokes, and I'll see you on Wednesday morning."

He slung his tennis bag strap over his shoulder and strolled off around the house.

What did he mean? I wondered as I showered. *Difficult? It seemed like he didn't like Timothy very much.*

I'm not sure what it says about me as a person, but it raised my spirits a bit to know that not everyone thought Timothy was *perfect.*

Minette, of course, was a godsend. I showered her with affection, and she more than returned it. Whenever I was feeling lonely, all I had to do was call her and she would come on the run, tongue hanging out and panting, and would jump all over me and lick me to death. She would follow me everywhere if I would let her. She slept in the bed with me, curling up on the pillow next to mine, and that made me feel somewhat less lonely. Several times a day I would put her leash on her and we would go for a walk around the grounds. The sound of me getting the leash always excited her, and I couldn't help but smile at her delight. Seriously, how could anyone be depressed or sad with such an adorable dog who was so clearly delighted to be in your company?

Every time I hugged her and she licked my face, I wondered what I would do without her.

On Tuesday morning we were out for our usual walk when I heard dogs barking on the other side of the hedge, from the house on the east side. I wasn't paying attention. I was lost in thought, going over the grips and strokes in my head again. Minette never really tugged on the leash, so I'd gotten into the habit of holding on to it loosely—but as soon as the dogs began barking next door she leaped forward. She pulled the leash right out of my hand and took off across the lawn toward the hedge and the barking dogs. Calling her name, I ran after her, but wasn't able to catch her before she wiggled under the hedges and into the neighboring yard. I couldn't fit underneath—there was barely enough room for Minette—and cursing under my breath, I forced my way through thick branches that slashed at my arms and face. When I made it through, I saw Minette happily playing with two other spaniels with the same coloring.

"Well, there you are at last," sniffed the older woman holding the leashes of the other two dogs. "Minette! Hetty! Charlie! Sit!"

All three dogs immediately stopped playing and sat, staring at her with their heads cocked to one side.

"I'm so sorry," I said, grabbing Minette's leash and pulling her away from the other dogs. Minette gave me such a sad, mournful look that I felt like a monster.

"For heaven's sake," the old woman snapped, clearly exasperated. "I wasn't talking about Minette—she's always welcome here. These are her parents, you foolish young man."

"Oh." I felt myself blushing again. "I'm sorry—"

"You're the new husband, aren't you?" She peered at me over the top of her glasses. She stepped forward and stuck out her right hand. "Eleanor Chamberlain, but my friends call me Nell."

I shook her hand and told her my name.

She was remarkably tall, and her white hair was tucked into a bun perched on the back of her head. Her glasses were thick, making her brown eyes seem much more enormous than they actually were. Her face was wrinkled, and some loose skin hung from underneath her chin. Her hands were brown with protruding blue veins, but her nails were perfectly manicured. She was wearing a loose-fitting dress of white cotton, but her figure was still quite trim and her bare legs looked strong. She was wearing brown leather sandals on her feet.

She was still peering at me like I was a bug under a microscope. "You're quite a bit different than the last one, aren't you?" she finally said with a snort, just as the silence was getting a bit uncomfortable. "I suppose Carlo wanted something different. Lord knows he wasn't going to find another Timothy Burke! That one was far too good-looking for his own good, if you ask me. But he certainly went pretty far in the other direction."

I could feel the blood rushing to my face.

She noticed, and rolled her eyes. "I didn't mean that the way it sounded—I'm an old bitch, but I'm not that mean." She reached down and unhooked her dogs from their leashes. "There you go— you wanted off so badly, go on with you now!" She looked over at me. "You can unhook Minette—they just want to run and play, you know."

I knelt down and unhooked Minette's collar from her leash, and the three dogs took off for the beach, barking and playing.

"Come on up to the house with me and have some tea," she commanded, tucking her hand through my arm. "I've been dying of curiosity ever since I heard the news that Carlo had remarried. I knew his parents, you know," she went on, "I've known him and that sister of his since they were babies, and I've watched them grow up. Seems like just yesterday Joyce brought that fortune-hunting gigolo home." She laughed, and it was a nice sound.

We sat down at a table on her back veranda, and she pressed an intercom button and ordered a pitcher of iced tea. She smiled at me. "So how are you finding life here in the Hamptons? It must be a bit overwhelming for you." She clicked her tongue at me, narrowing her eyes. "Dorian Castlemaine was insisting that you must be some kind of gold digger yesterday when we were playing bridge, and that is, I'm afraid, the general consensus around here. But Dorian can be a nasty bitch—a bit of a snob, that one is, always seems to forget she wasn't exactly born with a silver spoon in her mouth either—it was her curves and her pretty face that landed her a rich husband and a house in the Hamptons, not her pedigree." She peered at me again over her glasses. "But with you right here in front of me, I'm afraid I just can't see that. No, you're not a gold digger at all, are you, young man?"

"No." I bristled a little bit. "I had a job—"

"Working for that dreadful magazine in the city," she cut me off. "But then, all magazines are dreadful these days—and one must make a living, I suppose, when one doesn't come from money." She smiled at me. "I know it's rude and terribly snobbish, but people with money always assume people only marry into our class for money. As I pointed out to that rude bitch—who, like I said, married for money herself and is no better than she should be—Carlo Romaniello is a very handsome man, what the young people would call a hunk, so the probability of love was very high, even if you only knew him for a week before getting married."

"It was rather quick," I admitted. "But I do love him. I don't care so much about the money, to be honest. I'd almost rather he didn't have quite so much."

"Don't be ridiculous, young man. The story that money can't buy happiness is a lie told by people who don't have any money so they can feel better about their little lives. Don't ever turn your nose up at money." She laughed again. "It definitely has its advantages."

I shook my head. "I'm not used to, you know, not having to look at price tags. Carlo thinks its funny. And living in Spindrift is like living in a hotel."

"You'll get used to it—you'll be surprised at how quickly," she replied as a uniformed woman brought a tray out and set it down on the table in front of us. "That's all, Doris, thank you." The woman nodded and went back inside the house. "Be a dear boy and pour us a glass, will you? This damned arthritis is brutal on my hands."

I obliged. The tea was delicious, and I said so.

"You'd think one couldn't ruin iced tea, but you'd be surprised," she commented. She glanced at the watch on her arm. "I'd offer you something stronger but it's still too early." She peered off toward the Beach. "I'm glad Minette has you now. Since Timothy died"—she paused for a moment, and cleared her throat—"since Timothy died no one's really had time for her, you know. I don't think Carlo much cares for dogs—he's never had one, which is all I need to know—and I've worried about her over there with no one to play with her or keep her company. I've thought about asking Carlo for her, you know, to take her back—Charlie and Hetty would be delighted to have one of their pups back, and I love dogs, can't get enough of them—but he's been hardly back at Spindrift since—well, since you know." She fixed her eyes on me again. "But now you're there, and you clearly love her, so I don't have to worry about her anymore."

I smiled back at her but didn't say anything.

Of course, I was thinking, *of course the dog was Timothy's. Everything was his before it was mine.*

"I didn't realize Minette was—was his." I said.

"It doesn't make a difference, does it?" she asked.

"No, of course not."

"Then forget about it." She waved her hand. "He wanted one of Hetty and Charlie's pups in the worst way—and then once he had her, he never seemed to have any time for her. If I'd known—" She made a face. "But now she has you—and I can tell, you love her. And that's all that matters."

"She's wonderful," I replied, taking a sip of the tea. "She—she makes me feel less lonely, since Carlo's away."

"So, what did you think of your tennis lesson?" she asked.

"How did you—"

She laughed and pointed upward. "The widow's walk. I can see everything that goes on at your house from up there. I like to go up there and watch the neighborhood sometimes—it keeps me from feeling lonely."

My heart went out to her. "Oh, dear, do you get lonely?"

She made a face. "Don't be feeling sorry for me, boy." She rapped the table with her knuckles. "My husband's dead this many years and my children are grown and moved away, but I have plenty of friends in this town."

I smiled back at her. "So you use loneliness as an excuse to go up there and spy on your neighbors?"

She laughed. "I like you, boy, I think I'm going to like you a lot." She leaned forward and narrowed her eyes. "But you didn't answer my question. Did you enjoy your tennis lesson?"

"Chris is a good teacher," I replied with a smile. "I learned a lot, and I'm really looking forward to the next lesson."

"See that tennis is all that he teaches you." She made a face.

"What do you mean?"

She sniffed. "You surely can't be that naïve, can you?"

I gaped at her. "Are you saying…"

"I wonder sometimes if Chris Thoresson was the one who killed

Timothy," she mused, resting her chin on her hands and leaning forward.

My heart flipped over inside my chest. "But Timothy drowned—he went for a swim in the ocean and—"

"You don't believe that ridiculous story?" She chortled, and went into a laughing spasm. When she finally was able to get herself under control, she gave me a shrewd look. "Timothy knew how to swim, child. He worked as a lifeguard as a teenager—he trained with the Olympics in mind when he was young. How does someone like that drown?" She shook her head. "No, Timothy was murdered, as sure as we're sitting here. Was it coincidence that *all* the servants at Spindrift—even that awful Carson—had the day off the day he drowned?"

"But—the autopsy—the coroner ruled it an accident."

"His body had been in the water for over a week when it washed ashore." She replied, whistling for the dogs. "The fish had been at him. There's no telling what kind of evidence the coroner missed—or the water ruined. Have you ever heard the phrase 'the rich are different from you and me'?"

I nodded. "F. Scott Fitzgerald."

"There's a different kind of justice for the rich than for most people." She stood up as the dogs came running up. She opened the door and let Hetty and Charlie into the house, while Minette jumped up into my lap. Her legs were wet—the dogs had been in the water.

"I walk the dogs at this time every day—you're more than welcome to join us if you like," she said as she shut the door, dismissing me.

I put Minette's leash back on her and walked the length of the hedge down to the beach. My heart was pounding. Timothy—*murdered*? It couldn't be possible. She'd also alluded that Chris and Timothy had been more than teacher and student.

Who would want him dead?

I froze as I came around the hedge.

If Timothy had been having an affair—and Carlo found out about it…

"Don't even think like that," I scolded myself. "She doesn't know what she's talking about. Timothy drowned, and it was an accident. Even the best swimmers get cramps."

I couldn't help but look up, though—and I could see the widow's walk on top of her house. Yes, anyone up there had a clear sight line into Spindrift's backyard.

Had she—*seen* something the day he died?

Minette started pulling at her leash, and I looked down at her. "What is it, girl?" I asked, and followed her sight line.

A man I didn't recognize was opening the door to the— *Timothy's*—studio.

Curious, I let her pull me along in the direction of the studio. I peered in through one of the windows, but it was tinted dark so I couldn't see in. I turned the knob and opened the door. "What are you doing here?" I asked, only then realizing it might be foolish to confront a trespassing stranger.

But rather than barking, Minette was whimpering and going into paroxysms of such joy that it was obvious she knew the man.

"And who," he asked, standing up to his full height, "might you be?"

I caught my breath as I got a good look at him. He was an extremely good-looking man—if you liked that type. He had thick, wavy blond hair that was darker underneath and at the roots, wide green eyes, a heavy brow over a strong nose, and broad shoulders. His lips were thick, and he had a crooked front tooth. He was also tall—he had to be around six three or four. He was wearing a black cable-knit pullover shirt that stretched tightly across his strong chest, and khaki shorts that exposed tan, well-muscled legs.

Before I could answer, he smiled and said, in a rather nasty tone, "Let me guess—you must be the *new* Mrs. Romaniello." He cocked his head to one side. "Not much like the old one, are you?"

Minette had been straining at her leash since we'd gone inside the studio, so I let go of her leash. My face started getting hot, and the traitorous spaniel dashed across the room and leaped on the stranger. He knelt down to let her lick his face and he scratched her back. He looked back up at me. "I'm sorry—that was offensive, and the last thing in the world I want is to offend you—you simply caught me off guard." He stood back up, and Minette came back over to me, wagging her tail and her tongue sticking out. He walked over to me and extended his hand. "My name is Taylor Hudson."

I told him my name as I took his enormous, strong hand in mine. He shook it gravely, his eyes twinkling. "It's nice to meet you, Mr. Hudson," I replied. "But you still haven't told me what you're doing here. You *are* trespassing, you know."

"Yes, I suppose I am now," he replied, scratching his forehead. "I've been away for over a year, and I suppose I need to get used to the idea that I may not be as welcome at Spindrift as I used to be. Your husband was never particularly fond of me—he made that very clear on more than one occasion. I was a friend of Timothy's, you know, and I kind of got used to coming and going as I pleased. Timothy and I went way back."

I stiffened at the mention of Timothy. "How long did you know him?"

"Since we were kids," he said with a smile. "You could say we grew up together in a one-horse town in the Florida panhandle." He sat down on a sofa and crossed his legs. "I got back to town just this past weekend."

"I'm sorry, his death must have been quite a shock for you."

"Yes, it was." He shook his head. "I'm still trying to wrap my mind around it, frankly. It's bad enough that he's dead—but I just can't believe Timothy drowned. He was at home in the water as a fish, you know."

This was the second time in less than fifteen minutes someone had said this to me, but I kept my face rigid as I sat down on a chair. Minette jumped up into my lap. I started stroking her silky fur, careful not to let him see or notice how nervous I was. "Where have you been for the last year? You didn't come back for the funeral?"

He smiled. "Timothy got me a gig as a personal companion to a lady he knew from his modeling days in New York, and we were touring the world." His face darkened. "I got the news about him when we were in Paris, and of course I would have rushed back, but," he shrugged his massive shoulders, "I hardly saw any point. He was dead, and he never put much store by funerals and memorials and that sort of thing." He looked around the room. "If you ever happen to come across a gold medallion with a dolphin on it, would you mind returning it to me? It was on a chain of gold links." He looked sad. "I won it in a swim meet when I was a teenager—but I gave it to Timothy because if he hadn't been sick he would have won it. We used to give it back and forth to each other, but he had it when he died and I was, of course, in Europe."

I bit my lower lip. I *knew* the medallion he was talking about— Timothy had often been photographed wearing it. "If I see it, of course," I said.

"I can almost feel him here, you know." He got up, walked over to a stack of framed prints against a wall, and started flipping through them. "He loved this place." He smiled and pulled one out, turning it so I could see it.

It was a black-and-white print of a nude man lying in the sand while a wave broke around him. It took me a few moments to realize it was Taylor.

I blushed and looked away from the photo.

"Timothy wanted everyone to pose for him," he said, picking it up and looking at it. "Would you mind if I took this?"

"I—I'm sure no one would mind," I stammered, careful not to look at it again.

"Well, I'd best be on my way," he replied, tucking the print under his arm. "If you find that medallion, please let me know."

"How would I reach you?"

He placed a business card on the desk. "This has my cell phone number and my e-mail address. It was quite a pleasure to meet you." He winked and walked out the door.

I stayed there for a few minutes after he walked out.

I knew what he meant about feeling Timothy—the sense of him was very strong in this place.

When I couldn't stand it anymore, I grabbed the dog and headed back to the house.

CHAPTER EIGHT

I had just come back in from taking Minette for her morning walk and was sitting down to breakfast when Carlo got back from his trip.

I was exhausted. I hadn't slept well, tossing and turning the entire night. I couldn't put what Nell Chamberlain had said out of my mind—much as I wanted to dismiss her implications, I just couldn't. Of course, that would have been much easier to do had Taylor Hudson not confirmed her statement about Timothy being a great swimmer. I'd taken dinner in my room, and spent the night online reading everything about Timothy and his death that I could find. Nowhere was there the slightest indication that anyone suspected his death had been anything other than a tragic accident. I was able to download a PDF of the autopsy from a gossip site, and while most of it was unintelligible medical jargon to me, it was clear that the cause of death was from drowning—his lungs had been full of water. Unfortunately, the autopsy report was also full of exhaustive detail about what had happened to his body while it was in the water for the eight days—his eyes were gone, and the fish had eaten his fingers and toes, and been at other parts of his body as well.

There was one thing that didn't make sense to me—when his body had washed ashore, he'd been wearing knee-length board shorts.

Timothy had given up his modeling career except for his own underwear line—it seemed odd to me that he wouldn't have cared about the tan line he would have gotten from board shorts. On the other hand, he wasn't tanning in them—he'd just gone for a swim. I also knew, from photo shoots at *Street Talk*, there were a lot of ways to cover up the wrong kind of tan lines.

Getting nowhere with that, I Googled Taylor Hudson. He'd been honest with me—he was from the same small town in the Florida panhandle as Timothy. They'd been friends, and after Timothy had started getting some fame as a model, he'd helped Taylor get started in the business, getting him signed with the same agency. They'd even done some shoots together—but Taylor's career never quite caught fire the way Timothy's had. He wasn't as photogenic or handsome, and when Timothy had stopped modeling after marrying Carlo, Taylor's career pretty much dried up.

I couldn't help wondering why Taylor had never had his crooked front teeth fixed. In almost all of the images I was able to find of him online from his modeling days, he never showed his teeth. That had to have held him back somewhat.

I finally went to bed around midnight, trying to no avail to sleep, finally giving up when Minette started whimpering to go out around seven. I threw on some clothes, washed my face and brushed my teeth and hair, and took her down to the beach. I took off her leash and let her run free while I simply stared out at the ocean, wondering what happened to Timothy out there that fateful day.

I made up my mind to question Nell a little more thoroughly that afternoon.

When I took her back inside, I gulped down a quick cup of coffee and loaded up a plate. Carlo walked in just as I sat down with my second cup. Minette went crazy, wagging her tail, barking and running around him.

"Quiet, dog!" he snapped at her, kissing me on the cheek with a flourish and a smile as he sat down opposite me at the table. Minette looked stricken, and she cowered down. I was about to call her when she fled the room, her tail between her legs and her ears drooping. My dismay must have shown on my face, because he immediately apologized. "I'm sorry, Mouse, but I'm just not a dog person, and I should have probably given her away after…" He bit his lower lip. "And she always reminds me of…" His voice trailed off and he poured himself a cup of coffee hurriedly. "Anyway, I'm glad to be back here with you, Mouse. I missed you so much."

I made a mental note to keep Minette out of his sight. The last thing I wanted for him was even more reminders of Timothy—reminders that I wasn't him. "I've kept myself busy," I said, wiping my mouth with my napkin. I spread strawberry preserves on my buttered toast and took another swig of my coffee. I stifled a yawn. I was definitely going to have to take a nap at some point.

"Yes, Joyce told me she'd been by to meet you and had already set you up with tennis lessons," he said with a wink. "Don't let her bully you—she's a fanatic about tennis and will have you on the courts all day every day if you let her."

"I like her," I replied. "She's fun to be around, frankly."

"Good, because I've invited them to dinner tonight—don't worry, I've already let Delia know, and asked her to make a prime rib—it's Frank's favorite." He smiled at Juana as she brought him a plate of food. He speared a link sausage and popped it into his mouth. "Have you met anyone else? Been exploring the town or anything? Shopping? What have you been doing besides taking tennis lessons?"

"I met Nell Chamberlain." I smiled at him. "Yesterday afternoon, when I was walking Minette."

"Ah, Nell does love her dogs." He beamed at me. "She's something, isn't she? Speaks her mind and doesn't care whose feelings she hurts. The advantage of age, I suppose."

"I also met Taylor Hudson yesterday," I said, keeping my voice casual and watching his face as I took another drink from my coffee cup.

His face froze, and a muscle in his right jaw began working as his broad smile faded. "I wasn't aware he was back," he remarked, keeping his voice level. "Where did you run into him?"

"He was on the grounds when I came back from visiting Nell," I said, my heart sinking as the expression on his face became more thunderous.

"He was trespassing?" His eyebrows met over his nose, and his lips tightened.

I took a deep breath and went on. "He was looking for something in—in the studio. He didn't find it—he asked me if I could keep an eye out for it." I hesitated, biting my lower lip. The look on his face was scaring me, and I could feel the coffee churning into acid in my stomach. I looked down.

"And what was he looking for?"

I exhaled. "A gold medallion on a chain, a swimming medal of some sort." I looked up.

Carlo's face drained of both color and anger. He looked like he'd been punched in the stomach. His mouth opened and closed a few times, and he pushed his chair back. "That—that was buried with Timothy." he said in a quiet, stricken voice. He daubed at his lips with his napkin and stood up, placing his hands on the table for support. He shook his head and took a few deep breaths before giving me a weak smile. "I—I seem to have lost my appetite, Mouse, if you'll excuse me...I—I believe I'll go lie down for a while. I got up obscenely early this morning." He walked around the table and kissed me absently on the cheek before leaving the room.

I sat there, mortified, not knowing what to do or say. I felt tears swimming up in my eyes. *He's obviously still not over Timothy, so what do I do? Like an idiot, the minute he comes back home the first thing I do is throw Timothy back in his face. Will I ever learn?*

My appetite gone, I pushed my plate away.

Minette came trotting back into the room and placed her front paws on my leg and whimpered. I looked at her, her tail wagging slightly and the mournful look on her face. I leaned down and hugged her, hiding my tears in her fur. "Oh, Minette, why am I so stupid?" I whispered. She responded by licking my face, and I couldn't help but smile back at her. I slipped Minette a couple of the sausages left on my plate, and she gulped them down quite happily and looked up at me hopefully, obviously wanting more. Instead, I got up from my chair. "Come on, girl," I said to her. "Let's go hide out upstairs."

But when we walked out of the dining room, she took off running to my right. "Minette!" I called after her, but she ran on. Annoyed, I followed as she ran up the staircase to the east wing. When I reached the top of the stairs she was sitting in front of the mysterious locked door. She looked at me and stood up, putting her paws on the door. "Bad girl!" I said, and she gave me a mournful look.

But as I drew nearer to the door, I could hear the unmistakable sound of someone crying on the other side.

I paused, listening. I lifted my hand to knock—but stopped myself, not wanting to intrude. Instead, I whispered to Minette, "Come on," and she followed me all the way back to my room. Olivia was just finishing making the bed when Minette jumped up and lay down on what I'd come to think of as her pillow.

"I was just finishing up," Olivia said with her bright smile. "I'll be getting out of your way now, sir."

"I have a question for you, Olivia." I closed my eyes and took a deep breath. "In the east wing, on the second floor, there's a locked door."

She got a fearful look on her face. "Yes?"

"What is that room, and why is the door locked?"

She looked out into the hallway, her eyes wide, and stepped forward so she was closer. She said, in a very low voice, "That's Mr. Timothy's suite, sir. The door has been kept locked since"—she swallowed—"since he died, sir. The only person allowed in there is Carson, sir—the rest of us have been forbidden."

"Forbidden? Why?"

She looked uncomfortable. She closed her eyes and took a deep breath. "Mr. Timothy's suite—it's been kept exactly the same as it was the day he died, sir. All of his things are still there, no one's been allowed to clean it out or anything, sir."

Of course—just like his studio—shrines to the wonderful, irreplaceable, beautiful Timothy.

Somehow I managed to say, "Ah, thank you, Olivia. That'll be all." My voice sounded strange and hollow to me. There was a roaring in my ears, and my stomach was churning, everything I'd had for breakfast threatening to come back up.

She fled, closing the door behind her. I walked into the bathroom and splashed cold water on my face.

It must have been Carlo in there, crying behind a locked door.

Who else could it have been? *Of course* it was Carlo. I'd reminded him of Timothy yet again, and he'd gone straight up to his suite of rooms, to weep over his loss all over again.

I had been right. Carlo wasn't over him yet—maybe he would *never* be over him.

I buried my face in my hands.

I was a fool.

I heard Valerie's voice in my head again, sneering, "What did you expect? Did you think someone like *you* could make him forget the love of his life?"

I pushed her voice out of my head, and splashed more cold water in my face. I took some deep breaths, and calmed myself down.

I stared at my plain face in the mirror. "I may not be Timothy, and Carlo may not ever love me the way he loved him, but I *can* make him as happy as I can. I may not be able to make him completely forget him, but I can do everything I can to make him happy."

My mind made up, I walked back into the bedroom and sat down at my desk. I went through my e-mails quickly and spent the rest of the morning reading an art history book I'd taken from the library until it was time for lunch.

As I walked into the dining room, I heard Carson's unmistakable voice saying, "Sir, I'm afraid I have no other choice but to find a new cleaning service."

Carlo put down his newspaper and looked up at Carson as I slid into my chair across the table from him. He didn't acknowledge me. "What do you mean, Carson?" He frowned.

Carson folded his hands together in front of him. "Yesterday I had occasion to go into the office, sir, and immediately I couldn't help but notice that the antique china spaniel statue was missing. I looked around for it, thinking perhaps it might have been misplaced or moved when the service was cleaning the office. You can imagine my surprise when I found it, broken in pieces, in the bottom drawer of the desk."

My cheeks began to burn, and I squirmed in my chair.

"So, quite naturally I called the service, but they all denied breaking it." He sighed. "It is one thing to break a priceless antique, sir, which is, of course, a terrible accident. Upsetting as that is, sir, it is understandable—these kinds of things do happen. However, the attempt to hide the broken pieces and the refusal to take responsibility for it is quite untenable and inexcusable. I advised the service I would have no choice but to recommend to you we terminate their services and find a new service."

Carlo's face was unreadable. "You handled that perfectly, Carson. Yes, find a new cleaning service immediately." He started to pick up his newspaper again.

"I broke it," I said in a small voice.

Both heads swiveled to me. Carson's lips pursed and his eyes narrowed a bit, but he didn't say anything.

"You broke the statue?" Carlo asked, his eyebrows coming together over his nose. "Why didn't you say something? Why did you hide the pieces? I'm afraid I don't understand, Mouse."

"I—I don't know," I replied, quite miserable and embarrassed. It wasn't the truth, of course—I knew exactly why I hadn't said anything, and why I'd hid the pieces. "I—I panicked...I mean, it was clearly valuable and I was—"

"Obviously I shall have to apologize to the service," Carson cut me off, his voice dripping scorn. He didn't even look at me, instead giving his full attention to Carlo. "I shall take care of that at once. My apologies, sir, for disturbing your lunch." Without another word, he swept out of the room noiselessly.

Carlo was still staring at me with that strange expression on his face. "I keep forgetting what a child you are," he finally said, and I squirmed again in my chair, mortified. "All that fuss over nothing. Yes, the dog was an irreplaceable antique, and valuable, but Mouse—you don't need to feel afraid. Accidents do happen, you know, and they can't be helped. This is your home now, everything in it belongs to you as much as it belongs to me." He blinked at me a few times before continuing, "And you caused Carson a ridiculous amount of stress and worry for no reason. In the future, if you break something you simply need to let Carson know. That could have created a rather awkward situation, with us falsely accusing the service. It's just a china dog, after all. Perhaps it can be fixed." He shrugged, and picked up his paper again, the subject closed in his mind.

I don't really remember what we had for lunch that day, but not another word was spoken during the meal. His disappointment in me was palpable. Once the dishes were cleared Carlo made some excuses about work that needed to be done and disappeared back into his office without another word to me. Embarrassed, humiliated, and wishing I were dead, I slunk back up to my rooms, where Minette was still sleeping on the bed. Why had I been so stupid about the dog? I kept berating myself.

Because I'd assumed, of course, that it was *his*, Timothy's. It was his old office, after all, complete with his stationery and his cards still in the center drawer, like he was going to walk back in at any moment. Everything in there was exactly the way it was when he went for his final swim in the sea, just like his studio and his suite in the east wing.

"Stop it," I said to myself. "What's done is done. You made a mistake, and nothing can be done about it now. Move on."

Resolutely, I put the leash on Minette and took her back out to the back lawn. There was a strong breeze from the ocean, and whitecaps were breaking everywhere in the sea. It was hot, though, and the sun was shining as I walked down to the studio, stopping every so often for Minette to sniff something. It was probably a mistake to go there—Carlo had acted very strangely when I brought up the medallion Taylor had been looking for. He had been angry about Taylor being in the studio—but he'd changed at the mention of the medallion, cutting off the conversation quickly and leaving the room.

Maybe there was more to it than just the reminder of Timothy.

Certainly it was possible for a good swimmer to drown—it happened all the time. He could have gotten tired, been caught by an undertow, developed a cramp—any number of things could have happened to him out there. And the autopsy report had been pretty definite about the cause of death.

Nell's suspicions had to be wrong.

Besides, who would have wanted to kill him? Everyone had loved Timothy. He was handsome and sexy and witty and charming.

If Nell was wrong about Timothy being murdered, then she was probably wrong about him having an affair with Chris.

That made sense, I reasoned as I reached the studio. Nell was just a bored old woman who entertained herself by reaching her own conclusions about what went on next door. Carlo had said she said whatever she pleased, regardless of how much it might hurt the listener. She'd probably just been trying to provoke a reaction from me—and it had certainly worked.

Besides, I didn't know her well enough to take everything she said as gospel.

I hesitated outside the studio and glanced back at the house. I saw no one, and looked over next door. The widow's walk on top of Nell's house was vacant—but she certainly did have a clear view of almost every part of our property from up there. It was possible she'd seen something—

I pushed that thought out of my head and pushed open the studio door. Minette ran inside as I reached for the switch to turn on the overhead light. Minette jumped onto the sofa and sniffed around for a moment or two, before turning around a few times and falling asleep. I stood there in the center of the room for a few moments, trying to figure out what I was doing there besides acting like a fool. The studio was silent, and I looked around, catching more detail than I had when I'd surprised Taylor inside.

The entire space was maybe a little larger than my suite in the main house. There was a large desk with a chair, a couch and various chairs and little tables scattered about. The floor was polished dark hardwood, and there were various easels stacked against the wall, as well as several stacks of canvases and framed prints. There was a small area in the back corner that looked like it might have served as a darkroom for developing film, and I could see camera equipment on a table near there—and several expensive-looking cameras, as well.

I walked over to the nearest stack of framed prints, which was the one Taylor had been looking through. On top was a black-and-white print of a muscular man in wet white underwear that didn't really hide anything. He was on his knees on a beach, with water rushing in from the tide around him. He had his left hand running through his wet hair, his eyes closed and his face looking out to sea. His remarkably muscular torso was beaded with water. On closer inspection, I saw the brand name on the elastic waistband of the underwear—TIMOTHY.

The shot was amazing.

Timothy had a good eye.

I started flipping through the stack.

The images were all of men in various states of undress.

It wasn't really all that surprising he was a good photographer. Timothy had been a successful model for years; he knew all about camera angles and lighting—and all of his models were incredibly beautiful men. But as I kept looking through the pictures, I started noticing others things about them besides the models. In a color shot of a tall gorgeous redhead, for example, standing in a doorway with the sea in the distance behind him, I realized with a start that he was standing in the doorway out to the balcony in my room.

The next print was a well-built Latino looking man lying in the bed in my room. He was completely nude, and this wasn't an artistic shot—he had an erection, and his left hand was gripping it. He was looking at the camera with a seductive expression.

The next one was even more graphic—it was the same Latino man, only this time he was on his hands and knees, and the picture was taken from behind. He had his ass cheeks spread apart—

I let the stack fall back.

I took a deep breath.

That picture was *pornographic*.

Why on earth was Timothy taking such graphic nude photos? It didn't make any sense to me. The earlier images, while nudes or semi-nudes, had an artistic aesthetic to them—the lighting, the poses, the lines—they were the kind of nudes that could be hung and sold in an expensive gallery in Manhattan. The less revealing ones— like the model kneeling in the sand with the wave crashing around him—could have easily been an ad campaign for his underwear company.

I could think of no reason for the more graphic images—or for framing such enormous prints.

There was so much about him I didn't know.

"You're just as obsessed with him as Carlo," I said out loud. Minette opened her eyes and looked at me, then sighed and closed them again. I crossed the room to another stack of prints. I frowned and tilted my head. The print was on its side, and I turned it so I could view it the way it was intended.

It was also a black-and-white shot of a nude man reclining on his back on what was clearly the big table in the formal dining room. His face was in profile, and his left leg was discreetly bent and raised in such a way that only some of his upper pubic hair could be seen.

If it wasn't Chris Thoresson, my tennis pro, then he had an identical twin.

I bit my lower lip.

Chris had posed for Timothy's camera—it wasn't much of a stretch to assume they'd been lovers.

"It means no such thing," I said out loud. Lots of photographers focused on male nudes—it didn't mean they slept with their models.

But the Latino—the pornographic shots of him pretty much suggested he, at least, had been intimate with Timothy.

Did Carlo know about this?

People often kill people they love—that's why they call them crimes of passion.

I pushed that thought away. That was ridiculous. Carlo had loved Timothy—and still wasn't over losing him.

I was letting Nell's suggestions get to me—which was probably what she wanted, why she'd said it to me in the first place.

Timothy had drowned, period. It was a senseless accident, nothing more.

I started flipping through the rest of the prints. None of these were in the least bit pornographic, and I didn't recognize any of the models. These were all black and whites, definitely more in the artistic vein. He had been good—he could have been a successful photographer had he chosen to be.

Of course, he was good at everything—everything came easy to people like Timothy.

"Stop it," I scolded myself, "it's crazy to be jealous of someone who's dead."

I reached the last print and gasped.

It was Timothy, in all his glory, his head tilted back to one side with his eyes slightly open and looking suggestively at the camera. Part of the reason Timothy had been such a successful underwear model was because of the hint of what was underneath the underwear, the tantalizingly big bulge in the front and the perfectly shaped round buttocks in the back.

But in this image he was reclining in the sand, the white sand in stark contrast to the dark tan of his skin. I could see the veins in his arms, his lower abs, and his legs. His hair was wet, and beads of water dribbled down the remarkably deep valley between his perfectly shaped pectoral muscles. His big round nipples were erect.

I looked over at the mirror, and back to the picture.

I wasn't even remotely in the same league as Timothy Burke.

Why had Carlo married me, what could he have possibly seen in me that he would marry me, someone who was practically a stranger, and bring me back to this incredible house where Timothy's memory still lived on, where he was everywhere I looked but just out of sight—like there in the corner of my eye but when I turned my head to see him he wasn't there anymore.

If it was like this for me—who hadn't known him, hadn't loved him—it must be ever so much worse for Carlo.

No wonder he could hardly stand to look at me.

He knew he'd made a terrible mistake and was trying to make the best of a bad bargain.

I don't know how long I was there in the studio, but by the time I finally snapped out of whatever it was I was experiencing and walked Minette back to the house, it was almost time for dinner. I took a shower and looked at my sad, pathetic body in the mirror.

Surely there must be some trainer I could hire to come teach me how to work out—to put the weights in the exercise room to good use? I could ask Chris when he came for my next tennis lesson.

Feeling somewhat better, I got dressed and went downstairs. Carlo, Joyce, and a man I assumed was her husband Frank were enjoying martinis in the drawing room. I heard their laughter as I came down the hall, and couldn't help but feel my own spirits lift. I loved Carlo and was determined to show him he hadn't made a mistake.

I accepted a martini from Frank, who was finishing mixing a fresh batch in a tall crystal pitcher. I took a sip and felt the vodka burn all the way down to my stomach. But there was a sweet aftertaste to it that I kind of liked, and I smiled at him.

I was feeling a bit of a buzz by the time we sat down to dinner. They were talking about things I didn't know anything about, so I simply listened to them.

I was slicing my prime rib when Joyce said, "PLEASE tell me you're GOING to have the Independence Ball THIS year, Carlo. I mean, EVERYONE'S wondering whether you're GOING to have it again—they ALL understand why you didn't have it LAST year, obviously, but NOW that you've married again—everyone's DYING to meet him, you know—and what BETTER way than the Independence Ball?"

I paused and didn't raise my head, but moved my eyes so they were on Carlo.

His face was impassive.

I knew what the Independence Ball was, of course. It was the big costume ball Carlo and Timothy had hosted every summer over the Fourth of July weekend, the big fund-raiser for the Gay Men's Health Crisis in New York City—it had raised something like ten million dollars ever since they'd started having it. Last summer, of course, it hadn't happened because Timothy had drowned.

After what seemed an eternity of awkward silence, his rigid face broke into a smile. "What do you think, Mouse?"

Three sets of eyes turned to me, and I swallowed. "Well, it is a good cause," I said, terrified I'd say the wrong thing, "but I don't have the slightest idea of how to throw a party like that. I'd be completely useless."

"Don't WORRY your pretty little head about A THING," Joyce enthused. "I'll take CARE of everything, of course with Carson's help. All YOU need to WORRY about is a costume."

"As the host I claim prerogative in not wearing one," Carlo replied.

"You're so DULL," Joyce shook her head, winking at me. "He HATES to wear costumes, even when we were CHILDREN he wouldn't dress up for Halloween."

"If Carlo isn't going to wear one—" I started to say, but she cut me off.

"Oh, no, you aren't BOTH going to be DULLARDS." Joyce shook her head. "It's WHAT, six weeks? You have PLENTY of time to COME up with a costume—and I'll set YOU up with the COSTUMER in the city I use."

I looked around the table at three smiling faces and nodded. "Okay."

Joyce clapped her hands in delight. "Wonderful. THAT'S settled." And she began making plans—really, thinking out loud, about music and decorations and the invitations and everything.

And at one point I looked up to see Carson standing in the doorway, looking at me.

When our eyes met, the corners of his lips twitched before he bowed his head and walked away.

CHAPTER NINE

It goes without saying Carlo did not come to my suite that night. It was foolish of me to expect him, after everything that had happened during the day—especially my idiocy about the china dog—but I waited up for him until it was clear to me, around midnight, he wasn't going to join me. I turned off the light and got under the covers, trying not to cry as I made excuses for him—he was tired after his trip, and Frank and Joyce had stayed rather late.

Minette, of course, sensed my distress and cuddled up to me in the bed.

I don't know what time it was I finally was able to fall asleep. I was worn out both physically and emotionally, but it still seemed to take a long time for me to drift off. I do know I was woken up at three in the morning when a storm front rolled in from the ocean. A crack of thunder startled me right out of a strange dream. Minette was whimpering and shivering, so I let her climb into my lap and started petting her and murmuring soothing words to her. Rain was pelting down against the French doors and windows, and I could hear the wind howling around the house. Lightning lit up the room, and the thunder that followed was so loud the house shook. That was all Minette could handle—she dove out of my arms and scampered under the bed.

I got out of bed and walked over to the French doors. The rain was pouring down, and in the dark it was almost impossible to see. A gust of wind rattled the door, and involuntarily I stepped back. There was about an inch of water on my balcony. I was about to reach for the balcony light switch when I noticed there was a light on in the studio. I looked back at my alarm clock. The red digital numbers glowed 3:04 in the darkened room.

Who could be out there at this hour, in this weather? I wondered. But as I watched, the light went out. I peered through the darkness, but couldn't see anything.

There was another bright, blinding flash, followed almost immediately by the roar of thunder. The wind was whipping around the house, and I shivered. The swimming pool was filled with whitecaps and breaking waves, and just beyond the pool I could see the hedges on that side bending and being whipped around by the wind. Over the incessant pounding of the rain I could hear the sea waves pounding away at the shore. I pressed my face against the glass, watching the studio, but I didn't see anything or anyone in the darkness.

Finally, I gave up and went back to bed, deciding to check it out in the morning in daylight.

But the rain didn't let up for several days, and the gloom was depressing. I got an umbrella and sloshed through the rain to the studio the next morning, but everything looked the same as it had the day before.

I tried to take Minette with me, but she flatly refused to go outside. I tried again later in the day, but she would have none of it, refusing to budge. Olivia advised me to just put down newspapers in my bathroom—which made sense, since Minette seemed determined to spend most of her time cowering underneath my bed.

Things with Carlo were going better, the incident of the dog apparently forgotten. It wasn't the way things had been in Miami and Manhattan, but it was better. Every evening after dinner we would watch a movie in the rec room together on the big flat screen television—he liked old black-and-white movies, which was fine with me since I hadn't seen any of them. Afterward, he would come up to my bedroom with me—and I would have to close Minette up in the bathroom. I would fall asleep in his arms, but when I woke up the next morning I was alone, other than Minette curled up next to me.

I spent most of my time during the day either in the library reading art books or trying to figure out what costume to wear to the Independence Ball. I was going crazy from boredom—my tennis lessons had been canceled, obviously, so I started Googling images from past balls to try to get costume ideas.

My father didn't believe in Halloween when I was a child. He always turned off the porch light so trick-or-treaters wouldn't disturb us. Sometimes I'd spent the evening staring out my bedroom window at the kids in their costumes with their bags, going around collecting candy. I so envied them, and the ones whose parents dressed them in costumes to wear to school. I never knew exactly what my father had against Halloween—but there was always a reason. I had always wanted to wear a costume, and since this was my first opportunity to wear one, I wanted something clever and original, something no one had ever done before. I was excited and spent hours Googling costume ideas and looking at pictures.

"I don't know WHY you won't let ME help you," Joyce groused at me one afternoon when she'd come by to plan the ball. "I'm wonderful at costumes. Frank would be LOST without my HELP, and people ALWAYS comment on how BRILLIANT our costumes are. I'd LOVE to help you."

"I want to do this on my own," I insisted, even though I was beginning to weaken. I couldn't think of anything, and my costume searches weren't helping.

Joyce was as good as her word. She took charge of the ball planning with a vengeance, and I quickly learned that it was best to stay out of her way. All she needed from me was my approval— Carlo just waved her off whenever she tried to present her plans to him. So, every day I met her in the library to approve her thoughts on food and hors d'oeuvres, music and alcohol, decorations and color schemes, music and little details I would have never thought of in a million years. Obviously, I couldn't help with the guest list—so I told her to just invite the people who usually were invited.

She made a weird sound when I said that, and I looked up from the book about eighteenth-century fashions I was paging through, hoping for any inspiration about what to wear.

She was gnawing her lower lip, and looked uncomfortable. "What's wrong?" I asked.

She closed her eyes. "Well, Mouse, you see—" She paused again. "Timothy always took care of the ball invitations." Her voice was small and sounded embarrassed.

Of course he did, and he probably always had the best costume, I thought, feeling the familiar knot forming in my stomach. "Then there's probably a list somewhere—I'm sure Carson knows where it is." I looked down at my book again so she couldn't see my face reddening.

"Yes, of course." She hurried out of the library.

I walked down to the office, not wanting to be there when she got back. I knew I was behaving childishly—he was dead, for God's sake, I shouldn't feel so threatened by a dead man. I sat down at the desk, and buried my face in my hands. It was still raining; maybe it was just the gloom of the past few days getting to me. I felt trapped in the house. And Carlo was leaving again in the morning—this time to London for a few days—and of course, he'd told me I would just be "bored" if I went with him.

Like I would ever be bored in London—but he refused to even discuss it.

He's ashamed of you—he doesn't want to be seen with you in public. He feels like he's making a mistake.

Someone cleared their throat in the doorway.

I looked up and saw Carson standing there, his face impassive as always.

"Yes, Carson?" I asked wearily. The last thing I wanted to do was deal with his contempt in my current mood. "Mrs. Sullivan was just looking for you."

"She found me, thank you, sir." He entered the room. "The guest list for the last ball should be located in the bottom drawer of the file cabinet, sir."

I waved my hand. "Then get it for her, Carson."

He walked past me and I heard a drawer of the filing cabinet open and shut behind me. Noiselessly he passed out of the room again, but he paused in the door. "Please forgive my asking, sir, but have you had any success in deciding upon a costume for the ball?"

"No," I replied. "And I'm about to just give up and not wear one. If Carlo can get away without a costume, there's no reason for me to wear one."

"Perhaps I might be of some use to you?"

Slowly, I looked up at him in wonder. He was smiling at me—or at least what passed for a smile from Carson. "Why would you want to help me?"

He tentatively stepped back into the office and pulled the door shut behind him. He cleared his throat again. "Sir, I feel that I owe you an apology."

I just stared at him, dumbfounded, unable to think of a thing to say in response.

"You see, sir, I was very devoted to Mr. Timothy," his face colored, "and—and I didn't like the thought of anyone trying to take his place. I deeply resented you, sir, and it wasn't my place. I'm terribly sorry, sir, and must humbly ask for your forgiveness. Could you possibly find it in your heart to forgive me, sir, and perhaps we could start over?"

I opened my mouth and closed it again. I was so stunned I couldn't speak, so I simply nodded.

"You see, I helped Mr. Timothy with his costumes for the ball every year—it was I who came up with the ideas for them, sir. And I would be more than happy to do the same for you this year."

Somehow I managed to say, "That would be very kind of you, Carson."

"Are you going to be here in your office for a while, sir?"

"Actually, I should get upstairs and check on Minette," I said with a glance out the windows. The rain seemed to finally be passing, and the sun was shining on the sea. "She hasn't been exercised since the rain began."

"Oh, please, sir, wait for me in your rooms while I drop this list off to Mrs. Sullivan. I can meet you up there in a few minutes. I have some pictures—ideas, really—in my room that could be very useful to you."

"Fine, Carson, I'll wait for you there."

"Very good, sir." He gave me a slight bow and walked away.

As I climbed the stairs, I had to resist the urge to whistle. Carson was coming around! I couldn't deny that having him dislike me so much had been bothering me. But if he was coming around—and if things with Carlo weren't quite the way they'd been in Miami and Manhattan, well, at least we were spending some time together before he left on his trip. He enjoyed watching his favorite old films with me, often explaining to me information about the actors or the director that I didn't know.

By the time I reached my bedroom the sky had completely cleared, and it seemed like a sign to me. Carson was coming around—the sun had come out and everything was right with the world. Even Minette greeted me cheerfully and looked happier than I'd seen her in days. I knelt down and scratched her ears. "Yes, we'll go for a nice long walk in a little bit, Minette, would you like that? But we're going to have wait—I have something to talk about with Carson first, and then we can spend as much time as we want outside, okay, girl?"

She seemed to smile at me in that way spaniels have, and I sat down at my desk.

I was checking my e-mail when Carson knocked on my door. "Come in," I called, turning in the swivel chair. Carson entered, carrying a manila file folder stuffed full of clippings. He closed the door behind him and walked noiselessly over to the desk. He was smiling that odd little smile of his when he handed me the folder.

"Let's see what we have here," I murmured, opening the folder. The first clipping I immediately dismissed as impractical—it was a man in a merman costume. Carson was standing next to me as I went through the clippings. He had never been so close to me before, and I could smell him—a strange combination of clove and antiseptic. I wanted to ask him to step a little bit away from me—but since we were now on a friendly basis I didn't want to risk offending him. I rejected each costume possibility until I reached the image of an angel.

I stared at it, amazed.

The costume was beautiful, and so was the man wearing it. He was dark, with curly dark hair. He had big full white wings and was wearing a skimpy pair of white square-cut swim trunks. A golden halo rested on his hair.

I sighed. "That's absolutely lovely, but I could never wear anything quite so revealing."

"But why not, sir?" Carson asked, his eyebrows going up. "I think you would look rather appealing in this costume."

"Thank you, but I don't have the kind of build that someone would need to wear this costume," I replied with a little laugh. "I mean, look at his body, Carson. There's no fat on him anywhere. And that muscle tone!" I shook my head. "No, I'm soft and have no muscles. People would laugh at me if I dared wear something like that."

"I think you're being too hard on yourself, sir," he said slowly, conviction in his tone. "You're very slender, sir, if you don't mind my saying so, and there's still almost six full weeks before the ball. There's absolutely no reason why you couldn't get yourself into that kind of shape by then. Perhaps not this kind of shape," he touched the clipping, "but you just need to put on a little bit of muscle and perhaps some definition, and you would be the sensation of the ball, sir." He tapped his fingers against his chin. "In fact, there's a wonderful trainer you could hire—he's done wonders with his clients. He worked with Mr. Timothy whenever he had a photo shoot coming up—and I'm sure you've seen the results! His name is Brad Collins. You could work with him several times a week, and of course, he would work with Delia to come up with an eating plan for you, to maximize the effects of the exercise." He snapped his fingers. "And all you'd need is to get a little sun—you could use the tanning bed in the exercise room; I can call them to come make sure it's working properly—it hasn't been used in over a year. Yes, you would definitely be the hit of the ball if you wore that costume."

"Do you think so?" I asked dubiously. "I'd hate to have the costume made and then not look good enough to wear it."

"You look good enough to wear it now, sir," he insisted. "I

really don't think it would be an issue. This is your debut, sir, and you really want to make a splash, don't you?"

I stared down at the picture and bit my lip. I remember the long board shorts I'd bought in Miami to wear on the beach to hide my body from everyone else. I remembered the shame and embarrassment of changing in the locker room for gym class in high school. I pictured myself coming down the grand staircase in that costume, with my halo draped over my hair, the enormous feathered wings attached to my back with a harness. I pictured the faces of everyone turning up to me as I paused for effect on the landing. I imagined the look of pride on Carlo's face as he introduced me to his friends as his spouse.

My excitement began growing. "Thank you, Carson. Can you get me the trainer's phone number so I can make an appointment?"

"I'll take care of it for you, sir." He smiled, gathering up all the other clippings and shoving them back into the folder, leaving the angel image on my desk. "Leave it all to me."

The door shut behind him, and I grabbed Minette's leash, which sent her into paroxysms of joy. "Did you hear that, Minette? I'm going to be the belle of the ball!"

I floated on a cloud of excitement and happiness the rest of the day. Even the fact that Carlo was leaving for a week the following morning wasn't enough to bring me down from it. There was no sign of Nell and her dogs next door, even though Minette and I stayed out for over an hour in the yard. The storm had done some damage—branches were down, and a lot of leaves had been stripped from the hedges. The pool was filled with debris and dirt and sand. I even took Minette out on the pier all the way to the end where the boathouse sat.

It was a glorious afternoon.

Joyce and Frank came over for dinner that evening, and I was very pleased to tell them I'd finally solved my costume dilemma.

"Oh, WHAT are you going to BE?" Joyce asked, her face alight with her curiosity, "Tell me, Mouse! I'm DYING here!"

"I'm not going to tell—you're just going to have to wait like everyone else," I replied with a laugh. "It's a surprise—but I think everyone is going to love it." I glanced over at Carlo, who winked at me.

"Oh, COME on!" she pleaded. "I can't WAIT until the ball to FIND out! I shall simply die of curiosity!"

"Now, now, Joyce, don't press him." Carlo gave me an indulgent smile and a bit of a wink. "Isn't the whole point of a costume that it's a surprise? And if Mouse wants to surprise us, we should let him, don't you think?"

"Oh, all right," Joyce said begrudgingly. She gave me a sly look. "But if you need some help with it—"

"Joyce!" Frank warned her, and she rolled her eyes.

And that apparently closed the subject.

The next morning I kissed Carlo good-bye just before he drove off for the airport. I stood on the front gallery and watched until the gate closed. "I won't be sad, I won't be sad," I said to myself as I went back inside to have breakfast.

"Brad will be here at eleven, sir," Carson said as I sat down with another cup of coffee in the dining room. "And I've taken the liberty of making an appointment for you in the city with the costume designer, for two o'clock tomorrow. I also," he bowed his head, "took the liberty of arranging tickets for you to see that new musical everyone is talking about, Roberts can drive you in and drive you back the following morning. Is that all right with you, sir?"

"Why, thank you, Carson, that was very kind of you." I smiled at him, genuinely touched. He was clearly trying to make up for his behavior. He gave me a smile, and bowed before walking out of the room.

I walked Minette after my coffee—the landscaping team was cleaning up the yard from the aftermath of the storm, and I wanted to make sure she was walked and back inside before they started running the mowers. She was absolutely terrified of the mowers—and after the days of thunderstorms I didn't want to traumatize her any further. I checked next door from the beach but there was no sign of Nell. I considered walking up and knocking on her back door, but finally decided it was better to not bother her. Obviously, her comment about Timothy being murdered had just been meant to rattle me—she wanted to see how I reacted—and so there was no point in bringing it up ever again. I hesitated when we walked past the studio—but decided ultimately to forget about it. Maybe when Carlo came back I'd talk to him about clearing out Timothy's things from there, so the little building could be put to some kind of use.

Of course, it was much easier to think about discussing Timothy with Carlo when he was out of town.

Brad Collins arrived promptly at eleven, and he looked vaguely familiar to me. He was wearing a string tank top that exposed enormous muscles, and his legs were like tree trunks. He was fair-skinned with curly auburn hair and startlingly light blue eyes, and he had more freckles than anyone I'd ever seen. He gripped my hand tightly when I introduced myself, and veins popped out in his forearms as he shook my hand.

"Thank you for squeezing me into your schedule," I said as we walked down the hallway to the workout room. "I need to get in better shape for the Independence Ball—my costume is going to be a little bit daring. But you need to know I am terribly uncoordinated, and I've never lifted a weight in my life."

He grinned, showing big strong even white teeth, and two dimples sank into his cheeks. His smile was exceptional—his entire face lit up when he smiled. "Not to worry—it's much easier to put on weight than it is to lose it in six weeks."

I opened the door to the exercise room, which I'd only peeked my head inside of once. Like all the other rooms in the main section of the house, there were enormous windows with an extraordinary view of the ocean and the backyard. The room was a fully equipped gym—we'd done a photo shoot for *Street Talk* at one of the most popular gyms in Manhattan once, and there wasn't anything that health club had that wasn't in the Spindrift exercise room. There were a couple of treadmills, elliptical machines, and stationary bicycles lined up against one wall. Every wall was covered with mirrors, and there were full sets of weights and dumbbells. There was every conceivable kind of bench, as well as squat racks.

"The most important thing," he said once I'd closed the door behind us, "is for you to build muscle and burn fat in the most efficient and healthy way possible. You said you've never lifted weights before—have you ever done any kind of physical activity?"

"Outside of walking the dog before you got here—never," I replied, embarrassed. "I mean, I always used to walk to school when I was growing up, and even to college, Mr. Collins, but—"

"Just call me Brad." He smiled. "And it's not a big deal—I actually prefer my clients to have no preconceived notions about exercise—people always think they know more than I do, and there's nothing I hate more than arguing with people about proper diet and technique. Just from looking at you, and what you've told me—and what Carson said on the phone about your goals, I don't really think it's going to be that difficult to get you ripped in six weeks. It is six weeks, right?" When I nodded, he nodded. "Okay, let's get your shirt off so I can assess your body."

I hesitated for a moment, and flashed back to high school gym class my freshman year. It was the first time I'd ever had to change clothes in front of anyone other than my doctor, and I remember one of the football players laughing at me. After that, I always hid somewhere when I had to change.

Brad smiled. "You have a bad experience in school? Yeah, me too." He shrugged, the muscles in his massive shoulders rippling underneath the skin. "I used to get picked on something fierce, man. I started bodybuilding when I was a junior because, you know, I got sick of getting picked on and never looked back." He flexed one of his arms, and the biceps muscle peaked. "Nobody fucks with you when you have guns, you know. So, go on, I'm not going to make fun of you. It's just an assessment, so I know what kind of program we need to put together to get the results you want."

"I don't want to get really big," I replied, slipping my shirt over my head. I stood there, holding my right elbow with my left hand, shifting from one foot to the other.

He walked around me, viewing me critically. "Well, you've got a pretty decent frame—small, so no, you don't want to put on a lot of muscle, it wouldn't look proportional…" He reached out and pinched the skin at my waist. "You're a bit soft, and you don't have a lot of fat, so with eating properly and exercising with weights, a full body workout, and two days of cardio a week, in six weeks you'll be amazed at the difference in your body. Do you drink a lot of soda?" When I nodded, he shook his head. "You need to cut that out—not entirely, but try not to have more than one a day, and drink a lot of water. Remember when I pinched your skin? A lot of that is water retention—there's a lot of sodium in soft drinks—so you get thirstier the more you drink so you'll drink more. And that sodium makes you retain water, which makes your skin puffy."

He took me through the entire workout, beginning with a thorough body stretch, using light weights "so you won't get sore, this way your body gets used to the movement and then when you start lifting heavier, you'll be able to get out of bed the next day," and we finished with several different variations of crunches.

When we finished, he sprang up to his feet and offered me his hand. I took it and he pulled me up to my feet like I didn't weigh anything at all. "You can do crunches every day," he said. "Your abs are the only muscles you can safely work out every day. You don't have to, but it'll help you with getting your heart rate up—so try to do your abs every day. Now, when do you want to see me again?"

"I'm going into the city for a costume fitting tomorrow morning, and I should be back the following afternoon—do you have anything available?"

He dug out a cell phone from his bag and started searching through it. "What is your costume?"

"It's a secret."

He looked up and winked. "How about three that afternoon?"

I nodded, and he entered the information into his phone. As I watched him, I realized where I'd seen him before.

He was one of the models for Timothy's prints.

"Carson said you used to train Timothy whenever he had a photo shoot coming up," I said, trying to keep my voice casual. "Did you know him well?"

He put the phone back into his bag. He looked at me suspiciously. "Well enough, why do you ask?"

"I was in his studio the other day—I was curious, and was

going through some of his prints—and there were some where you were the model." I felt myself turning red as he stared at me.

"Oh, those." He shook his head. "I'd forgotten about those." He rolled his eyes. "Look, I don't want any trouble, okay?"

"Trouble?" I gaped at him. "What do you mean?"

"I'm going to come clean with you, okay?" He took a deep breath. "I'm probably crazy for saying anything, but Timothy— Timothy was an asshole." His lips tightened. "Yeah, I used to train him. Sometimes whenever he had to do a shoot, yeah, or whenever he thought he'd gained an inch or two in the waist and freaked out about it." He laughed bitterly. "Almost from the very first time I came here, he was trying to get in my pants, okay? I wouldn't—it's really poor form for a trainer to fuck one of his clients—the word gets out, you know. He wasn't used to being turned down."

I nodded. "Yeah, I can believe that."

"So it became like a thing with him. He pursued me." He sighed. "Look, I'm a gay guy, and he was gorgeous. It's not like I wasn't tempted, you know? Finally, he just gave up. That was that—I figured he got the message. Then after about a year, he starts scheduling appointments with me again. He tells me he's thinking about taking the marketing for his company in a different direction."

"The underwear?"

He laughed harshly. "Yeah—he was thinking of doing something different. Every underwear company uses lean, ripped models, so he was thinking using a big muscle guy would make a splash, would make his ads stand out."

"And he thought you could do it."

He nodded. "I was perfect, he said. It would be a quarter of a million dollar per year contract—who can say no to money like that? I was an idiot. So, yeah, I posed for him. And I let him seduce me, like an idiot. It lasted for maybe two weeks…and then he tells me they're going to go in a different direction with the new ad campaign."

"So, he just—"

"Used it to get me into bed? Yeah." Brad threw the strap of his bag over his shoulder. "I wasn't sorry when he drowned, let me tell you. Good riddance to bad rubbish, you know what I mean?"

I nodded.

"All right, man," he said, his face still flushed from anger, "I'll see you in a couple of days—and I'd appreciate it if you didn't tell anyone about that little lapse on my part."

I walked him to the front door and watched him drive off in his Jeep.

As I went back into the house, I said to myself, *Nell said Chris Thoresson slept with Timothy—and now I know Brad did as well, and wasn't happy about it.*

Maybe he *was* murdered after all.

CHAPTER TEN

I was so tired I almost fell asleep at the dinner table and could barely make it up the stairs to my room.

It was early, so I tried to stay up, but I could barely focus on the book I was reading. Somehow, I managed to make it until ten, at which point I surrendered to the inevitable, undressed and turned off the lights.

I was asleep almost the moment my head hit the pillow.

I had a very strange dream that night, which wasn't surprising.

In the dream, I was standing underneath the grand staircase, staring out the back door to the beach. Minette ran out between my legs and started barking excitedly by the pool—which I couldn't see from where I was standing. I called to her, but she ignored me and continued barking. Annoyed at her disobedience, I walked out the back doors to the gallery, calling and whistling. My voice died in my throat as soon as I could see the swimming pool. Minette was barking and wagging her tail at a man with his back to me, wearing nothing more than a skimpy bright yellow bikini that barely covered his ample buttocks. The yellow made his deeply tanned skin look even darker, and there were beads of water on his back. His muscular legs were perfectly smooth—no sign of body hair anywhere. His bluish-black hair was wet and plastered to the sides of his head. *But he's dead* was all I could think as he raised his hands over straight over his head, the muscles in his back rippling, bent at the knees, and dove into the pool. He surfaced, shaking his head so drops of water flew in every direction from his curly hair. He smiled and waved me over as he held on to the side of the pool. Hesitantly, my heart in my throat, I walked down the gallery stairs and across the lawn toward the pool. He was even more beautiful in person than he'd been in the magazine ads and the underwear boxes, but I couldn't understand or wrap my mind around the notion that he was somehow still alive. He was smiling at me, but as I got closer I realized it wasn't a nice smile at all—it was more of a nasty smirk.

Did you really think I'd let someone like you take my place? As master of Spindrift? Did you honestly think someone like you could ever replace me in Carlo's bed? In his life? At his side? He mocked me, throwing his head back as he started laughing.

I stopped, my heart ripping in half, unable to even get the words out to beg him to stop.

But as he laughed and I struggled to say something, anything, two hands came out of the water from behind him and shoved his head under. He cried out in surprise but the cry was cut short as he submerged. I moved closer to the side of the pool, horrified, and screamed for help. My voice echoed, and I knew I had to get into the water to help him, else he would drown, but I was frozen in place, unable to move, as air bubbles rose to the surface and I could see Timothy struggling under the water…and when I finally could move again his struggles ceased, his body floating back up to the surface, face-down and limp, his arms floating up at the sides but his legs dangling toward the bottom. I opened my mouth to scream as the man who'd held him under, who'd killed him, rose up from the water and smiled at me. I couldn't make out his face—he was wearing some kind of mask over it so I couldn't make out his features. He was also wearing a bikini, only his was white, and like Timothy's had left very little to the imagination. He held a finger up to his lips and whispered, "shhhh." I tried desperately to make out his features through the gauze or whatever it was he had over his face, but couldn't. I couldn't move at all, couldn't do a damned thing as he leaned back over the water and grabbed one of Timothy's limp arms. The man dragged his body through the water over to the side of the pool, and pulled Timothy out of the water like he didn't weigh an ounce. He hoisted the limp, dripping body into his arms and walked toward me. I could tell he was smiling underneath whatever it was that masked his features.

Isn't this what you wanted? he asked. *He's dead, and now you have no rival. With him out of the way you can have everything.*

I couldn't move, I couldn't scream—it was like my feet had grown roots, immobilizing me permanently to that spot in the grass. And as the man carrying the corpse drew nearer, his features became clearer to me despite the mask, which was just some kind of nylon stocking. My heart started racing, and in that moment I knew absolute terror.

And just when I was almost able to recognize him—

I sat up in bed, gasping. I glanced over at the digital clock. My heart was pounding so hard I could hear it, and I was dripping with sweat—according to the clock it was about ten minutes to six. I'd set the alarm for six—I had told Roberts we would be leaving for the city at seven, which I figured gave me enough time to shower and grab some breakfast first. There being no point in staying in bed, I stood up, rubbing my eyes. Minette opened her eyes and thumped the bed with her tail, but didn't get up. I walked into the bathroom and turned on the shower.

I stared into the mirror. My eyes were bloodshot and my hair damp. The dream had been so disturbing—although I shouldn't wonder I dreamed about witnessing Timothy's murder.

"He wasn't murdered. It was an accident," I said loudly to my reflection. "He had sea water in his lungs—the autopsy showed quite clearly he'd drowned."

But as I opened the glass door into the shower, I remembered that Spindrift's pool was salt water.

And wasn't it odd that all the servants had been given the night off? How often was Timothy—or anyone, for that matter—ever in this big house all alone?

Resolutely I put that out of my mind and focused on my day.

I showered quickly. I had packed one of my suits, a shirt, and some other clothing into a rolling suitcase the day before. I shoved my laptop and its power cord into a computer bag, and went downstairs, pulling the rolling suitcase behind me. I left both bags near the front door and wandered into the kitchen.

Delia was yawning when I walked into the enormous kitchen. She nodded at me as I walked over to the coffeemaker and poured myself an enormous mug.

Delia Leatherman was in her late thirties, and barely over five feet tall. She always wore flat shoes and sometimes had to stand on a small stool to get into the cabinets. She had dishwater blond hair she always pulled up into a bun, and always had a chef's cap on her head. She was a little on the stocky side and was an amazing cook. Everything she made was amazing—her grilled cheese sandwiches were works of culinary art. She'd trained at the Cordon Bleu, but had told me once she preferred being a personal chef rather than running a restaurant. "This is much easier," she'd said with a wink.

"I can just eat in here," I said, sitting down at the big butcher block island in the center of the enormous room. The coffee was incredible—she made the best coffee I'd ever had. "I'm sorry to get you up so early. I could have scrambled some eggs for myself, and made some toast." I stifled a yawn.

She waved her hand wearily. "It's no problem, I told you. With you and Mr. Romaniello out of the house, I got some extra time off. Believe me, once you're on your way into the city I'm going back to bed and plan on sleeping till about noon or so." She grinned at me. "So, pancakes? Waffles? Oh, wait." She opened a drawer and pulled out a computer printout. "None of that for you—I forgot you're on a diet now! Brad e-mailed me your new meal plan." She stared at the printout and grimaced. "Well, this stuff is all bland, but nothing some spices and good vegetables can't make tasty. Sit down and relax, your breakfast will be ready in a jiffy." She shook her head. "I'll make you a snack to take with you into the city—this says you're supposed to eat every three hours."

The egg white omelette she made was delicious, and she also prepared a thermos of coffee for me to take in the car. She also gave me a plastic container with sliced fruit—berries, bananas, peaches, and apples—for the prescribed snack on my eating plan. I was pretty full from breakfast, but Brad had told me it didn't matter—when it was time to eat, I had to eat. It didn't make a lot of sense to me—why eat if you weren't hungry—but he was the expert.

When I made my way back to the front door of the house, my bags were gone. I opened the front door and saw Roberts was waiting for me in the car. I got in the backseat, and we headed for the city.

I couldn't get the dream out of my mind, or the possibility that Timothy's death might not have been an accident.

There's a different kind of justice for the rich than for most people, I heard Nell saying again.

The implication being rich people could get away with murder, and the police would just look the other way?

As much as I hated to admit it, Nell was right about that. The rich got a different kind of justice than anyone else—I'd read enough of Maureen Drury's articles in *Street Talk* to know that.

Maureen Drury.

I fumbled my cell phone out of my bag and scrolled through the contacts. I smiled to myself—her number was there; I'd had to call her any number of times on Valerie's behalf. She was the perfect person to talk to.

Maureen Drury had been an actress when she was younger, had been nominated for a couple of Oscars in the supporting actress category, and had starred in her own television series for a few years, adding a pair of Emmy Awards to her résumé. But she retired when the show was canceled—she married a poor relation of an old society family, and wanted to be a wife and mother. She turned to writing, and her first play had won a Tony and a Pulitzer Prize. She developed and produced television series—she had an uncanny knack for knowing what viewers wanted, and she became a bit of an empire. Her husband died young, and she never remarried, focusing on her two children, both of whom followed her into the acting profession. Her daughter was killed by a stalker when she was merely twenty-two and her career just starting to take off; it was an extremely notorious case, made even more notorious when her killer was sentenced to a few years in a mental hospital.

This shocking lack of justice turned Maureen into an avenging angel. She sold her production company at an enormous profit and began writing about crime. She wrote a couple of novels based on true stories where a wealthy killer got away with their crime, which became huge bestsellers and were made into enormously popular television miniseries. As a member of society through her marriage, she had access to the upper echelons of society that most writers couldn't achieve—and people talked to her. She became *Street Talk*'s crime reporter, covering the trials of the rich and famous, while also still writing her bestselling novels. She was also a big advocate for victims' rights, and started a foundation in her daughter's name to help crime victims through their ordeal.

She'd always been gracious and kind to me—she'd sent me a lovely arrangement of roses to Spindrift to congratulate me on my marriage. It was a nice gesture, but I knew there was more to it than that. She was hoping to use me as one of her sources—which I didn't have a problem with, frankly. No, the real problem was I hadn't exactly made a lot of friends out there, so I didn't have anything to tell her.

I knew she'd be more than happy to share anything she knew with me—she'd want me to be in her debt. But I would have to be careful—I didn't want her writing anything about Timothy or Spindrift.

Not now, at any rate—later things might be different.

I dialed her number. She answered on the second ring. "It's about time you called me, you dreadful little beast," she said.

"Did you get the card I sent you? The flowers were lovely. It was very kind of you." I replied.

"Of course I got the card—I was hoping you'd call so we could dish," she replied with her standard hoarse laugh, "and since you no longer work for the magazine, I'm hoping this call means you have some juicy gossip from the Hamptons for me? You know I'm always looking for new sources—and I never name names." It was true—it was why people would still talk to her; she never used a source's name in any of her pieces. She would always just say, "A source close to the family said" or "Several ladies discussed the case over cocktails one afternoon, and…"

I'd always wondered about that—after all, wasn't it possible some people would use her to get negative things into print about people they didn't like? Things that weren't true?

"I was wondering if you had some free time this afternoon? I'm coming into the city today to run some errands, and I'd love to buy you a coffee or a drink or something," I said cautiously.

She snorted. "Just come by the brownstone, and I'll make coffee. I'm stuck on the new book and am pretty much giving up on the day as lost. Maybe some gossip from out there will do me some good, give me some inspiration or something." She sighed. "It's been a pretty dry summer, you know, for murder amongst the rich and famous."

"I'll be there around one," I said, after consulting my watch and estimating how long I'd be with the costume designer. "You do know we're putting on the Independence Ball again this year?"

"I'd heard something to that effect," she replied. "I'd better be on the guest list."

"Of course," I replied, hanging up. I took a deep breath.

Once we reached the city, I had Roberts take me to the costume designer's. Her studio was in the old meatpacking district, and after being buzzed in I found myself inside a big open space, with racks and racks of costumes as far as the eye could see. I could hear sewing machines running in the back. Joyce had told me that Mendelbaum Costumes' primary income came from making and renting costumes to stage, television, and film productions in the city. As soon as I spoke to the receptionist, a Goth-looking young man with dyed black hair and black fingernail polish and more piercings in his face than I'd even seen before, he called back and before long a small woman came walking hurriedly toward us through the racks of clothes.

Ruth Mendelbaum was legendary in theater circles, having dressed every major Broadway diva and having won any number of Tony Awards for her costumes. In person she was short with thick iron-gray hair, almost skeletally thin, and was wearing a black T-shirt and baggy black pants. Her eyes peered myopically at me from behind steel-rimmed glasses. She could have been any age between fifty and eighty. She looked me up and down, and signaled for me to turn around. She snapped her fingers. "Follow me," she said in a raspy voice that sounded like too many cigarettes and even more bourbon. She started walking and I fell into step behind her. She led me to an office where a cigarette burned in an enormous ashtray filled with ash and smashed butts smeared with lipstick. She shut the door and took an enormous puff before grinding the cigarette out. She folded her arms. "So, what are you thinking?"

"I—"

"Come, come, I don't have all day," she snapped. "Spit it out."

I pulled the folded picture out and handed it over to her. She examined it, looked at me, then back at the picture again. "Of course this is doable," she said, tossing the picture back onto her desk. "Get undressed."

"Um—"

"I don't have all day!" She spat the words out, snapping her fingers at me. "Get undressed! I need to take your measurements and I can't do that with your clothes on. Are you planning on wearing your clothes underneath your costume? No? Good, because that would look ridiculous. Okay then, get undressed." She lit another cigarette, expelling a plume of bluish smoke toward the ceiling. "You can leave your underwear on, of course."

A little cowed, I undressed, folding my clothes and placing them neatly on a chair. Once I was standing there in my underwear, shifting nervously from foot to foot, she grabbed a measuring tape and started measuring me. "I've just started working with a trainer, and he put me on a diet," I explained as she took notes on a notepad. "So I'll look better in my costume."

"The trunks will be white lined Lycra-cotton blend, so your junk won't show—the cotton will help it breathe so you won't sweat through it, and the Lycra will make it shiny so it'll catch the light and be more flattering." She sniffed, crushing the cigarette out and tossing the notepad onto her cluttered desk. "The Lycra will also stretch, so if I make it to fit with a give-or-take a size up and a size down from where you're at now, it'll still fit and be flattering. And the harness that'll keep the wings on will be made of white leather, and it'll be adjustable. So don't worry your pretty little head about it." She made a face at me. "But if you're going to wear white, I'd suggest you work on your tan." She waved her hand. "It'll be delivered the week of the ball. It shouldn't need any fittings."

I got dressed and fled.

From there, I had Roberts take me to Maureen's brownstone in the village. "You can just take my things to the apartment," I instructed him as I got out, "and I'll either take a cab or the subway over there when I'm finished here. I won't need you again until it's time to go to the theater."

I shut the door and he drove off, and I crossed the street and rang the bell. I had been to Maureen's once before, to drop off proofs of one of her articles. It had already been vetted by the magazine's lawyers, but Maureen always wanted to see the proofs and sign off on them before the magazine could go to press. Early in her career at *Street Talk*, a major error in one of her articles had resulted in an out-of-court settlement for an undisclosed amount of money—and since then Maureen insisted on seeing the page proofs. I hadn't been allowed inside—she'd simply answered the door and took the pouch from me. I'd waited in a coffee shop nearby until she'd looked them over and initialed them so I could pick them up and return them.

This time, she led me into the courtyard behind her brownstone. It was a jungle. Maureen was of medium height and was now approaching seventy. She dyed her hair black, but even in the worn-out sweat suit she was wearing, she gave off an air of dignity and class. She poured me a cup of coffee from an insulated carafe, and then one for herself. She took a sip and sighed in satisfaction. She then looked at me shrewdly.

"I have to congratulate you," she said with a slight nod. "I would have never in a million years believed you'd wind up married to Carlo Romaniello."

"You're not alone," I replied.

That made her laugh. "I'm sure Valerie had a few choice things to say, bitch that she is." She shook her head. "When she told me, she was still swearing. I don't know why it bothered her so much—but I told her she'd been a fool if she'd offended you." She winked at me. "She'd give anything to get in with society, that one would—always hounding me to see if I can get her invited to the right parties." She shook her head. "I told her she should be kissing your ass—since you could get her an invitation to the Independence Ball. I'll be there, of course. I always spend July in the Hamptons visiting Dorian Castlemaine—she was a cousin of my husband's."

The one who called me a gold digger to Nell, I thought, keeping my face impassive. *Maybe I should get her disinvited.*

"But that's not why you're here." She poured herself another cup of coffee. "And you clearly don't have any gossip for me—I just talked to Dorian, and she's said no one's seen or met you since Carlo brought you to Spindrift. So why are you here?"

"Someone said something to me the other day, and I can't get it out of my head," I said slowly. I took a deep breath and plunged ahead. "It's probably nothing, but—someone told me that Timothy Burke's death wasn't an accident."

She didn't reply at first. She just looked at me and sat back in her chair. "Well, well, well," she finally said, crossing her legs and lighting a cigarette. "They certainly didn't waste time, did they? Are you afraid you married Bluebeard?"

"Bluebeard?" I stared at her as her meaning took root in my mind. "Carlo? Carlo didn't kill Timothy. Carlo loved Timothy."

"The first person the police look at when someone is murdered is their spouse or partner."

"Carlo wouldn't have done it," I replied vehemently. "That's absurd."

"If you say so." She inhaled on the cigarette and gave me a wry look. "Are you afraid someone unbalanced is in love with Carlo and kills off his husbands?"

That hadn't occurred to me. "You think that's possible?"

She laughed, but her eyes were still shrewd. "Anything's possible, young man, as you'll know when you're as old as I am." She shrugged. "I suppose you're here wondering if I've heard anything." She tapped her ash into a full glass ashtray. "Obviously, last July when I stayed with Dorian, all the Hamptons gossip was about Timothy's drowning. I'd never heard anything bad about him, you know, until he was dead. For some reason which I've never quite understood, it was after he died that the gloves came off—which was quite unusual in that circle, you know." She gave me a brittle smile. "I heard he was actually quite active sexually, cheating on Carlo. That 'studio' of his was apparently one of his favorite places to meet lovers—and of course, he would often come into the city and use the penthouse. I didn't believe any of it—I've known Carlo Romaniello for years, and he would have to have been a fool to not know what was going on almost right under his nose—and if there's one thing Carlo Romaniello is not, it's a fool. And I can't imagine he would tolerate any of this, can you?"

"You think Carlo would have killed him?" I asked hesitantly.

"Carlo would have thrown his ass out. No, it doesn't make any sense." She shook her head. "Mind you, I never much cared for Timothy Burke. There was something about him—it was like chewing tinfoil."

I shuddered involuntarily.

She went on, "Oh, he had excellent manners and he was charming and witty and handsome as all get-out, but there was something about him that seemed off to me. He was very clever—not smart clever. He'd used his looks all his life to get what he wanted—a successful career, a wealthy husband, his own business—but he wouldn't risk that. He wasn't that stupid. If Carlo threw him out, he'd have *nothing*." She started ticking things off on her fingers. "No money. No company—Carlo put up the money for that underwear business of his. No big house in the Hamptons. No penthouse on Central Park West. Nothing. But then—" She paused. "There are none so blind as those who will not see. It's possible Carlo turned a blind eye to all of it because he didn't want to know."

"I know that he slept with his trainer."

"That would be Brad Collins?" She flashed a smile at me. "I heard it was that friend of his, that gigolo Taylor Hudson, or the tennis pro. But no one—not one person out there—whispered that his death was anything other than an accident."

I exhaled. "Thank you for talking to me, Maureen. I don't know why this was bothering me so much, but it was."

She stood up. "Was it Nell Chamberlain who told you?"

Startled, I nodded.

"Don't look so surprised, dear. It was a pretty educated guess—she lives next door to you." She walked me to the door. "Nell hated him, you know. Something to do with one of those damned spaniels." She shook her head. "She's quite unreasonable when it comes to those dogs—they're like her children." She opened the front door for me. "I'll listen, though, and ask some discreet questions, if you'd like. It would make for a good story." The door shut behind me.

I stood there, staring at the door in horror. The last thing in the world I wanted was for her to write a story about Timothy.

I gave up on a cab after two zoomed past me, and took the subway uptown. Once the horror died, I began to think such a piece on *Street Talk* might not be such a bad thing.

It felt strange being in the penthouse without Carlo. I mixed myself a martini the way Joyce had showed me, and relaxed on the deck, listening to the city sounds as the day came to a close.

Then again, I finally decided, if Timothy hadn't been murdered—which now seemed more and more likely to be the case—there was no story.

And on that note, I went inside to get ready for the theater.

The musical was terrible. I left during the intermission and hailed a cab.

I was an hour and a half or so early for my dinner reservations, but the host managed to squeeze me into a small table in the crowded restaurant, which I appreciated. I ordered, and was nursing a very dry martini when I heard someone say my name.

I knew that voice.

"Valerie," I said, getting out of my chair and forcing a smile onto my face. "What a coincidence to run into you here." I knew damned well it wasn't a coincidence—Maureen had ratted me out. She'd gotten here early so she could ambush me—but leaving the show early had ruined that for her. "Please, have a seat and join me for a drink. We need to catch up."

I couldn't think of anything I'd rather do less than have a drink with Valerie, but there was no way around it that I could see—and maybe I could do something to defuse whatever she was thinking.

A busboy brought a chair over and she sat down across the table from me. "Oh, I'm waiting for my own table, but bring me a Manhattan," she said, waving off the menu the waiter tried to hand her. He bowed and hurried off. She smiled at me—what I always thought of as her piranha smile. "I had an interesting conversation with Maureen Drury this afternoon," she said, carefully smoothing out her skirt. "I have to say, it caught me a little off guard."

Mentally I made a note to tell Joyce to cross Maureen and her cousin off the guest list for the Independence Ball. I smiled back across the table at Valerie and hoped my face didn't betray how fast my heart was beating. "Did it?" I said, surprised at how smooth my voice sounded. "I don't see how it concerns you, though."

"You don't?" She raised her eyebrows and tilted her head slightly to one side. I knew that look. It was a tactic I'd seen her use any number of times on people she wanted something from, when she thought she had the upper hand, was sitting in the catbird seat. But unfortunately for Valerie Franklin, I was quite familiar with all of her tricks. "I should think an investigative journalist like Maureen Drury looking into Timothy's strange death would be the last thing in the world the Romaniello family would want."

"*We* have nothing to hide." She flinched at my emphasis on the word "we," which made me smile a little. "Maureen is seeing things where there's nothing to see. My neighbor, Nell Chamberlain, mentioned to me the other day that she didn't believe Timothy's death was an accident, and I was curious if there was any other gossip—and who better to ask than the biggest gossip in the city?"

She clearly didn't believe me. She made an odd little noise, and her smile widened. "If that's how you want to play it—"

"I'm not playing." I replied evenly. "If Maureen misunderstood our conversation, I can't help that." My waiter was hovering with my dinner. "And if you'll excuse me, my dinner's here."

She narrowed her eyes, but she got up and headed to the bar. I hurried through my dinner, paid the check, and escaped.

The next morning, Roberts drove me back to Spindrift.

CHAPTER ELEVEN

Maureen e-mailed me an apology the next morning. I read it on my phone in the car on my way back to Spindrift. I got up early, wanting to get back as early as possible—I missed Minette, and decided the next time I came into the city I was bringing her with me.

Her e-mail was succinct and to the point.

Darling,

I only just now discovered that some careless words I uttered to Valerie yesterday regarding the information you and I discussed at my home were, unfortunately, taken as gospel truth by the woman. She informed me this morning that she spoke to you last evening about it. I most humbly ask your forgiveness. I had no idea she was planning on tracking you down and harassing you, and I certainly made it quite clear, just now on the telephone, that there is nothing factual to suggest that Timothy's death was anything other than an unfortunate accident, and she certainly couldn't risk publishing anything quite so slanderous.

I am so terribly sorry, I don't know what I was thinking in mentioning any of this to her. I certainly had no idea she would behave so atrociously, or I wouldn't have mentioned anything.

Please accept my apology, and if there is anything,
anything at ALL, that I can do to make up for this egregious
abuse of your trust, do let me know.
    Sincerely,
    Maureen

I couldn't help but smile to myself as I put my phone back away. Maureen was clearly afraid she might not be on the guest list for the Independence Ball.

By the time we arrived at the house, I was feeling very confident and sure of myself, more so than I had at any time since I first moved in. Carson was waiting for me in the entryway when I walked in the front door, with some minor issues he needed me to go over and some checks to sign. We went into my office and shut the door behind us while I went over the receipts and signed the checks he'd already filled out for me. He bowed his head politely, gathered up everything, and was almost to the door when I stopped him.

"Carson, I've been meaning to ask you." I leaned back in the chair and watched him carefully. "There's a locked door on the second floor of the west wing. Do you know anything about that?"

His mouth tightened a little, and a muscle started jumping in his right cheek. "Yes, sir. Mr. Carlo has asked that the door be kept locked."

I had already figured out the answer to my next question, but wanted confirmation. "And why is that, Carson?"

"I cannot tell you the reason, as I do not know, and anything I might say would only be speculation," he replied, closing his eyes carefully and lowering his head a bit. "But those were Mr. Timothy's rooms, sir." He said nothing else, but I could see the sly gleam in his eyes.

"I'd like to see them," I replied.

"Of course, sir." He nodded again. "Let me put these things away, and I shall meet you up there." He backed out of the room.

I took a deep breath and stood up. I walked over to the windows and watched the waves in the distance, coming ashore. A rush of nervousness came over me, but I tamped it down quickly. As master of Spindrift, I had every right to go in there and take a look around. Even if Carlo was still in love with Timothy, I was married to him now, and this was my home. If I wanted the room stripped and fumigated, so be it.

And as I climbed the grand staircase I thought, *And maybe what this entire house needs is an exorcism. Facing the ghosts in the west wing is surely a good start.*

Yet as I reached the top of the stairs and entered the west wing, I could feel my heart beginning to pound loudly and my nerve start to desert me. It took all of my willpower to keep walking forward— especially after I noticed that the door to his rooms was open. I took a deep breath, lifted my chin, and walked in.

The entire room was done in shades of red. The bed was a four-poster, just like mine, but it was enormous—five people could sleep comfortably in it, I estimated. The carpet was thick and plush, also a deep shade of red, a cross between crimson and maroon. The curtains hanging around the bed were a rich red velvet—and there were matching curtains on the windows. A rolltop desk similar to the one in my room sat in the exact same place—but directly over it was a framed black-and-white print of the most famous photo of Timothy when he was a model. I couldn't help myself, I walked over to it and stared up at it.

He was leaning back against a brick wall, and the photographer had taken the picture in front and from an angle just slightly below, shooting the picture up. The end result was that all the shadows from the lighting made the deep cuts in Timothy's abdomen stand out like they were carved from solid rock—and of course, the bulge in the front of the tight white briefs looked enormous. There was no real expression on his face, other than the raised eyebrow and the slight tilt of the head that made the pose provocative, as though he were inviting a caress from anyone viewing him, daring the viewer to touch him. I had seen this picture any number of times in ads in magazines, but at this enormous size, without the ad copy or the brand name written across the bottom, it was different. Rather than selling underwear, it was an extraordinarily artistic shot; one that could be hung as a piece of art or sold in a gallery.

"He was quite beautiful," Carson said, his tone quiet and winsome.

I hadn't heard him come up behind me, and I hadn't seen him when I walked into the room. "Yes," I replied hollowly, "yes, he was."

"After he died, Mr. Carlo asked me to lock the door to this room and keep it locked," Carson said, walking past me and staring up at the print. He wiped some dust off a corner of the frame. "He wanted it left exactly as it was, and I was to be the only person allowed in here to keep it clean."

I tore my eyes away from the print and walked over to the door that led to the closet. I opened it, and it was full of clothes—from several tuxedos to slacks to shirts in an array of colors. Shoes were lined up neatly underneath the hanging clothes. I could feel my breakfast turning to acid in my stomach.

It looked ready for him, like he was going to walk in through the door at any moment.

I closed the closet door and took a few deep breaths. I felt more than nauseous. This entire room—it was a shrine to Timothy. And the night I'd heard a man crying in here? It had to be Carlo.

"Thank you, Carson," I somehow managed to say, and carefully walked out of the room, my head still held high as my insecurities ran rampant through my mind. I don't know how I managed to simply walk all the way back to my rooms in the east wing without running or having to hold on to the wall for support.

He's still in love with Timothy. No matter what I do, I cannot compete with that. I'm not in the same league as him. Marrying me and bringing me here was a huge mistake, and if he hasn't realized that already, he will soon, and will ask me to leave, and then what am I going to do?

Minette leaped on me the moment I opened my door, and I knelt down and hugged my precious, beautiful spaniel. And as she licked my face, her tail wagging madly, I managed to calm down.

I wouldn't speak to Carlo about Timothy's room. It could stay as it was, carefully locked against intruders. I would never bring it up, or anything about him. I was alive, after all; Timothy was dead—and it was my bed that Carlo came to at night. As I buried my hair in the neck of my wonderful dog, I made up my mind. I was going to be the best I could be. I wanted to be a writer, so damn it, I was going to write. I would take my tennis lessons seriously and would become a good player. I would do what my trainer told me, and I would tighten up my body and make it more beautiful than it was.

I would be the best husband Carlo could have ever asked for, and eventually, he would have to forget all about my predecessor.

I felt better, and stronger. I put Minette's leash on her and took her out for a walk.

My life soon fell into a pattern, a routine I began to enjoy. Each morning I would take Minette for her walk, take a shower, and go downstairs for breakfast. Three days a week I worked out with Brad in the exercise room. The two days I didn't work out with him, I took a tennis lesson from Chris. I used the tanning bed every day for ten minutes, and my skin began to darken. Between the weight training and the tennis, my body was beginning to change. I could see it in the mirror—veins were starting to appear in my arms, muscles were starting to poke their way through my skin, and my only wish was that my body would progress faster somehow.

I also spent several hours every afternoon writing on my laptop. Sometimes I took it out to my balcony and wrote with the sea breeze in my face and the sound of the gulls in my ears. I wrote short stories—I had no ideas for a novel, but plenty of ideas for short stories. None of them were any good, of course, but I kept trying. I would always spend an hour or so after dinner revising and editing stories I'd already written. I wasn't ready to submit anything anywhere yet, or to even show them to anyone, but I could see a steady improvement in them as the weeks passed—just as there was in my body.

Every morning Joyce came by to go over preparations for the ball and for my input on the decorations, the music, the food, the invitations, the guest list—everything. I helped her as much as I possibly could—she wanted my opinion on everything, which I really appreciated, but I knew she could have done the entire thing without any input or assistance from me. She clearly enjoyed the planning and preparations, and I said as much to her one morning after we'd decided on the invitations and what kind of hors d'oeuvres to serve.

"Don't FOOL yourself for a MINUTE, darling," she replied with a wink. "Next year, YOU'LL be doing this on YOUR own, with ME to help out as NEEDED. And the year after? ON YOUR OWN."

Carlo, of course, was in and out—board meetings and problems kept him traveling. Much as I didn't like him going off and leaving me alone, I kept my mouth shut and didn't say a word. The last thing I wanted for the time we had together was for me to whine and complain. He thought I'd be bored on these trips and so it was left at that. He did frequently promise to take me away once all the business was settled—he told me over and over that the summer was the busiest time for him and we would spend September in Paris if that was what I wanted to do.

I spent a lot of time researching Paris, figuring out what I wanted to do and see when we got there.

When he was at Spindrift, we settled into an easy routine together. If our life together wasn't quite the same as it had been when we were in Miami, it was easy and comfortable. We had an ease with each other I came to deeply appreciate—we enjoyed each other's company and I wasn't quite so insecure anymore. Maybe he didn't say he loved me as often as I would have liked, and maybe there were times when I felt like he was dismissing me from his life, but what we had seemed to be working. After all, I'd never been in a relationship before, and my mother had died when I was too young to have any memory of her—so I didn't have the example of my parents' marriage to go by, either.

My interactions with Carson were also better. I wasn't so foolish as to think he would ever approve of me completely, but he'd been so helpful over the matter of my costume—and his manner with me seemed to be much easier since he'd shown me Timothy's rooms. We met once a week to discuss the flowers and the menus for meals, and I found myself no longer quite as intimidated as I'd been. There were times when I would catch him watching me, a strange expression on his face, but I had no idea what it meant, and dismissed it. Carson was just Carson, and that's all there was to it.

My newfound confidence in myself and my role at Spindrift was noticeable, and both Carlo and Joyce commented on it.

Several times a week I went over to Nell's so Minette could visit with Charlie and Hetty, and we always had iced tea while the dogs romped together. The subject of Timothy never came up again—I wasn't about to mention him, and she seemed to no longer have any interest in the subject. We never talked about anything personal—only about the dogs, or the approaching costume ball. She did try on several occasions to get me to tell her what I was going to wear as my costume, but I flatly refused to tell her anything. I was keeping it a secret from everyone, even her.

It was the afternoon of the ball when she brought Timothy up again.

I took Minette for a walk, glad for any excuse to escape the madness of the house. Workers were everywhere, decorating and moving furniture, and deliveries were coming and going, and I just couldn't take it anymore. Carlo had taken refuge in his room after breakfast, and I grabbed Minette's leash and headed next door.

"It's so strange to have the ball without Timothy being there," Nell said after a long silence while we watched the dogs playing. "He is so associated with this party in my head—and so many others, I'm sure…it must be very strange for Carlo." She fixed her eyes on me. "You do know most people are coming tonight more out of curiosity than anything else."

"Yes, I kind of figured that. And Carlo's holding up just fine," I replied, looking her right in the eye. It wasn't true—Carlo had returned from Buenos Aires a few days earlier in a very strange mood, and his moodiness had increased with each day. He hadn't come to my suite since he'd returned, and rather than our usual evenings of watching black-and-white movies, every night after dinner he excused himself and went up to his rooms.

I knew the party was triggering memories for him. The last time the ball had been given at Spindrift, Timothy had been the host.

I'd found the pictures—Timothy had come as Michael Phelps, the Olympic swimmer, in a very skimpy stars and stripes Speedo with faux Olympic medals around his neck. One of them had been real, though—the gold medal Taylor had asked me about.

But rather than allowing my insecurities to come to the fore again, I reminded myself that it was only natural he'd be haunted by his memories. This was the first time the ball had been held since Timothy died, and it was an essential part of the healing process. Once Carlo made it through the ball this time, it would be easier the next. I was determined to make sure we had a wonderful time—so the new memories could crowd out the old.

I was finished with being jealous of a dead man. I was focusing on the positive and moving forward—and leaving Timothy's shadow far behind us.

"I'm sorry—it must bother you to have me bring him up," She reached across the table and patted my hand. "That's why I haven't since that first time you stopped by here, you know. I could see that it upset you."

"It's fine, Nell, really." I insisted. "I can't pretend like he never existed. He did, and Carlo loved him. But he's dead, and I'm alive. That's what I hold on to now."

"He was murdered, you know," she said in a quiet voice. "But he deserved to be killed. What he was doing to Carlo was unforgivable." She looked off into the distance. "I used to see him from the widow's walk. There was"—she shook her head—"there was a time when I was having trouble sleeping every night. I didn't want pills—my sister had a problem with sleeping pills, you know, and I was already taking enough pills as it was, so I said no thank you, I'm not taking more—and so I used to go up to the widow's walk to sit and breathe the night air and listen to the sea until I got sleepy. And of course from up there I could see everything that went on over at Spindrift—I have a clear view of his studio." Her lips compressed tightly together. "Studio, he called it." She sniffed disdainfully. "He'd have his men meet him out there. I used to see him waiting for them…and poor Carlo had no idea. One of them killed him, I'd be willing to bet on that."

"You're so certain he was murdered," I said after a moment.

"Someone took the *Rhiannon* out that night," she replied.

At first I didn't know what she was talking about—but then I remembered the *Rhiannon* was the yacht in the boathouse. It was sitting there in dry dock, unused. I'd asked about it once, and Carlo simply replied he'd lost interest in boating. I'd let it go.

"I was up on the roof," she went on, her hands shaking as she put her glass of tea down, "and I saw it leave. I didn't think anything of it, of course, but I had a very clear view of the beach—and there wasn't anything there, like they said there was, later. No towel, no bag, nothing. I did think it was an odd time for the boat to go out—it was almost dusk—but it was none of my business, and if Carlo or whoever wanted to take the boat out at that time of day, it didn't matter to me. I went down into the house and didn't see it come back." She looked at me, her eyes wet. "And then, of course, the next morning I heard about Timothy…and then I wondered if maybe it did matter after all."

We sat there in silence, the only sounds the waves in the distance and the dogs playing. She wiped at her eyes.

When I spoke again, my voice was unsteady. "Why didn't you say anything?"

"We don't talk to the police, don't you know that by now?" She stood up. "And have to testify in court, and be fodder for the gossip columnists and the tabloids and those horrible programs on television? No, we don't talk to the police, my friend." She whistled for her dogs. They came on the run, their tongues out, barking and yapping around. "I'd best be getting inside." She smiled at me. "I may not be coming tonight after all—I'm not so sure I'm up to it. Give Carlo and Joyce my regrets."

"Nell—"

The door shut behind her. I sat there for a moment, petting Minette, my mind racing.

Someone had taken the boat out that night.

But the autopsy showed Timothy had drowned—he had sea water in his lungs. And he was a strong swimmer—surely if someone had tried to drown him…

I stood up, a little shaky, and walked Minette back to the madness at Spindrift.

I put everything Nell had said out of my mind. I pitched in and helped a crazed Joyce with the finishing touches on the house before she left to go put on her own costume. Carlo was in a remarkably good mood, teasing me about my mysterious costume, and I was relieved to see it. He seemed like his old self again—as though he'd managed to put his painful memories behind him and wanted to enjoy himself.

My plan to help him forget was clearly working.

I was still in my afternoon clothing when Frank and Joyce arrived, several hours early. They were staying overnight—I'd had Olivia prepare the Lavender Suite for them—and I had suggested they just come early and get dressed at Spindrift. But Joyce wouldn't hear of it—and I couldn't help myself. I started laughing when they came through the front doors—Joyce was dressed as Little Bo Peep, complete with thick pancake makeup, thick mascara, and rouged cheeks.

Frank was one of her sheep.

"Go ahead and laugh," Frank groused at me. "I need a drink." He stormed off to where a bar had been set up in the formal dining room.

"Frank, I'm sorry," I called after him. "I love your costume, really!"

"Don't worry about him," Joyce said rather crossly. "He always complains about his costumes. I always tell him if he hates the costumes I come up with so much he's more than welcome to come up with his own ideas—but he won't do that. He just likes to complain. Where's Carlo?"

"Getting dressed," I replied, and was pleased to see Frank returning with a drink, a twinkle in his eye.

He handed Joyce a rather large martini. "Not sure how I'm supposed to go to the bathroom in this stupid outfit, so there just might be an accident later." He winked at me and took a big drink from his own glass.

Joyce gave him a dirty look and turned to me. "Don't you think you should be getting dressed yourself?" she groused as Frank handed her a glass of red wine.

"All right, I was just waiting for you two to arrive in case someone showed up early." I bowed and dashed up the grand staircase.

My costume had been delivered that morning, and I had immediately hidden it inside my closet. As I unzipped the big bag, I gasped in pleasure at the sight of the wings. Ruth had done a great job on them—the real white feathers were soft and beautiful, and the halo itself was round and covered with gold glitter that caught the light and reflected it beautifully. I took my shower and shaved, and after drying myself I walked back into the bedroom. I pulled the pure white trunks on and looked at myself in the mirror. They fit snugly, like a second skin. They were also a little briefer than I would have liked, but it was too late to do anything about it now. I stared at my reflection. I turned and checked out my backside. The trunks delineated the crack of my ass—and I hesitated for a second. *Maybe it's too much? Too risqué?*

Don't be ridiculous, I reminded myself. *New experiences, and confidence. You can pull this outfit off.*

I faced myself again in the mirror and smiled. My body looked good—I wasn't Timothy, but that hadn't been the idea anyway. No matter how much I worked I would never be that. But my muscles looked nice, my skin was nicely tanned, and the white of the trunks made my tan look even deeper than it really was. I put on a pair of socks and laced up the white leather boots that reached my knees. Once again, with the laces tied tightly, I examined myself in the mirror.

I looked really good. Better than I could have hoped for.

Carlo is going to be speechless, I thought with a big grin.

I slipped my arms through the harness and snapped everything together in the front. The wings looked beautiful, and I slipped the halo on the top of my head.

I looked—*beautiful.*

"Wow," I said out loud, reaching out and touching the mirror's surface.

I put my other hand over my mouth and felt tears forming in my eyes.

All those years of loneliness, of being nobody, of being a shy, quiet person, of being ignored and looked over were in the past.

I was now married to a great man who loved me, and I lived in a castle. And I looked amazing—and tonight I was going to be the belle of the ball.

I felt like Cinderella.

I couldn't stop looking at myself in the mirror.

This was going to be the greatest night of my life.

I felt like I could fly, if I really wanted to.

There was a knock on the door, and Olivia poked her head in. "Sir, the guests are starting to arrive and Mr. Carlo—oh." She stopped talking and her eyes goggled in her head.

"How do I look, Olivia?" I spun around for her, the wings rustling.

She'd gone pale, and she stammered out, "You look really good."

"Then why are you acting like you've seen a ghost?"

"They're waiting for you downstairs," she gasped out, and hurried away.

That was certainly odd, I thought as I took one last look at myself in the mirror. I closed my door and started walking down the hallway. I was going to make a grand entrance down the grand staircase, debuting my wonderful costume and my amazing new look. I could already imagine the looks on their faces when they saw me… The thought brought a grin to my face, and a delighted laugh burst out of me. I could hear car doors shutting outside, and I started hurrying even faster. I wanted everyone who walked in through the front door to see me, I wanted them to look at me and think, *Why, he's not Timothy, of course, but I don't know why everyone was saying he was so plain, he's rather attractive, and that costume looks wonderful on him.* I wanted to see the lusty gleam in Carlo's eyes as he looked me up and down and for the first time could truly see how my body had changed, how different I was from that little Mouse he'd met in Miami.

I looked like someone who belonged at Spindrift now.

I reached the stairs and placed my left hand on the banister and majestically started walking down the steps. I could hear the feathers rustling softly and feel them brushing gently against the skin of my back. My smile was so big my cheeks were starting to ache. I paused when I reached the landing, and took a deep breath. *Prepare yourselves for a big surprise*, I thought.

I went around the corner of the landing and could see them all standing there, just inside the front door.

I cleared my throat and they all looked up.

They all gasped at the same time.

I smiled and, holding my head high, gracefully glided down the stairs.

"What do you think?" I said when I reached them. I turned around for them. "Isn't it beautiful?"

It was then, and only then, that I saw the looks on their faces—and they weren't what I'd been hoping to see.

Frank looked embarrassed, Joyce mortified. Carlo's face was red, his eyebrows knit together, and a muscle in his jaw was jumping.

No one said anything.

And it was at that inopportune moment that some guests arrived. They greeted Frank and Joyce and a wooden Carlo and were introduced to me, but I was so worried and concerned I didn't catch their names or what they were saying to me. All I could think was Carlo was angry, somehow I'd done something wrong, maybe the costume was too revealing or I didn't look good in it.

The woman was smiling at me—she was dressed as Cleopatra, and she was saying something about how good I looked in my costume, and then she and her husband were gone, on their way to the bar.

Carlo strode off without a word.

Helplessly, I turned back to Joyce and Frank.

And I heard Cleopatra saying to her husband in a loud whisper she surely intended for me to hear, 'What incredibly poor taste! Can you believe he had the nerve to wear the costume Timothy was going to wear last year? He's certainly no Timothy, that's for sure."

I felt like throwing up.

I turned to Joyce, who had tears in her eyes, her hand over her mouth.

"I didn't know," I whispered, and turned and ran up the stairs as quickly as I could.

And when I reached the top of the stairs, there stood Carson, a smirk on his face.

Without a word, he turned and walked noiselessly down the hall.

Chapter Twelve

I staggered along the upstairs hallway, my eyes filled with tears of humiliation. I couldn't get the look on Carlo's face out of my mind—or the contempt and barely controlled anger in his voice. I started fumbling with the buckle on the front of the harness. I kept my eyes on the floor—the faces in the paintings on the walls all seemed to viewing me with scorn and contempt. Outside, I heard the music playing—I vaguely remembered Joyce telling me he was the hottest deejay in the gay clubs of the city—and wondered how I was ever going to be able to go downstairs again and face our guests.

Somehow, I had to. I had to summon up the courage from somewhere and go down there and pretend like nothing was wrong—even though what I wanted to do was get dressed, pack a bag, and run as far away from Spindrift as I could.

I laughed at myself contemptuously. *You don't have a way to leave if you had the guts to walk out—you don't have a car, you don't even know how to drive. What are you going to do, walk to the nearest train station?*

And what would it ultimately prove, anyway? That everyone who thought Carlo made a mistake in marrying me was right?

I opened the door to my room and closed it behind me. I finished unbuckling the harness and shrugged the straps off my shoulders. They fell to the floor and I picked them up, tossing them into the corner. Some of the feathers bent or broke, but what did it matter? I was never going to wear them again.

I resisted the urge to set them on fire.

I sat down on the edge of the bed and started untying and unlacing the boots. My hands were shaking and the tears finally started flowing out of my eyes. My nose started running, but I kept unlacing the boots, trying to focus; focusing on the task at hand was what was keeping me together. Once the boots were unlaced, I yanked them off and threw them into the same corner as the wings.

Minette shoved her head under my hand and gave me such a sad, mournful look that my heart broke. Her tail thumped against the bed, and she climbed into lap and tried to lick my face.

That was the final straw. The dam broke and the misery completely overwhelmed me. I hugged her, burying my face in her neck and let go, giving way to the sobs.

I don't know how long I cried—but it seemed like hours passed before I was all cried out. I gently pushed Minette out of my lap and walked into the bathroom.

I stared at my tearstained face and turned on the hot water spigot.

Let me just get through this damned party, I said to my reflection as the mirror started to steam up, *and I'll go away. Tomorrow, when my head is clearer, I'll figure out what to do. I'll pack some things, and maybe—maybe Carlo will help me get started somewhere far away from here. He owes me that, at the least. It isn't my fault he doesn't love me.*

That thought brought the tears back, but I splashed hot water on my face and got hold of myself. I washed my face thoroughly, and a terrible calm seemed to settle over me.

Of course Carlo will help me. It takes two to make a marriage fail, and I did my best, didn't I? I won't go back to New York—too many memories, and I am not going to go back to work for Valerie, but maybe he can help me find a job in Chicago or New Orleans or somewhere. He has to have connections in publishing, right?

I smiled at the mirror. My eyes were red, but other than that I looked okay. I could pull it off, I could go downstairs and smile and play host and be gracious. No one would have the slightest idea that anything was wrong. I was numb and deadened inside.

There was a knock on the bedroom door, and I called, "Come in!" I turned off the spigot and walked back in the bedroom just as Joyce opened the door.

"Are YOU all right, dear?" Despite the ridiculous pancake makeup on her face I could see she was concerned. "I came up as QUICKLY as I could—I am SO sorry." She crossed the room and grabbed both of my hands, peering into my face. "I don't know WHY Carlo can't control that TEMPER of his—he NEVER could, even when we were KIDS. PLEASE forget how BEASTLY he was to you and come back to the party."

"No need to worry, Joyce, I'm not going to give the gossips any fodder. As soon as I put on something else, I'll be down to pretend like everything's just marvelous," I said bitterly. I grabbed a pair of underwear out of my dresser and walked into my walk-in closet. I grabbed my white linen suit and placed it across the chair. I left the closet door ajar so we could still talk. "I won't shame the family name, Joyce." I peeled the tight trunks off, wadded them up into a ball, and tossed them in the little wicker garbage can—no need to keep them. I'd never wear them again. I pulled on the underwear and pulled out a dark blue silk shirt.

"Now, DARLING, Carlo undoubtedly feels like a complete ASS, and if I KNOW my brother, you can EXPECT a most EXPENSIVE apology gift," she called out.

I buckled my belt and walked back into the bedroom carrying a pair of socks and my suede Bass shoes. I sat down and slipped my feet into my socks. "I don't want an expensive gift."

"Darling, don't be ABSURD." She smiled at me, which looked rather bizarre given her Bo Peep makeup. "TRUST me, he'll be TERRIBLY contrite." She sighed. "I SHOULD have gotten another DRINK before I came up. You look quite NICE in that suit, dear."

"Thank you." I got up and straightened the color of my shirt in the mirror. "And I really appreciate what you're trying to do, Joyce.

But I think it's best that Carlo and I admit we made a mistake and split up."

She goggled at me. Her mouth opened and closed, no sound coming out. Finally, she said in a hoarse whisper, "Darling, WHAT are you talking ABOUT?"

I shrugged. "He goes on trips and doesn't want me to come with him. We sleep in separate rooms. Half the time he isn't here, and most of the time when he actually is here he can't be bothered with me. I don't know why he married me in the first place. Clearly, he isn't over Timothy, and I'm tired of him looking at me and being disappointed because I'm not *him*."

My voice was flat and devoid of emotion. The numbness had worn off, replaced by tired resignation. What was, was, and no matter how much I wanted it to be different it would never be.

"Oh, my dear," she whispered, and her eyes glistened with tears.

"I'll talk to Carlo about it in the morning," I went on. "And now, don't you think we need to get back downstairs before the guests start talking?" I checked myself out in the mirror again. "I think the story we tell people about my costume was that it tore, so of course I had to go change. They'll believe that, won't they?"

"Yes, of course." She dabbed at her eyes with a tissue. "We really need to be getting back down." She stood up, and blew her nose, smearing some of her makeup.

"Carlo might be angry with me for wearing Timothy's costume," I said, "but he'll be even angrier if everyone is talking about how I'm missing from the party, won't he?"

"Timothy's costume?" Joyce looked at me, clearly bewildered.

"That woman—the one dressed as Cleopatra—she said—"

"That was MIDGE HUNTLEY." Joyce waved a hand and sniffed disdainfully. "Ever since Timothy DIED, Midge has acted like they were BEST friends—which they were most definitely NOT. Timothy DISLIKED her. He used to IMITATE her in a MOST cruel way." She shook her head. "So she has NO idea what Timothy's costume WOULD have been last YEAR—he would have NEVER told HER. Besides, Timothy ALWAYS kept his costume a SECRET until the party."

I bit my lower lip. "Like I did this year?"

She sighed. "Yes, like you did THIS year. It was SO strange…" Her voice trailed off.

"Well, if I'd known he kept his costume a secret every year…"

"How WOULD you have known? None of us EVER talk about HIM." She shook her head and changed the subject. "Midge Huntley's a BITCH, and she *wanted* you to hear her say that." Her eyes took on a nasty gleam. "Don't WORRY, I know how to deal with HER."

"Then why was Carlo so angry?" I was confused. "If it wasn't the same costume…I don't understand."

"It DOES have to do WITH Timothy." She sighed, and sat down on the side of the bed. Minette hopped up next to her, shoving her head under Joyce's hand so she would pet her. Absently, Joyce began stroking her head. "Timothy ALWAYS wore SOMETHING like that—revealing. They FOUGHT about it EVERY year."

"That doesn't make sense," I replied. "He was an underwear model. Everyone saw him in his underwear, all the time."

"Yes, WELL, that was Carlo's POINT. I know, it doesn't MAKE sense, but Carlo…" She let her voice trail off, trying to think of the right words. "Carlo THOUGHT it was INAPPROPRIATE. And when YOU came down those STAIRS…well, it WAS quite a SHOCK to ALL of us. I SWEAR my first THOUGHT was dear GOD, he's risen from the DEAD…"

Carson, I thought, *he knew, and did this deliberately. Every costume in that folder—all of them were revealing, something Timothy would have worn. He had to have known Carlo disapproved—he knew everything that went on around here.* But I was still too numb to feel anything—even anger. Yes, Carson had deliberately set me up—to create problems between Carlo and me. He still hated me, wanted me gone. But I'd think about that some other time—it couldn't be dealt with tonight, anyway.

"So, yes, Carlo WAS angry because it reminded HIM of

something Timothy WOULD have worn. I'm SURE he was caught off guard JUST as we were." She took my hand. "Darling, SURELY you understand? Had I KNOWN I would have STOPPED you."

"Of course." I pulled my hand away. "Because who would have ever thought someone like me would wear something like that?" My voice sounded more tired than bitter to me.

"Oh, darling, you mustn't think like that." Her voice was low and subdued. "You looked amazing. I knew you'd been training with Brad, but I had no idea you'd been working so hard. It's been quite a transformation. You should be very proud of yourself."

I leaned down and kissed her cheek. "You're a dear, Joyce, you really are. You've been so very kind to me...always. I appreciate it more than you'll ever know." And finally, I forced myself to say the words I'd always known were true but would never admit to anyone. "But I know he's still in love with Timothy and hasn't gotten over him—and I don't know if he ever will. I was just a poor replacement, some kind of experiment to see if he could move on—well, I guess we know the answer to that, don't we?" I laughed bitterly. "And no doubt seeing me in something like Timothy would have worn only brought that home all the more to Carlo."

She stared at me, her mouth open. After a moment, she said, "Is that *really* what you think? You can't really believe that! But my dear—"

I walked out of my room without waiting to hear the rest of it.

I took a deep breath and walked down the hall, my head held high. I glided down the grand staircase and smiled at Frank and Carlo as I walked up to them. "Sorry I was gone for so long," I said, managing to keep my voice even and light, almost cheerful. "Better late than never."

Carlo looked at me, his face expressionless, but before he could say anything a couple dressed as what I took to be George and Martha Washington walked through the front door and we turned to greet them. I don't remember their names—but right after they moved on to the party, Joyce came down the stairs and stood next to me. "Darling, we need to have a talk—a serious talk," she whispered under her breath as yet another group of people—dressed as Harry Potter and friends—came through the front door.

I just smiled at them.

Somehow, I managed to get through the ordeal of greeting the new arrivals. No one would have guessed that my heart was broken or that my marriage had ended earlier that night. I was polite and friendly, and made small talk with everyone who came into the great house—but it was all just a blur to me. I was on autopilot, careful not to let the emptiness and numbness I was feeling inside be seen by anyone. It was torture, sheer torture. The whole time Carlo stood next to me, but never said a word directly to me. With a big smile on his face he would introduce me, and I would just smile and nod, accept congratulations, shake hands, kiss cheeks. Every so often I would catch Joyce watching me, her eyes sad. The costumes were extraordinary, and some were incredibly clever, ranging from the Scooby gang to the Beatles to Lady Gaga to Tippi Hedron from *The Birds*. Some made me laugh out loud. Maureen showed up with a group of people, all dressed in costumes from *Dangerous Liaisons*, their faces powdered and wigs towering on the women's heads. Maureen tapped me with her fan and pulled me aside to whisper into my ear, "Find me later—I have some things to tell you." I just smiled at her. I no longer cared about how Timothy died.

All I cared about was somehow getting through this evening.

Around eleven Joyce decided we no longer needed to stay in the foyer and I escaped into the party as quickly as I could without a word to either of them. I made my way to the nearest bar, got a glass of red wine, and disappeared into the nearby shadows while I sipped at it, watching the guests milling about or dancing. After a few moments, I took a deep breath and entered the fray, a smile plastered on my face. I played host as best I could, wandering around and checking ashtrays and drinks, making sure the buffet table was stocked, smiling and nodding politely to people as I passed within their line of vision. I never stayed stationary long enough for anyone to engage me in conversation—though many tried. My role as cohost enabled me to make a quick escape, with a promise to come back to finish the conversation—promises I had no intention of keeping. "Lovely party," I was told over and over again, and I just smiled and nodded my thanks and kept moving, weaving my way in and out of the endless crowd of guests. I kept my eyes moving, trying to avoid Carlo and Joyce. The disc jockey was playing dance music at a rather high volume, and out on the dancing area there was a crowd of younger guests dancing madly.

I only saw Carson once, when he come out of the kitchen. He stood on the gallery, looking out over the party, an unreadable expression on his face. Was it triumph, celebration for what he had accomplished that night? I stared at him, wondering what drove him, what kind of person could take pleasure in seeing another suffer.

For just a moment, a spark of anger cut through the numbness, but it quickly faded away.

I might be finished at Spindrift, but before I left this house for good Carson would pay for what he'd done to me.

As long as I lived I would never forget the look of triumph— and hatred—on his face as I stumbled up the grand staircase in humiliation and disgrace.

And as long as I lived, I would never forgive him for it.

Finally, exhausted, I hid in the darkness just below the gallery, sitting down on a stone bench in the shadows, tired of people, tired of forcing the muscles of my face to smile. I just wanted to be get away from people, to catch my breath and recharge, relax for a moment and decompress.

Just above me, two women were talking in hushed tones— unaware that someone had just sat down below where they stood on the gallery.

"Well, I suppose one shouldn't have expected this ball to be as good as they used to be, when Timothy was alive," one woman said disdainfully. "Did you get a look at the replacement? Whatever was Carlo thinking! He's little more than a child. It's disgusting."

"Hush, Nicola!" the other woman whispered, but went on in her equally sly and smug voice, "You're right, though, he isn't much to look at, is he? Little wonder there's so much talk that Carlo's already tired of him and thinking he made a mistake." She sniffed dismissively. "I certainly hope he was smart enough to have the boy sign a prenup—but if he didn't he has no one to blame but himself."

"I don't think he's in Kansas anymore," the first woman deadpanned, and they both burst out in laughter. "Oh, I'm sure he's nice enough—he seemed like a sweet child—but to be married to Carlo Romaniello? To live in this house? He looks more like a schoolteacher or a paid assistant."

"That's what he was, you know—to Valerie Franklin, you know—the editor of that dreadful magazine? That's what he was doing when they met. Can you imagine?"

"If he looked like Timothy, I could. But that mousy child? Whatever was Carlo thinking?"

"Clearly, he wasn't." This was followed by more of the nasty laughter.

My stomach churned. I hadn't eaten anything since lunch and hadn't had anything stronger to drink than that one glass of red wine. I felt like I was going to throw up at any moment. I bit my lower lip and took a series of deep breaths, wiping the sudden wetness of hurt from my eyes. I glanced through the railing of the gallery—one of the women was dressed as Snow White, the other was Maleficent from *Sleeping Beauty*—a most appropriate costume for the bitch. I remembered meeting them when they arrived, but their names escaped me.

I knew I should stop listening, should go back to the party, but I couldn't tear myself away—like when I had an aching tooth and couldn't stop worrying it with my tongue.

"And that nonsense about his costume not fitting properly!" the one called Nicola, the one dressed as Snow White, was saying. "Midge told me he actually had the *nerve* to try to pull off the costume Timothy was going to wear last year, and Carlo would have none of it! Apparently there was a terrible scene, and Carlo ordered him to go upstairs and change!" Her laugh was a nasty sound. "Trouble in paradise—I don't give that marriage another three months!"

"Midge would know, I suppose," the other woman mused. "What did Carlo see in that boy? Do you think he was just lonely?"

I couldn't stand to listen to anymore, so I stood and turned to look at them. I was pleased to hear the two bitches gasp as it slowly dawned on them that I'd heard everything they'd said. "Ladies," I said, inclining my head ever so slightly. They gaped at me, unable to say anything. I smiled at them and walked across the lawn as quickly as I could, my head spinning and my stomach still tied in knots. I saw Cleopatra—Midge Huntley—standing near the pool, and it took all of my self-control to not go over and shove her into the deep end. Miserable, horrible woman!

As I made my way around the dance area, I could hear Valerie's words echoing in my head: *You have no idea what people in that circle are like—you have no experience with them and they will eat you alive.*

I smiled and nodded at people, uttered inanities that meant nothing when a response was required, but through it all I wasn't really listening. I didn't know where Carlo was and I didn't care. I didn't want to see him or talk to him.

"There you are," Maureen hissed, grabbing me by the arm and pulling me out of the light into the shadows. "I've been looking for you everywhere. Where can we go talk?"

Her wig was crooked, and I straightened it for her. "The studio?" I asked. I didn't want to hear what she had to say—it no longer mattered, after all—but it would get me away from the party. So when she nodded, I escorted her through the darkness to the studio. There were some people on the dock, and others on the beach talking, but all the lights in the studio were off. I didn't turn on the overhead lighting because even with the blinds and curtains closed people would be able to see the lights were on. I pulled out my cell phone and used the dim light from its screen to negotiate my way through the darkened studio, and turned on the desk lamp. Maureen stepped inside and shut the door behind her.

It was a small lamp, and I felt confident no one would be able to see it through the pulled curtains. I sank down on the sofa and buried my face in my hands. I felt completely drained—this emotional roller coaster was wearing me out, and all I wanted was for the interminable party to be over so I could go to bed.

"Is everything all right?" Maureen asked, sitting down beside me on the sofa with a rustle of her petticoats. "You seem—distressed."

I laughed. "You have no idea." I said brokenly.

She tapped my arm with her fan. "Well, I've done some asking around, and even though no one really wants to talk about it over a whisper, there *is* some talk about Timothy's death not being an accident."

I almost said *it doesn't make any difference,* but she kept talking.

"It was no secret, apparently, out here that Timothy wasn't faithful to Carlo—the only person who didn't know was Carlo," she went on. "And of course everyone talked about it, but no one would tell Carlo." She shook her head and reached up quickly to keep her wig from sliding off. "But there was a terrible scene at one of the restaurants in town the day before he died—Carlo was in the city, and Timothy was having dinner with the tennis pro—Chris Thoresson—and Taylor Hudson caused a scene."

That aroused me out of my torpor. "Taylor Hudson?" I heard his voice in my head: *I was in Europe when Timothy died.* "I thought he was out of the country when Timothy died."

"No," she replied with a grim little shake of her head. "He's been Hermione Delano's companion for the last few years, and they left for Europe the day after Timothy disappeared." She stood up. "So, there just might be some fire where you smelled smoke." She walked over to the door. "I'll let you know if I find out anything else." The door shut behind her.

I sat there for a few minutes, digesting what she'd told me—but finally just dismissing it. What did it matter, anyway? Carlo was still in love with Timothy—even if Timothy hadn't been faithful to him. There was no point in telling him now.

My situation was unchanged.

The door opened, and I jumped. A man wearing a mask slipped through the doorway and quickly closed the door behind him. He had come dressed as a zebra, and I realized as he turned around again to face me that he wasn't, in fact, wearing a body suit as I'd originally thought but actually had painted his body white with black stripes.

He was wearing a pair of square-cut trunks, similar to the white ones I'd intended to wear, that had also been painted to match the rest of his body, as were the knee high leather boots. Like my white ones, they really didn't leave much to the imagination. He slipped the zebra mask up, and I felt a chill go down my spine.

"What are you doing here?" I asked, the numbness giving way to fear. "I'm pretty certain you weren't invited."

"I was brought as a plus one." Taylor Hudson smirked at me. "And I saw you come in here with Maureen Drury, so I waited until she left so I could talk to you alone."

"Is that why you wore a mask? So Carlo wouldn't throw you out on your ear?" I needed to get away from him, but my mind was too drained and tired to think of what to do or say.

"How little you know your husband." Taylor turned a chair around and straddled it. "Carlo would never cause a scene at the Independence Ball." He laughed. "I think I would have preferred seeing you in your angel costume. I understand you're building up quite a nice little body—shame to cover it up with all those clothes."

My cheeks burned. Did *everyone* know about the goddamned angel costume?

"I don't suppose you ever found my gold medal," he went on. "I really need to find it."

"I asked Carlo about it, and he said Timothy was buried with it." I shook my head. "I'm sorry, I should have let you know. But—"

"You didn't want to rock the boat with your precious hubby." He mocked me. "It's okay, I'm very well aware of how Carlo feels about me. He doesn't hide his feelings very well. He must be a terrible poker player." He peered at me. "Like you. You might be fooling everyone else at this party, but you're not fooling me. You're miserable."

"That's none of your business." I stood up.

"So Carlo said Timothy was buried with the medal, interesting." He tapped his chin with his index finger. "He wasn't wearing it when his body washed ashore…"

"So? That doesn't mean he wasn't buried in it."

"I had a chat with the funeral home. Timothy wasn't buried with any jewelry. And there's something else rather curious about the body that was buried—the autopsy showed he had broken his arm as a child."

"So?"

"I knew Timothy his entire life—and he never broke a bone. We grew up together, remember? His family lived down the street from mine. I would know."

A chill went up my spine. "What are you trying to say?"

"The body that was buried in Timothy's grave wasn't Timothy."

I stood up. "You're crazy. Are you saying he's still alive? That's impossible."

"Maybe Timothy got tired of being in an abusive relationship, and faking his own death was the only way he could think of to get away from Carlo."

"What you're saying is Carlo identified the wrong body? Why would he do that?"

"Maybe he would do that if he killed Timothy and got rid of the body, and staged the whole little scene at the beach."

I heard Nell saying, *Someone took the boat out that night.*

I walked to the door, but he grabbed my arm. I tried to pull away from him but he was too strong. He shoved me up against the door and pushed his body up against me, getting body paint on my clothes. I struggled against him. "Let me go!"

He pressed his lips to mine, but I turned my head and finally brought my knee up between his legs. With a loud noise, he let go of me and staggered backward, dropping finally down to my knees. "If you ever touch me again like that I will kill you," I seethed.

"Your...husband...isn't...the...man...you...think...he...is," he gasped out, pulling himself up to his feet again.

I opened the door just as Carlo was reaching for the doorknob. He took one look at me, at the paint on my clothes, and then back at Taylor Hudson. His lip curled.

Without a word, he turned and walked away.

I closed the door to the studio behind me.

I went up to my room and changed my clothes yet again, and came back to the party to try to find Carlo. I wandered through the crowds of costumed people and didn't see him anywhere. I couldn't seem to find Frank or Joyce, either—until the party started winding down and the guests started leaving.

"Have you seen Carlo?" I asked Joyce when I finally found her.

"Not in hours," she replied. "I'm so exhausted."

"Everyone's gone," Frank said as he entered the den.

"We need to talk, Mouse, but I'm just too tired now." Joyce shook her head. "Come on, Frank, let's go up to bed."

They left me alone in the den.

I went upstairs and undressed.

I climbed into my bed, and Minette cuddled up to me.

I hoped I'd be able to sleep.

Chapter Thirteen

Despite the ease with which I fell asleep, I didn't sleep well—which wasn't really a surprise since I dreaded the coming of the morning.

It seemed like most of the night was spent in that horrible kind of half sleep where you're asleep yet still very aware—every tick of the clock, every wave on the shore, every time Minette moaned or groaned in her sleep and moved. And when I would finally fall into a deep sleep, I had the most horrible dreams. I'd wake up, panting and sweating, and sit up in the bed as the dream and the terror it evoked slowly faded from my memory. Minette would open her eyes and look at me, thump the bed with her tail a few times, and then close her eyes with a sigh and go back to sleep. I would lie back down, staring at the ceiling for a few moments before closing my eyes and drifting back into that horrible state that provided no rest for my exhausted body and mind.

The sun was starting to come up, my bedroom getting lighter, when the utter exhaustion finally overcame my tension and stress, enabling me to fall finally into a deep dreamless sleep.

My eyes opened again at just before ten, and I was wide awake. I didn't feel the least bit rested but knew I wasn't going to fall back asleep. I burrowed in deeper under the covers. The bed was so comfortable, and every muscle in my body was tired. My eyes were also tired and burned a little. I closed my eyes and rolled over onto my side. I just wanted to stay in bed—it certainly was preferable to facing the day I had in front of me.

I could just stay in my room, I reasoned, keeping my eyes firmly closed. *No one would think anything of it, and I'd be able to put everything off till tomorrow. I can deal with it better then—I can't face everyone and everything this morning when I haven't slept well.*

I knew it was cowardly, but if my marriage was indeed over, damaged beyond repair, couldn't facing that be put off for yet another day? What would it hurt? I liked the idea of simply hiding out in my room. I could more easily figure out how to deal with Carson's hideous betrayal with the extra time. I could more easily decide what to do about my marriage. Wasn't it, after all, better to let emotions cool and talk to Carlo about everything with a cooler head, rather than with my emotions out of control?

The more I thought about it, the better it sounded.

Unfortunately, Minette started whimpering and licking my face, her tail thumping hopefully against the bed. I knew far too well what that meant. No matter how much I wanted to stay in bed and hide, it wasn't going to happen—Minette would need to be walked, and it was my responsibility. I couldn't punish her because I was too much of a coward to leave my room. I hugged her and she kept licking my face, whimpering and trying to comfort me. "No matter what happens, Minette," I whispered to her, "you're coming with me."

I got up and pulled on my robe before walking over to the balcony doors and pulling the curtains open. It was gray outside, the sun hidden behind what looked like a ceiling of cotton balls. I closed my eyes and rested my forehead against the glass for a moment as I relived some of the horror of the previous night, the horrible gossiping women I'd overheard, the outright nastiness of that Midge Huntley woman. Surely, Carlo could be made to understand that I hadn't arranged to meet with that awful Taylor Hudson in the studio. My cheeks burned with embarrassment as I remembered the look on his face as he stood there in the doorway, that horrible body paint from Taylor smeared all over the front of my suit. I gave the pile of clothing I'd tossed aside last night as I undressed a look when I walked into the bathroom. I winced at the sight of the betraying paint on the front of my jacket.

Surely Carlo knows I would never betray him like that, I thought as I stared at myself in the bathroom mirror. I looked horrible. My eyes were red from lack of sleep, and there were dark purplish circles beneath them that looked like bruises. My hair was standing up in every direction in that weirdly fashionable way that a lot of men spent hours with gels and sprays trying to achieve. My mouth was dry, and it felt like fur had grown on my teeth overnight. I gave myself a tired, crooked smile and yawned as I turned on the spigots and reached for my toothbrush. As I brushed my teeth, scraping off the fur, I wondered why no one had bothered to wake me up. It was way past time for breakfast, after all, but maybe that was how things were the morning after the Independence Ball. It had been around three when the last guests had left, so maybe the Spindrift tradition of breakfast at seven had been suspended. I rinsed out my mouth and washed my face thoroughly, scrubbing away and getting the crud out of the corners of my eyes. I peered at my reflection and noticed an angry-looking enormous pimple forming on my chin that I hadn't noticed before. I put my brush under the faucet before running it through my hair, and the wetness managed to flatten my hair into something reasonably presentable. I still looked like I hadn't slept well, but at least it was an improvement. I threw on a T-shirt and a pair of shorts and retrieved Minette's leash, which excited her.

I knelt down to clip the leash to her collar. "You really have to go, don't you?" I whispered to her. "I'm sorry I'm such a bad daddy."

I opened the door and she ran out ahead of me into the hallway. As I followed her, I felt strangely intimidated by the size of the hallway. I'd always been aware it was enormous, but this particular morning it felt huge and empty and cold, as though the house itself were rejecting me as I walked, the sound of my moccasins slapping against the marble floor seeming to echo in the weird silence. How could I have ever thought I could be happy in this enormous mausoleum of a house?, I asked myself, the marble statuary in the little alcoves staring at me with their empty eyes as I walked past them, the vibrant colors of the oil paintings seeming to mock my stupidity. I had never belonged here, and never could have.

"We're going to stop in the kitchen for some coffee," I said to Minette as we walked down the grand staircase.

There was a lot of activity on the first floor—the cleaning service we used had apparently hired extra help. Furniture was being dusted, the rugs were being vacuumed, the exposed floors being mopped and polished. Minette ignored them as we walked past, her held regally high as we made our way down to the kitchen.

The kitchen was in chaos. Every sink was piled high with dishes and pots and pans, and enormous plastic bags of trash were piled into a corner, their ties pulled tight against the bulging contents within. Delia looked tired and out of sorts as she stood at the big island in the middle of the room, seasoning an enormous cut of meat—a roast of some sort. She looked up from what she was doing and scowled at me.

"Just want some coffee," I said with a smile, pouring myself an enormous mug while maintaining a strong hold on Minette's leash. The scent of the meat on the island was driving her mad with hunger and curiosity—and Delia relented, smiling at her and slicing off a tiny piece, which she gobbled down quickly. "Come along, Minette," I said, giving her leash a slight tug, and reluctantly Minette turned her attention away from Delia. I opened the back door and we stepped out onto the back gallery.

It was muggy outside—damp and clammy. The ocean breeze, usually so cool and refreshing, felt like a hot wet cloth being slapped over my face and body. A mist was also rolling in off the ocean, and in the distance it looked like a thick wall of fog was hanging over the water. Everywhere I looked, uniformed workers were busy cleaning up the mess from the party. I nodded and smiled at them politely as Minette and I passed by them. I wondered how long they'd been at work—the yard was still in ruins; I could only imagine how it must have looked before they started. Enormous plastic bags of trash were being piled against the hedge between Spindrift and Nell's estate. One of the crew was fishing trash out of the swimming pool with an enormous net, and it occurred to me that we'd probably have to have it drained and scrubbed. The worker was a Latino, and looked vaguely familiar to me when he looked over at me and smiled—he was young, perhaps my age, and rather handsome with strong white teeth and cinnamon skin. I nodded in response to his smile, but Minette and I kept walking. She was pulling at the leash, and I heard barking from the other side of the hedge. She clearly wanted to go romp with Hetty and Charlie, but I wasn't in the mood to deal with Nell just yet—she would be full of questions about the party, and God only knew what she'd been hearing about the party all morning long.

No, I could deal with her later.

As we walked through the damp grass, stopping every now and then for Minette to sniff around a bit and relieve herself, I shivered a little. Nell could be put off, but Carson and Carlo could not. I had to confront Carson about his duplicity and cruelty—even if today wound up being my last day at Spindrift. There was undoubtedly nothing to be gained from it other than my own satisfaction, but it had to be done. And after I was finished with Carson, I had to sit down with Carlo and pick through the wreckage of our marriage.

Last night I hadn't believed there was anything left worth saving—particularly after that terrible little scene at the studio.

The memory made me wince. Surely Carlo didn't think—he couldn't possibly think—that I was interested in that awful Taylor Hudson?

The coffee was chasing the dust out of my mind, and I felt my confidence starting to grow. Carlo knew what kind of person Taylor was, so he would believe me when I told him what really happened. I would also explain about the costume and apologize to him.

The truth was I didn't want to leave him. I loved him. I'd loved him almost from that very first day when Valerie had flagged him down and made him sit with us in that café. He was so kind to me, and had made me feel special. I'd never felt like that before—I'd never felt like that in my life. I wanted to get that feeling back, and while it had seemed so impossible last night, now, in the light of a new day, it seemed not only possible but probable. All it would take was a little work. I wanted to get that feeling back, the feeling we'd had in Miami and Manhattan, after we first met and fell in love and lived together, gotten married. It was possible, I was certain of it.

No, I didn't want to give up on my marriage—I wanted it to work. I was willing to do whatever it took to make it work.

But the only way it could work, the only way we could move forward, was if we were honest with each other.

And that meant talking about Timothy, no matter how painful it was. The only way Carlo could finally heal was to open up to me about his previous marriage. And no matter how much it hurt, no matter how little I wanted to hear about how much Carlo had loved Timothy, I had to listen. I had to listen and understand, and be comforting, and put my own feelings aside.

It was the only way to move on.

I heard Taylor Hudson's voice sneering his nasty accusations again, and quickly pushed them aside.

I didn't care what Taylor Hudson thought—I refused to believe Carlo had killed Timothy. He wouldn't have done such a thing—and he wasn't that kind of a person. It was far easier to believe that Taylor had killed him. They'd fought the day before in a public place, they'd been sleeping together, and the very day after Timothy disappeared he'd left the country and stayed gone for over a year.

That didn't sound like the behavior of someone who loved Timothy. It was actually rather suspicious, frankly.

And what was the deal with his obsession with that gold medal?

But the accusation that Carlo had deliberately identified the wrong body concerned me. If it was indeed true—and I'd seen the autopsy report, and it did say that Timothy had broken his arm when he was young—why would he have done so?

It could have simply been a mistake, I thought. He was distraught and the body had been in the water for over a week. It would have been an easy mistake to make—his stress and heartbreak and agony, and then having to look at a body that had been in the water for so long, that the fish had been at—it would have been incredibly traumatizing, and a mistake could easily have been made under those circumstances.

It should be easy enough to find out whether Timothy had ever broken his arm. I couldn't just take someone like Taylor Hudson's word for it.

I stopped walking, and Minette looked up at me, her face clearly expressing her puzzlement at my abrupt stop.

If Carlo hadn't identified the body, they would have tried to identify it by other means—dental records, bone breaks—things like that. But once he positively identified the body as Timothy, they wouldn't have looked any more.

So if the body hadn't been Timothy's, whose was it?

Someone else who'd disappeared around the same time, obviously.

I could do an Internet search and find out.

My head was starting to hurt as I walked the dog back toward the house. The mist was clearing and it was getting hotter. The Latino who'd been fishing things out of the pool was helping with one of the tents and had taken off his shirt—and I stopped short.

He was one of Timothy's models—that's where I've seen him before.

He smiled when he caught me looking at him, and winked suggestively. I looked away and started walking quickly back to the house.

I ran into Olivia when we reached the upstairs hallway. I asked her to bring some toast, fruit, and a pot of coffee up to my rooms.

Once safely back in my room, I took a long, hot shower. I felt much better once I was finished, and the confidence that began growing when I was walking the dog was now even stronger. This wasn't going to be my last day at Spindrift, everything was going to work out.

I was examining my clothes when Olivia knocked on the door. Once she'd set down my breakfast tray on my desk, I asked her if the clothes could be cleaned.

"Well, sir, it looks like greasepaint," she said, examining them critically. "You never can be sure, so I'll send them out to be dry-cleaned, sir, and we can hope for the best." She was leaving the room when Joyce almost knocked her down on her way in.

"That coffee smells heavenly—Olivia, would you be a dear and bring me a cup?" she asked with a large yawn. She sat down on the bed. "I'm exhausted," she said as she helped herself to a piece of toast from my tray and slathered strawberry preserves on it. "I don't know why I always forget I can't sleep in a bed other than my own. But I just couldn't face the drive home last night. Frank of course is snoring away like there's no tomorrow."

I gave her a weak smile.

"I'm sorry I was just too tired last night to talk to you—but then again, it was probably for the best anyway. One can't really talk about anything truly serious at a party." She yawned again and leaped to her feet when Olivia rapped on the open door. She carried in another carafe of coffee and a cup for Joyce, which she set down on the desk next to my tray.

"Shut the door, will you, Olivia?" I asked pleasantly.

Joyce quickly gulped down a cup of coffee and moaned in pleasure.

"I don't know what there is to talk about," I replied, pouring a second cup for myself. "Really, Joyce, everything's fine."

"Carlo was being a jackass last night, and he needs to apologize to you, that much is for certain." She sipped at her coffee and moaned again with pleasure. "My God, I wish my cook could make coffee half as good as Delia's! If Carlo wasn't my brother I'd steal her right out from under him."

"I'm fine, Joyce, really." I ate a piece of toast and swallowed it down with some coffee. "I was kind of a wreck last night, I admit, but you know, it was a rough night for me. But I have it under control this morning, really. Last night I was ready to pack up and get out of here. But this morning it doesn't seem nearly as hopeless as it did when I was caught up in all the emotions. I love Carlo, and I'm not giving up without a fight."

"I'm so glad to hear that," she replied. "Carlo really does love you, Mouse. I haven't seen him this happy in years. And as for Timothy—"

I stopped her. "Joyce, thank you and I appreciate your

concern—but I don't want to talk about Timothy with anyone other than Carlo." I took a deep breath. "All this time I've been too afraid to mention him or bring him up, but that's been the wrong approach. We need to bring everything out into the open, talk about it, and then we can move on."

"But you're all wrong—"

"The party was lovely, Joyce." I changed the subject firmly. "And thank you so much for taking charge the way you did. You did an excellent job."

"I—" She paused and looked at me, and held up her hands. "Okay, you win. But promise me you'll talk to Carlo about it today—that you're going to clear the air once and for all."

I smiled at her and raised my right hand, like I was swearing on a Bible to tell the truth, the whole truth, and nothing but the truth. "Joyce, I solemnly swear to you that I am going to get everything straightened out with my husband." I winked at her. "Now, can we change the subject?"

She nodded and gave me a relieved smile. "I thought the party went extremely well, don't you?"

I nodded, and she stood up, yawning. "I think I'm going to go shower now, and see if I can get Frank up." She smiled at me, and leaned down and kissed me on the cheek. "Seriously, Mouse, you ARE the best thing to HAPPEN to Spindrift in YEARS."

After she left, I finished my breakfast and changed into a yellow pullover shirt and a pair of jeans. I hugged Minette and took a deep breath. "Wish me luck, girl," I whispered to her, "I'm going to go face down the dragon."

She wagged her tail happily.

Olivia was in the hallway putting yellow roses into a vase when I walked out of my room. I took a deep breath and steeled my nerve. "Olivia, do you know where Carson is, by any chance?"

She smiled. "I believe he's in the east wing, sir."

"Thank you." I replied and started to walk away. But after taking a few steps, I stopped and turned back to her. "Olivia, I want to thank you."

She looked puzzled. "Whatever for, sir?"

"You've been wonderful ever since I came here," I replied sincerely. "And you do an amazing job. I just wanted you to know I've noticed, and I deeply appreciate it."

She colored. "Th-thank you, sir."

I turned and walked away, heading for the east wing.

I knew exactly where I'd find him, and I was right.

He was in Timothy's rooms.

The door was open, and he was changing the linens on the bed. I stood in the doorway and watched as he spread the covers back over the bed and tucked the red velvet bedspread underneath the pillows. I stepped over the threshold and slammed the door shut behind me.

He straightened up and turned to face me, raising an eyebrow. In his usual aloof, disdainful tone, he said, "Is there something you need, sir?"

I'd never hated anyone so thoroughly in my life as I hated Carson in that instant. I remembered every rude thing he'd said to me, the contemptuous way he spoke to me, the disdain in his every glance. I'd put up with his horrible behavior for far too long. The costume was the last straw. I wanted nothing more than to slap that look right off his face and hurl invectives at him. Instead, I maintained my own composure. "Yes, Carson." I walked over to the window and pulled the curtains back. I spun around and faced him, a big smile on my face. "I want this room emptied."

He paled, but his face was impassive. "Emptied, sir?"

"Yes, emptied." I walked over to the closet and threw the door open. "All these clothes—I want them bagged up and disposed of. Everything that was his—I want it all gone. I don't care what you do with these things. Give them to some charity, drag it all outside and burn it—I don't really care. But I want everything gone by Monday—and I am including the furniture in that. I want this room completely stripped down to bare bones—it's time for these rooms to come back to life, and the sooner the better."

He stepped closer to me. "You might think you're going to get rid of Mr. Timothy by getting rid of his things, but they're just that—things." He stroked the curtain hanging around the bed. "You'll never get him out of Mr. Carlo's heart, you know. This house—this room—will always be Mr. Timothy's. You'll never change that."

"Well, we'll just see about that, won't we?" I smiled brightly at him. "You seem to have forgotten something very important, Carson—Timothy's dead. And all this—" I waved my hands around. "Keeping his rooms ready for him, like he's going to walk back through the door at any minute? Dead means dead, Carson. He's gone and he's never coming back. And keeping the rooms like this is just sick."

He didn't react. He just kept standing there and looking at me.

"And by the way, I wanted to thank you for all your help with my costume for the ball."

He didn't say anything.

"You've hated me ever since I came here," I went on. "You've undermined me, treated me with contempt, and what you did last night was unforgivable."

The reserve broke. "Of course I hate you!" he snapped. "Coming here, to Mr. Timothy's house, trying to take his place. I won't have it." He walked over to the closet and got out a cashmere sweater. He held it to his face and smelled it. "You don't know anything. Mr. Timothy was everything you aren't. He was smart and funny and kind, stylish and—"

"A whore." I interrupted him. "He was nothing but a cheap little whore who couldn't keep his pants up."

His eyes blazed. "And what of it?" he sneered. "Mr. Timothy didn't care about any of those people. He thought it was fun to toy with them and their emotions. That idiot trainer, Taylor Hudson—he would come back from the studio after meeting one of them there, and he would laugh about how stupid they were, how easy it was to make them fall in love with him. It was all a game to him, and why shouldn't he have some fun with his life?" His voice broke. "And then he died because I wasn't here that day. I could have saved him had I been here. It wouldn't have happened if I had just been here."

Despite everything I couldn't help but feel sorry for him in his grief. "Carson—"

"And then he brings *you* here. To Mr. Timothy's house, like someone like you could ever take his place."

And my sympathy was gone in that instant.

"You're forgetting something, Carson," I said, allowing myself a little smile.

"What?"

"This is Carlo's house, not Timothy's. And now it's mine." I paused at the door. "I want all of his clothes gone by the end of today and this furniture out of here by Monday afternoon—or you're fired...and I'll see to it you never work again." I slammed the door behind me and walked down the hall.

By the time I reached the grand staircase I was close to hyperventilating. I stood there for a few moments, taking deep breaths and trying to get my heart rate to slow down.

That really wasn't so hard, I thought as I felt myself returning to normal. *You should have never put up with anything from him in the first place.*

There was a part of me that hoped he wouldn't clean out the room, so I could fire him.

As I walked down the stairs my confidence began rising again. I had done it, after all. And after Timothy's rooms were cleared out, the studio would be next. I would use it as an office, where I would work on my writing once the demons were exorcised. If Carson didn't like it, he could quit. I could run the house myself. I didn't need Carson—we didn't need him.

And now I was going to make everything right with my marriage.

Carlo was on the phone when I reached his office. He nodded to me as I entered and shut the door behind me. He looked pale.

"Uh-huh......yes...of course, yes...I understand...yes."

He hung up the phone and looked at me, his face incredibly sad. "Well, that's that." He laughed bitterly. "It's all over." He shook his head. "I owe you an apology, Mouse. I was rather beastly to you last night, and I'm terribly sorry—you have no idea how sorry I am, Mouse. The last thing in the world I would ever want to do is hurt you—and all I've done, over and over again, is hurt you."

"I don't mind, really." I started to walk toward him, but the look on his face stopped me. "What is it, Carlo? What was that phone call? You don't look well."

"I was stupid to think I could ever be happy again. I'm sorry, Mouse."

My heart dropped into my stomach. I opened my mouth but no words came out. I couldn't think of anything to say. I felt the tears rising in my eyes. He didn't love me, he wanted me to go. "Carlo—"

"I knew it would eventually come back, these things always do." He went on, pacing around the room. "It was always just a matter of time. I stayed away, thinking that would do the trick—but no, I couldn't forget. Always I remembered, always. And I tried everything I could think of to make me forget. But nothing worked and then I met you." He gave me a weak smile. "I thought—when I met you I thought we might be able to be happy together. You were sweet, such a sweet young boy so full of love with no one to give it to, and you made me smile, you made me forget for a time."

"Carlo, please." I finally said, trying to keep the tears back. "We can still be happy."

"No, Mouse, we can't." He gestured to the phone. "You asked who that was. It was the sheriff calling me to tell me. The call I always knew would come, the sword of Damocles that's been hanging over my head. You see, someone found him."

"Found who?"

"Timothy."

I sat down hard in a chair, unable to believe what I was hearing. "Timothy?" I was having trouble breathing.

"I always knew they would find him, you know." He sighed. "I'm so sorry, Mouse, I never should have married you and involved you in all of this."

"I know you loved him—"

"Loved him?" He stared at me in shock. "You aren't listening to me, Mouse. A fisherman found him a few days ago—tangled in his nets. They only were able to identify him this morning."

"I—I don't understand." I gaped at him. "What are you talking about?"

"I didn't love Timothy, Mouse—I hated him. I hated him as much as any human being can hate another human. I've been such an incredible fool." He rubbed his eyes. "A fisherman found him, Mouse, do you understand me? They found him, after all this time, like I always feared they would."

"I—"

"I hated him, Mouse. I hated him, and I killed him. And now they've found his body."

Chapter Fourteen

The room was silent.

I was very aware of the sound of my breathing, the beating of my heart. Outside in the far distance I could hear a lawn mower engine starting with a dull roar. Behind us I could still hear the workers talking and shouting to each other, sometimes laughing, as they kept up their efforts to return the back lawn to a semblance of normalcy, what it had been before the ball. If not for these distant sounds it seemed like time had somehow come to a stop, that we were frozen somehow outside of time and space, forever just staring at each for an eternity. I remember noticing there was thin coating of dust on the end table next to my chair, and idly thinking I would need to speak to Juana about it, and that there was stubble on Carlo's pale face.

I sat there, not saying anything, not knowing what if anything I could say in response, even though I could see the agony of suspense on his own face in addition to the anguish in his eyes. I was in some sort of shock. All I could do was sit there in my chair, looking at him, my mouth open like a fool, unable to think or say anything.

"How you must hate me now," he said finally, his voice soft and sad, "although I can't say that I blame you. But please, let me explain. May I at least tell you how it was for me, for the two of us in our marriage? Maybe then you can find some understanding—and maybe even some forgiveness—in your heart for me."

"Did you—did you ever love him?" I heard the words coming

out of my mouth. My voice sounded hollow and distant, like I was speaking in another room.

"Yes." His face became grim. "My parents were always very supportive of my sexuality, Mouse. I told them the truth when I was a teenager, and while they were clearly disappointed I wouldn't have any children, they also made it clear they loved me and would support me no matter what. They just wanted me to be happy— although I did wonder about that when they so clearly disapproved of Joyce's first marriage." He rubbed his eyes. "I dated, of course, but I never really felt anything for the men I was seeing. There was always an initial attraction that seemed to wane the better I got to know them. I was never into casual sex—I don't think there's anything wrong with it, of course, it's just not for me."

"Of course," I replied.

"And I was always on my guard whenever someone showed interest in me. I know I'm not unattractive, but—" He sighed. "When you have money and social position, you never can be sure whether people are actually interested in you for yourself or for what you can do for them. Obviously, actors and dancers were always throwing themselves at me, hoping I'd use my influence to get them parts in shows I was financing—which I of course would never do." He stood up and began pacing. "By the time I was in my thirties I had pretty much come to the conclusion I was destined to be alone for the rest of my life, that I would never find the kind of relationship I wanted, and I was fine with it, Mouse, really, I was. I wasn't looking to get involved with anyone." He walked over to the big window and put his hands on the sill, his back to me.

"How awful for you," I said, and I meant it. My heart went out to him. When I worked for Valerie, I'd learned very early on that many people thought that the best way to get to Valerie was through flattering me. As her assistant, I had access to her schedule and could slip someone in. They were stupid if they thought she ever listened to anything I had to say—Valerie always made up her own mind and never really listened to anyone else—but I never fooled myself that any of the minor celebrities who flattered me and sent me gifts and acted friendly actually cared anything about me. I was simply a means to an end.

Awful as that was, that was *business*. I couldn't imagine how much more awful it would feel never to be certain of anyone in your personal life.

"I, of course, knew who Timothy Burke was—who didn't in those days? His images were everywhere. He was one of the first male supermodels." He turned and walked over to the sideboard, clunking a few pieces of ice into a glass before pouring whiskey over them. "I knew he was beautiful—who didn't? But I'd never met him, never dreamed…" He took a drink from the whiskey and closed his eyes for a moment. "I'll never forget the night I met him. It was here, at the Independence Ball." He leaned against the sideboard, remembering. "He came with Dorothy Masters—she and her husband had an interest in the company he was modeling for." His face twisted and he looked off into the distance. "He had the most amazing costume; he came as Apollo, Greek god of the sun and music. His entire body had been painted gold, and he had golden rays coming out from his head. He was wearing skimpy shorts painted the exact same shade of gold and covered in glitter. He had somehow mixed glitter into the body paint so his entire body sparkled in the light. Even his hair had been painted the same shade of gold. His body was just extraordinary…I had never seen anyone like him before—oh, don't get me wrong, I'd dated and slept with plenty of men, plenty of beautiful men, but Timothy was different. He looked like Apollo come to life…my first look at him and my breath was taken away. I was spellbound, unable to take my eyes off him. And he was aware of his effect on me…he flirted with me… and I had to have him."

He polished off the glass of whiskey and poured himself another. "Looking back now, I can't believe I was such a fool. I wasn't thinking—all I could think about was Timothy. I couldn't stop thinking about him after that night at the ball. I pursued him… was obsessed with him. I asked him out on dates, and he kept me at arm's length, aloof and never giving me anything other than a chaste kiss on the cheek after the date was over. I was stupid enough to actually believe him when he said he wasn't the kind of man who slept with everyone he met—I actually admired him for his integrity. He always talked about his religious upbringing in Florida, and how even though he'd abandoned his faith when he came out, he hadn't abandoned his morality. He told me that he believed that casual sex was wrong, he would never do that unless he actually loved someone…was in a relationship. I bought him things—expensive gifts he would only accept if I understood his acceptance didn't mean I was buying his love." His voice turned bitter. "He was playing me. He was playing for keeps. The more he pushed me away, the more he denied me, the more I wanted him. I was such a damned fool. And as soon as Massachusetts legalized gay marriage, I asked him to marry me."

As his words washed over me, I realized I had been wrong, so wrong, so many times about so many different things, so many different times. What I thought was love for his dead husband—it must have been *guilt*.

"And you know, for the first year we were really happy—well, I should say that I was really happy that first year, and of course Timothy was happy—he had access to my fortune, and he loved being master of Spindrift." He ran his fingers through his hair and refilled his whiskey glass. "Timothy was the one who got me into actual activism—before I would always just write a check—but he convinced me that, with his fame and my money, we should do everything we could to promote gay rights—that we were in a unique position to advance the cause. And so we started doing all the speeches, and talks, and…" He shook his head. "And by the time I found out what he really was…well, it was too late."

"And what was he?" I leaned forward, almost afraid to hear the answer, but I knew I had to—otherwise there could never be any chance of healing.

Carlo's face darkened. "A monster. He was a monster wrapped in the most tender and beautiful flesh." He laughed harshly. "You know that stupid saying about beauty being skin deep? Timothy was the proof of its truth." He rubbed his eyes. "He had no conscience of any kind. I don't think he was capable of love, any more than a crocodile is. Nothing mattered to him except himself—he was utterly self-absorbed. It was when that Taylor Hudson came here to stay, at Timothy's invitation." He closed his eyes and took some deep breaths. "I never liked Hudson, but tolerated him for Timothy's sake…they'd grown up together, were childhood friends…Hudson tried to seduce my sister…"

"Joyce?"

"She and Frank were having some problems…Hudson saw his opportunity and tried to take advantage of the situation…he saw an heiress with a rather inconvenient husband…I told Timothy I would not permit it, and Hudson was no longer welcome at Spindrift."

He swallowed. "I'll never forget that night as long as I live. He was in the red suite, sitting at his desk and writing thank you notes. He sat there with his back to me and didn't say a word while I raged about Hudson…and when I finished, he sealed an envelope like I'd said nothing and turned around in his chair and laughed at me. He laughed at me…and then, he told me the truth of who he was…"

He proceeded to tell me of Timothy's darker desires, the passions that drove him, and what he turned the studio into. "The studio I had built for him, so he could pursue his artistic desires, in privacy away from the hustle and bustle and noise of Spindrift, so he could focus on his work and not be interrupted, he'd turned it into a place for orgies and sexual games of the darkest and most debased kind. I was sickened, horrified and appalled. All I could think as he told me what he'd kept hidden from me the entire first year of our marriage, through the entire year or so we'd dated, was how badly I wanted to kill him. I could feel my hands on his throat as I choked his miserable life out of him, as his oh-so-beautiful body went limp in my hands. The entire time…when I'd drop him off after a date and got a chaste kiss on the cheek—he would go up to his apartment for a night of debauchery, or off to a sex club…and he laughed at me. He laughed at me. The entire time, the entire time I'd been falling in love with him, imagining our future together, the entire time we'd been married, he'd been laughing at me with his lovers, laughing at me…"

I couldn't speak, I couldn't respond to the litany of perversions and horrors he'd recited, the things that had gone on in the studio. They sickened me yet at the same time they made me curious; even as they disgusted me I couldn't get the images out of my mind, the images of Timothy and that beautiful body, a lusty and lascivious look on his face as he played his games of sensuality and sexuality, satisfying his dark desires of dominance and humiliation, always trying to satisfy the lusts that drove him.

"He was smart, so much smarter than the fool he married," Carlo went on, sipping his whiskey, and giving me a sad look. "I hadn't made him sign a prenuptial agreement, of course, and in the crazy madness of love I put his name on the deed to Spindrift after we were married. He was smart, so very smart, and he manipulated me very neatly. I was a fool, Mouse, a total fool. If not for Spindrift I would have done it, I would have gotten rid of him, divorced him no matter how bad it looked for us to split up, in spite of the damage it might have done to the marriage equality cause…"

The house, I thought, *of course it was the house.*

"When I told him I didn't care, I wanted to divorce him, I would do it in New York and argue that the Massachusetts marriage law had no bearing on property in New York state, he laughed, oh how he laughed at me. I'll never forget the contempt and loathing on his face. 'You'll never get Spindrift back from me,' he said to me. 'I'll draw this out and make it as ugly and nasty as I possibly can. No prenuptial agreement, remember? By the time I'm finished I may not get a dime of the Romaniello money, but your name will be mud—and gay marriage? Not a chance—every time it comes up the haters will use us as an example of why we can't be permitted to marry. It will be the ugliest divorce in history. Why not? What do I have to lose? And think about your companies, and how the value of their stock will drop every day some new horror comes out in the press about your private life…are you willing to be that humiliated in public, Carlo?'"

I felt sick to my stomach, hoping it would end. It was horrible, all so horrible, so much worse than I ever could have imagined. Who would have ever thought such evil lived behind that beautiful face? But it wasn't over. Carlo kept talking.

And awful as it was, I had no choice, I had to listen to it all.

"We finally came to an arrangement—only on rare occasions would we ever be in the same residence at the same time. I bought the penthouse in New York—I'd been wanting to get a residence in the city for years anyway—and we negotiated a compromise about special events and things we'd need to appear at as a couple. He promised he would be discreet—there would be no whispers or talk or hints in the tabloids about his activity, and he even put it into writing that should any scandal ever be attached to his name, he would voluntarily give me a divorce, would take no money, and would surrender any claim to Spindrift. Oh, and I also had to fund his underwear company—but if it failed, it failed—I insisted on that—there would be no more money after my initial investment." He shook his head. "But of course it was a huge success. Everywhere, it seemed, that I would turn, there he was. Oh, he kept his word, of course—not a whisper of scandal, ever. We kept pretending we were happily married, and once the fund-raiser or the event was over, we went our separate ways. It galled me. I hated him so much, Mouse, you have no idea how much I hated him. We would stand there, at HRC dinners, posing for the cameras and smiling, and all I could think about was wanting to kill him, wishing he were dead. I thought about killing myself, I can't tell you how many times I thought about suicide, the times I took the *Rhiannon* out to sea and thought how easy it would be, to tie myself to a weight and jump overboard..."

"Why didn't you just—" I stopped myself.

"What?"

"Never mind, go on." *Why didn't you just hire a private detective to follow him, take photos of him doing the unspeakable things he was doing, and threaten to leak them to the tabloids? Use them to get him to leave once and for all?* was what I was going to say. But there was no point in saying anything—it was far too late for anything but guilt and recriminations—and even those feelings were pointless.

"The night it happened—well, no one was expecting me out here. I was in the city, and he called me around noon, said he needed to talk to me, in person, and could I come back out to the house? I didn't like the way his voice sounded—I'd never heard him that way before. He sounded desperate, almost frightened yet still so smug and triumphant. Much as I didn't want to, I drove out here. When I arrived the house was empty—all the servants were gone. I went up to his rooms, but he wasn't there. I looked out the window and I saw him walking out to the studio.

"So I followed him. I don't know what I was thinking, but with every step I took out there, all seven years of our sham marriage replayed in my mind, all the times I had to pretend to love him, all the things I'd had to do to keep the lie alive, and all the money of mine he'd spent. Of course, the underwear company was making him a lot of money and so he didn't use much of mine anymore, but I'd paid for that company. I remember asking myself as I walked out there, am I going to spend the rest of my life paying for him? There had to be a way—there had to be a way out somehow. I couldn't take it anymore.

"He was looking at his prints when I got there, and stood in the door. He smiled at me, and I couldn't help myself. I asked him, you've got the underwear company now, so why can't we get a divorce? I promised him as much money as he wanted, within reason of course, and all he did was laugh.

"'But you won't give me Spindrift, will you?' he said, still laughing at me. 'That's all I really want. The first time I saw it, I knew I would do whatever I had to marry you and make it my home. I fell in love with the house, not with you. I never loved you, Carlo, but you already knew that, didn't you?'

"'Why am I here? I asked him. Get to the point. I need to get back to the city.'

"'I want the house, Carlo,' he told me. 'We stayed married long enough—no one will think anything of it now if we end this mistake. But I want the house.' He laughed at me when I told him I would never let him have Spindrift. He told me he didn't care about the money—he had enough of his own now…but he wouldn't have any problem with airing everything, accusing me of physical and mental cruelty…

"I snapped, Mouse. And honestly, I don't know what happened in the next five minutes, it all happened so quickly…one minute he was laughing at me, the next I was standing there, holding the desk lamp, and he was lying on the floor, his skull smashed. I'd hit him with the lamp, and kept hitting him until the lamp was battered and he was lying on the floor dead. I didn't know what to do. And then I remembered…I remembered that no one was at the house, no one knew I was here. So I rolled him up in a sheet and carried his body down the dock to the *Rhiannon*, and took him out to sea. I tied some weights to him and rolled his body overboard. I threw the lamp overboard as well, and weighted the sheet and got rid of it as well. And then I headed back here. I went up to his room and got his robe and a beach towel and the little bag he always took with him down there, and made it look like he'd gone for a swim and hadn't come back. I went into the studio and cleaned up the blood with bleach. And then, when everything was the way I thought it should look, I drove back into the city. That was a horrible night, let me tell you. It was the next morning that Carson called and told me what they'd found down on the beach, and that he'd already alerted the Coast Guard. I rushed back out here…and you know the rest." He buried his face in his hands. "A week later, that body washed ashore at Montauk. I decided to identify it as Timothy—the face—the fish had been at it, and he was in good shape and wearing swim trunks…so, God help me, I said it was Timothy. And now…now they've found his actual body. And they know he was murdered—his skull… And I'm going to go to jail."

I sat there for a moment, not saying anything.

He was staring at me, waiting for me to say something. I could tell by the look on his face he was expecting me to reject him, to recoil from him in horror, to get up and run.

The man I loved, the man I married, was a murderer.

But I felt strangely calm.

And finally, I looked him right in the eyes and said, "But no one saw you, right? No one knew you were here that night, right?"

He gave me an odd look. "Yes."

I exhaled. "And they didn't find the lamp—and even if they did, it's been in the water so long they'd never be able to lift prints from it. So the only thing the police know for sure is that Timothy was actually murdered and you incorrectly identified the wrong body." I shrugged. "That's not even enough evidence for an arrest—even if you weren't an incredibly wealthy and powerful man."

He stared at me, his face shocked, like he couldn't believe what I was saying. "What are you saying, Mouse?" he asked, his voice strangely quiet and confused.

"I'm telling you any decent lawyer would get any charges dismissed on such flimsy evidence." I shook my head and laughed harshly. "Haven't you ever read Maureen Drury's articles in *Street Talk* magazine? There's a different justice for the rich than there is for everyone else, Carlo. And you certainly can afford the best criminal attorneys in the country. All you did was wrongly identify a body. And who could blame you, under the circumstances?" I stood up. My hands were shaking, so I shoved them in my pants pocket. I couldn't believe my voice wasn't shaking. "You were traumatized by the unexpected death of your husband. The body'd been in the water for a week...any lawyer could make a jury understand you made a mistake, you weren't in your right mind."

He just kept staring at me as I talked, his mouth open, and when I finished, his expression changed to one I'd never seen before from him—wonder. "You—you don't hate me, Mouse?"

"Hate you?" I couldn't help it—I started laughing and within seconds it turned into sobbing, tears running down my face, my nose running. I wiped feverishly at my face with both hands as I managed to choke out, "Oh, Carlo—all this time—it's just—I thought you still loved *him*, that you were always comparing me to him...but all this time..."

"Oh, my poor Mouse." He crossed the room in a few strides and swept me up into his arms, kissing my neck and holding me so tightly I could barely breathe—but I didn't mind, I didn't want him to ever let me go. "I love you so much. Almost from the moment I saw you in that café—all I could do was think about you, and how kind you were, and how you were everything Timothy wasn't. I thought, after all the guilt and nightmares since the night I—I killed him, I thought, maybe he can make me forget, maybe I can be happy again." He was shaking, and I realized he was crying. I started stroking his head. "And I thought for sure—I thought for sure once you knew the truth, you'd hate me."

"I could never hate you, Carlo," I whispered, and I knew it was true. Now that I knew for sure that he loved me, I knew I would do anything I could to protect him. "I love you."

"And when I saw you last night—wearing something he would have worn—it was so horrifying—I thought—I thought you were turning into him, if you can believe that. That's—that's why I was so upset."

I bit my lip and blinked my eyes to clear the tears that were welling up in them. "We can be happy, my darling, we can start over—we can be like we were back in Miami, would you like that?" I whispered. "We just have to get through this somehow."

He nodded, and kissed me again. "I do love you, Mouse."

As he held on to me, I couldn't believe how stupid I'd been for so long. What I'd mistaken for obsessive love had been guilt, Carlo punishing himself. He'd kept Timothy's rooms and studio and office the way they'd always been, preserved like a shrine, as a reminder to himself of what he'd done.

And now, now it was time to exorcise Timothy's ghost and his malevolent presence from Spindrift once and for all.

We sat down together on the couch and talked for what seemed like hours, in low voices so no one could hear us. We talked about our future and what we had to do to make sure that Timothy couldn't hurt us any longer.

And when the sheriff arrived, we were ready for him.

Sheriff Tate was an older man, either in his late fifties or early sixties. His hairline was receding, and what was left was iron gray. His eyes were a dark brown, and his face was lined. His teeth were yellowed from nicotine, and he smelled slightly of cigarette smoke. He was still in pretty decent shape, maybe carrying some extra weight around the middle. He was wearing his brown uniform and was clearly uncomfortable.

He sat down in a chair on the other side of a coffee table from where we sat on the couch. We rose and shook hands, and Carlo offered him coffee or something to drink.

"No thank you, gentlemen," he said, pulling out a small spiral notebook out of a pocket as he sat down. "I don't want to take up too much of your time." He took a deep breath. "A commercial fisherman from over in East Patchogue was doing some net fishing, and his net caught on something. He had to get help to haul it up, and of course, when he and his men got the net up, there was the, um, corpse. They immediately radioed the Coast Guard, and long and short of it, the body was brought in on Wednesday. There was nothing on it to identify it—all that was really left was the skeleton, and some rusted weights that had been tied to the feet—that's why it was so hard for the net to come up, the weights were still chained to the ankles. The skull had been cracked—and the coroner pretty much determined that was the cause of death. I don't mind telling you, Mr. Romaniello, everyone pretty much thought it was a mob hit of some sort. So, they did some dental impressions…and it took a few days for the identification to come back—it just came back this morning and they called me." He swallowed. "You can imagine, Mr. Romaniello, how horrified I was to hear that it was positively Mr. Burke's body."

"There's no chance it was a mistake?" I asked calmly, placing my hand on Carlo's leg.

"Dental records are pretty conclusive," Sheriff Tate replied.

Carlo's response was measured and cool, with just the right touch of sadness and horror. "I don't know how I could have possibly made such a terrible mistake."

"Well, sir, it's understandable," the sheriff went on. "The face was pretty messed up, as I recall, and you were expecting it to be him…we all kind of were, to be honest…it made sense, didn't it? A man had gone missing off the beach and then a body washed up on shore…and it was a pretty bad time for you, sir." He closed his little notebook and stood up. "It's going to be hard, sir, to solve this crime after all this time…but we'll do our best."

"I would appreciate that, Sheriff."

"Can you think of anyone who had any reason to want Mr. Burke dead?"

"No, I can't." Carlo told the lie as smoothly as if he were telling the truth. "And as you remember, he'd given the servants the day off and he was all alone here at the house."

Sheriff Tate stood up with a heavy sigh. "I remember it all too well, Mr. Romaniello. I don't mind telling you I don't have the slightest idea how to even get started with this. But we're going to do our best, sir, you can be sure of that. If I have to get help from the state troopers, I will. I won't rest until we find out the truth."

"Thank you, Sheriff," Carlo said and walked him out to the door.

And that was when I remembered there actually was someone who'd been around that night, and knew more than anyone else.

Nell had seen the *Rhiannon* go out that night, after all.

CHAPTER FIFTEEN

I let myself out the back door to Carlo's office and walked down the gallery steps to the back lawn. The weather had almost completely changed while I as in the office with Carlo—I had no idea how much time had actually passed, but it seemed like an eternity; it seemed like an entirely different day. I laughed at myself and had just a moment of doubt about everything as I stepped off the bottom step.

Knowing what had happened between Carlo and Timothy that day in the studio hadn't changed the way I felt about Carlo at all. If anything, I loved him more than I had before. I couldn't imagine how awful it would be to fall in love with someone and marry them—only then to discover they were a completely different person, someone awful who made your life a living hell. I didn't believe for a moment Carlo had gone out to the studio intending to kill him. It had been an accident, a spur-of-the-moment, heat-of-passion thing—and not something that should ruin the rest of his life.

Who are you to play judge and jury? To decide that Timothy's death was justifiable?

Dark clouds were blowing in from the sea, and the air felt chilly and damp. The wind was so strong it was an effort to walk against it. I put my head down and kept going. The hedges were swaying, and sand was blowing up from the beach. There was a storm coming—I could see lightning flashes far out to sea, and it was going to be really nasty when it did finally reach land. It was fortunate, I thought, that the cleanup crew had already finished with the yard—they would have had to quit if they hadn't. The back lawn looked almost normal again—it was like the party had never happened, other than the places where the grass had been leveled and flattened by people walking or dancing. The ball seemed now like it had happened a hundred years ago, in a different time and place. My memories didn't seem quite real—it was like last night had happened to someone else entirely.

Now that I knew for sure that Carlo really and truly loved me, I had a new lease on my life.

As I walked and fought against the gale force winds, I felt eerily like someone was watching me. So when I reached the beach and the end of the hedge, I turned back to see Carson standing on what I now knew to be Timothy's balcony. There was now no question in my mind—we would have to fire him for certain. *We just can't have anyone who was so devoted to Timothy still in the house—he definitely is going to have to go.*

The thought brought a smile to my face. It wouldn't be hard to convince Carlo, and I could certainly run the house until we hired someone else. *Once we get through this investigation*, I thought, *I'll give Carson his notice.*

I walked around the end of the hedges and into Nell's backyard. The wind was picking up sand and blasting it against my skin. It stung, and I hurried away from it until I was about halfway across her lawn. I stopped and looked up at the house. It wasn't as big or as beautiful as Spindrift, of course—nothing was—but it was still a lovely home. I happened to look up and saw Nell, standing on the widow's walk at the top of the house. I waved to her and she waved back, and then disappeared. I started walking up to the house, reaching the back deck just as she opened the sliding glass door.

"Come in!" she said over the wind, which was getting even stronger by the moment. "I was wondering if I'd see you today."

Gratefully, I stepped inside and realized this was the first time Nell had ever allowed me inside her house—we'd always sat on the patio deck.

The room was a den, comfortably furnished with sofas and

chairs and tables. The three other walls had built-in bookshelves that ran from the floor all the way up to the ceiling, and each shelf was crammed full with books. Ordinarily, I would have immediately started looking at the titles, but this wasn't a friendly visit. I could resist my book lover's urges and leave the books for another day.

"Please, sit." She switched on another lamp, and sat down on a reclining chair, crossing her legs. She was wearing a navy blue sweatshirt with *Hamptons Yacht Club* written on the front, and a pair of khaki shorts. Her feet were bare, and as always her thick hair was pulled back into a French braid. She picked up a phone and asked someone to bring a pitcher of iced tea and two glasses to her sitting room. "What brings you out to visit an old woman on such a blustery day?"

I opened my mouth but closed it as the door opened and her maid brought in a tray with a pitcher of tea and two tall glasses. She set them down on the table in between where we were sitting, and Nell waved her hand to dismiss her. She closed the door behind her.

"I need to talk to you about something," I said, but now that the time had come I didn't know what to say, or how to even bring it up. She peered at me shrewdly and reached for the pitcher. She filled both glasses and handed one of them to me.

"All right, then. Why don't you tell me about the ball, while you're trying to figure out how to ask me what you want to ask me?" She took a drink from her glass and leaned back in her chair while she swallowed it. "It was pretty noisy over there, you know, but when you're old like me you can pretty much sleep through anything. When I'm tired, I'm tired. My husband used to say I could sleep through a nuclear war if I was tired enough."

"It was an interesting evening," I replied, taking a drink from my own glass. My hand was shaking slightly, and I hoped she wouldn't notice it.

"Midge Huntley called me this morning," she said with a sly look. "Couldn't wait to tell me her thoughts about Carlo's new husband." She laughed. "Wasn't very good, I don't mind telling you."

My cheeks flushed. "Midge Huntley—"

"Is a nasty old bitch with a mean streak as wide as Long Island, and I told her so right before I hung up on her," Nell sniffed. "I never liked that woman, but I put up with her to be polite for years. But if she thinks she's going to call me and say terrible things about you, my young friend, someone I actually care for, she's got another think coming." She sniffed again. "She's got plenty of room to talk. She wasn't nobody until she fooled Skip Huntley into marrying her in the first place. Little better than a prostitute over in the city, is what she was, and if she don't want to remember that well, I'll be more than happy to remind her every once in a while." Her eyes glittered. "Once a whore, always a whore, I say."

"Good to know," I said, raising my glass as if in a toast to her. She did the same with her glass before taking another sip out of it.

"What's on your mind? You didn't come here to ask me about Midge Huntley." She put her glass back down and pushed her glasses up her nose. "I can see you've got something on your mind. Out with it! You don't have to beat around the bush with me, you know."

"Nell," I said carefully, "I felt like I should come over and tell you before the story gets out. I wanted you to hear it from me first."

Her eyes narrowed, and her face lost all expression. "Hear what first? Out with already."

I cleared my throat. "Apparently, some fishermen found Timothy's body a few days ago."

"I wasn't aware it had gone missing," she said, her face still like stone. "I think I'd have heard that someone was stealing bodies from graves. Is that what you're trying to tell me—there's a grave robber in the Hamptons?"

"No—no, that's not it at all." I took a deep breath. "As it turns out, Nell, apparently Carlo was wrong when he identified that body last year as Timothy's." I gave a little shrug. It sounded strange to say it out loud. "He was obviously distraught and not in his right mind. An easy mistake—the body had been damaged by it's time in the water, you know."

"Well, isn't that—*interesting*," she replied without any expression in either her tone or her face. "Looks like there's a nasty storm coming." She refilled her tea glass and then looked back over at me. "So, the real body has turned up, you said?"

I nodded. "Apparently, you were right all along. Someone killed him, apparently with a blow to the head. Whoever killed him weighted his body and dumped it at sea. A few mornings ago, the body got tangled up in a fisherman's net, and his skull had been caved in." I took another deep breath. "So, when you saw the *Rhiannon* got out that night, it was probably the killer going out to dump Timothy's body."

She didn't answer, and we sat in silence for a while. The wind was now blowing so strongly I could hear it whipping and whistling around the house. I shivered—she had the air-conditioning on, and it was terribly cold inside. I looked back outside and could see the storm was getting closer to shore. I needed to get back to Spindrift before the storm arrived.

But I couldn't leave until I knew precisely what kind of danger she was to Carlo.

"Midge Huntley wasn't the only person to call me this morning," she finally said, her voice impassive. "She wasn't even the first person to call me, for that matter—Maureen Drury was." She turned her head and peered at me with those cold eyes. She raised and dropped her shoulders in a slight shrug. "You know her, of course—you used to work for that magazine that publishes her trash."

I wasn't even aware I'd been holding my breath until I let it out in a rush.

"I didn't tell her anything, of course." Nell shook her head. "I can't imagine why she thought I would tell her anything even if I knew anything. I guess she thought because a lot of those stupid biddies out here like to tell her things for her articles, I'd be thrilled to talk to her. She no longer thinks so." She gave me a brittle smile. "In my day, we didn't talk to the press, and we certainly didn't talk to the police."

"What did she think you knew?" My voice was so soft I could barely hear it myself.

"I'm afraid I already knew about Timothy's body before you told me," she replied, equally softly. "I also knew that he'd been murdered—but I already knew that before she called. I knew that last year." She made a face. "But I told that trashy bitch I didn't know anything. As I said, I do not talk to the press, nor do I talk to the police. What I know, I know, and it's nobody's damned business but my own."

I swallowed. "Nell—"

Her eyes narrowed and she leaned forward.

"How did you know Timothy had been murdered?" I blurted out. "If all you knew for sure was that someone had taken the *Rhiannon* out to sea that night—it doesn't necessarily follow that Timothy was murdered. But you told me he had been—how did you know?"

"I told you, I don't talk to the police." She stood up and walked over to the door. "Anything I saw that night, my young friend, is my secret to keep." She cracked a smile. "I'm an old woman, after all, and I do wear glasses. Any lawyer would make mincemeat of me on the stand should I try to identify the man I saw carrying something out to the boat all wrapped up in a sheet."

My blood froze, and my mouth opened and closed for just a moment.

She reached out and touched the doorknob, and paused, turning back to look at me. "You seemed like such a nice boy when I first met you—and you've done nothing since then to change my opinion. You always made time for a lonely old woman—so I told you what I saw, and what I knew. You didn't make an informed decision when you got married—so I thought you should know. Timothy wasn't a good person, but I suspect, from the look on your face, that you already knew that." Her face cracked into a smile. "You don't need to worry, my friend. All I saw was the boat go out that night—and I'm not even sure about that now. I'm an old lady, of course—it's entirely possible I may not have the day right, either." She shrugged.

"Was it the same night? Maybe it was, maybe it wasn't." Her right eye closed in a wink.

The door closed behind her.

I sat there for a few moments, trying to deal with the relief that was washing over me. I hadn't realized how tense I'd been since I'd left Spindrift to come over here. When I tried to stand up, my legs were wobbly and I had to hold on to the arms of my chair to keep from falling. I took some deep breaths until the sensation passed, and let myself out through the sliding glass door. The storm was getting closer, and the wind was insanely powerful. As I headed down to the beach, I put one hand over my eyes to keep the blowing sand out of my eyes. It felt like the wind was trying to sandpaper my skin right off my bones. I ducked my head and tried to walk faster, fighting the wind for every step I took forward. The waves were crashing against the beach, and when I dared to look up I could see that the sea was angry and gray, the waves higher than I'd ever seen them, whitecaps breaking in the water as far as I could see in the grayness. The water was also washing farther up on the beach than I'd ever seen it before. I shivered because the temperature kept dropping, and finally I reached the edge of the hedge.

I had just managed to make it around the end of the hedge when the storm rolled in. The sky simply opened, and it was like someone had turned a hose on me. Within seconds I was completely soaked, and the raindrops stung as they pelted me. I couldn't even see two feet in front of me, and the ground was quickly turning to mud underneath my feet. My teeth started chattering, and I decided that the wind was too cold for me to try to make it to all the way across the back lawn to the house. I was completely soaked and freezing, so I decided to run over to the studio. The wind was still blowing as hard as it had been, and I slipped and fell into the wet grass and mud several times. But finally I made it to the studio and opened the door, switching on the overhead lights and stepping inside.

My teeth were still chattering, so I made my way across the room to the other side to the bathroom. I opened the door and found a stack of enormous towels in the linen closet. There was also a blanket on one of the shelves, so I grabbed it as well, and the heavy robe hanging on a hook inside. I stripped off my wet clothes and hung them over the shower curtain rod. I rubbed myself dry with the towel, still shivering, and slipped the white robe on. I caught a glimpse of myself in the mirror.

On the left breast pocket of the robe, a letter *T* was written in red script.

The robe was Timothy's.

Well, of course it was, I told myself, resisting the urge to take it back off and throw it into the trash. *Whose else would it be? This is his studio, after all.*

I carried the blanket back into the main room and, my teeth still chattering, headed over to the little kitchen galley. There was still coffee in the canister, and so I filled the coffeemaker, pouring myself a cup as soon as there was enough in the pot. I closed my shaking hands around it for warmth and walked over to the sofa. I sat down, wrapped the blanket around my legs, and sipped the coffee, its welcoming warmth slowly spreading through my body.

The rain was still pelting down the roof of the little studio, and the wind was still howling outside. This close to the beach, the sound of the crashing waves was so loud I could barely hear myself think. I felt a little strange, and I looked down at the floor in front of the couch.

Was that where Timothy's body had lain after Carlo killed him?

The thought brought back the goose bumps.

Your husband is a murderer.

"Stop it," I said out loud, finishing the cup of coffee and heading back to refill it. My stomach growled, and I went through the cabinets looking for something—anything—to eat when I realized I hadn't had anything since breakfast. The storm certainly didn't look like it was going to let up any time soon, so I was going to be marooned in the studio for a little while. The cabinets were empty for the most part—there was more coffee, and some bread that had gone stale months earlier, but I did finally manage to find an unopened package of Goldfish crackers. I closed the cabinet doors and walked back over to the couch.

As I walked, I remembered the first time I'd run in Taylor Hudson in here—searching for his medal.

What is the significance of the medal? Sentimentality? I wondered, sitting down on the couch. But Taylor didn't exactly strike me as the sentimental type—he'd left the country for a year the day after his lifelong friend went missing.

Carlo said Timothy had been buried with it—but Taylor said the funeral director had said he hadn't been. Of course, Taylor could have lied—but why? For that matter, why would Carlo have lied about burying Timothy with it?

It didn't make any sense to me, no matter how much I tried to wrap my mind around it. I looked around as I stood there. This would make a nice writing studio. The previous times I'd been in here I'd had such a strong sense of Timothy—but now that I knew the truth about him, it was just a studio. I'd want to get rid of all the furniture in here and redecorate, so that nothing of his was left behind, of course. He might not be a shadow in between Carlo and me anymore, but there was no reason for me to keep his things.

It would be a shame, though, to just throw the prints away.

I tore the packaging open and put a handful of Goldfish in my mouth. They were still fresh—which made me wonder about what kind of preservatives had been used to make them.

The storm kept raging outside, and I wished I had a book or something to read. It was cozy in the studio—and I remembered this was where Timothy always met his lovers.

This was where he'd had his orgies, where he'd indulged his darkest fantasies.

I walked over to the stack of prints and started going through them. He really had been a good photographer. There was definitely some artistic merit to the prints. Maybe I could show them to a gallery dealer, have a little show, sell them and give the money away to charity? The Gay Men's Health Crisis would certainly not turn away another donation, and making it in Timothy's name would avert any suspicion from us—well, Carlo.

I wasn't going to be a suspect.

I walked back over to the couch and stumbled, dropping the bag of goldfish. They scattered everywhere. Swearing, I started picking them up, more than a little annoyed at my clumsiness. I reached under the coach to make sure none had gone under there—and my hand touched something cold and metal.

I pulled it out and stared at a round gold medal with blood crusted on it. There was a broken gold chain still running through the loop, and the chain itself was also crusted with blood.

I turned it over, and I saw what was engraved on the back.

Timothy I will always love you you deserve this Taylor.

That was the significance of the medal, then. That's all it was—a talisman of their friendship.

I dropped it into the pocket of my robe just as the door flew open again. Startled, I turned to see Taylor Hudson standing in the door.

Lightning temporarily blinded me, and the roar of thunder that followed was almost deafening. "What are you doing here?" I demanded. "And shut the damned door!"

Taylor smiled as he closed his umbrella, shutting the door behind him. His bare legs were wet, and his smile chilled me. It was predatory, and made me uncomfortable. I remembered him pushing himself on me last night when we were in here. He was bigger and stronger than I—what would have happened had Carlo not shown up when he did?

No one knows I'm out here, alone with him, I thought, and struggled to keep my rising fear under control. I couldn't let him see that I was afraid or even the slightest bit nervous to be alone with him.

"I told you why I come here." He set the umbrella against the wall and crossed his arms. "I'm looking for my medal."

"In a storm like this?" I replied sharply, sitting back down on the sofa. "And you aren't welcome here, as you well know."

He shrugged and smiled at me, and I felt my nerves tingling. "I don't think of this cottage as Carlo's, so what he wants doesn't matter to me. This was Timothy's place, and I was always welcome here. I'll come here whenever I damned well please."

"Timothy's dead," I reminded him. "And you're trespassing. I could have you arrested."

"You wouldn't do that." He stepped closer to me, the predatory smile getting bigger. I took a step backward. "I feel close to him here. Would you and Carlo begrudge me that? We were friends our whole lives. Surely you can't mind me coming here to commune with my dear old friend."

I took another step backward. "You were more than friends. You were one of his lovers, weren't you?"

He stopped walking toward me and shook his head. "So Carlo finally told you? I didn't think he ever would." Taylor laughed. "Carlo was always such a fool. Timothy and I laughed at him when we were in bed together, you know. Timothy slipped away from Carlo the night of their wedding to be with me—and how we laughed at him!" He started walking toward me again, and I backed up some more, well aware the studio was very small and I was going to run out of room soon…I bit my lower lip as he kept talking. "But the moment Timothy walked through the front doors of Spindrift, he wanted it, you know. When Carlo turned out to be gay—and a complete fool—it was almost like it was meant to be. Timothy made up his mind that very night that he was going to have Carlo and everything Carlo owned."

"You really need to leave," I replied, unable to keep the quiver out of my voice.

"I thought once Carlo knew the truth about the man he married, that would be the end of it all," he went on. "But Timothy had thought of everything. He was really far too clever for his own good. I couldn't believe he managed to have his cake and eat it too—but I always told him he had to be careful—it was a dangerous game he was playing, and if he wasn't careful he could end up dead. Which he did, of course."

"You lied to me, you weren't out of the country when Timothy died."

He made a face. "And now they've found Timothy's actual body." He laughed again. "I knew he hadn't drowned. He couldn't have drowned, he was too good a swimmer—didn't I tell you that? I knew he had to have been murdered, and I was right, wasn't I? Carlo killed him, didn't he?"

"Don't be absurd." My voice rose. I laughed hollowly, the medal burning a hole in my pocket. I couldn't give it to him—not with the blood caked on it. I didn't know if it was evidence that could work against Carlo in court—but I was not going to let Taylor have it. Or the police, either, for that matter. "People like Carlo don't kill people. They *hire* people to do it for them," I went on. "Rich people don't dirty their hands that way. You should know that."

One of his eyebrows arched upward. "So you're saying Carlo had him killed?"

"That's not what I said," I replied. "And even if he had, it wasn't like Timothy didn't deserve to be killed." I backed up again and felt the counter of the kitchenette against my back. I was suddenly very aware I was nude beneath the robe, and I was alone in the studio during a storm with a bigger, stronger man who'd already tried to force himself on me once.

Lightning stuck so close the entire room went white, and the power in the studio went out as the thunder rolled—and it seemed to go on forever.

There was a flash as Taylor struck a match and lit a candle. His face—in the candlelight his eyes looked scary, like I was his prey and he was stalking me.

Give him the medal, that'll distract him and maybe you can make a break for it.

He walked closer to me. "I can see what Carlo sees in you." His smile broadened as he moved toward me, the flickering light from the candle reflecting in his eyes.

"Stay away from me," I warned, but my voice sounded frightened to me. "Stay away!"

"Carlo took Timothy away," he said in a hoarse whisper. "First, he took him away from me by marrying him, and then he took him away permanently by killing him, and you know it's the truth even if you won't admit it to yourself. I may never be able to prove it, but we both know it's the truth, don't we?" He moved closer to me, and I kept backing up. "And no one knows either one of us is here, do they?" He laughed, and it was a horrible sound that sent a chill down my spine. "I could kill you and get clean away in this storm—they'd never know I was ever even here. And then Carlo would know how horrible it is to lose someone you love, to have them taken away from you suddenly and unexpectedly, to suffer and be lonely for the rest of your life."

"I said, stay away from me." I reached behind me onto the counter of the kitchenette. I fumbled for something—anything—I could use to defend myself with if it came down to that—and I suspected it was going to, very soon.

He was almost right on top of me. I could smell his cologne, feel the heat from his skin as he grabbed me and pushed his face against mine. I twisted my head from side to side but he was too strong for me, and finally he pushed his lips against mine.

"Stop," I gasped out.

He laughed. "Don't you know I always get what I want? And I want to defile you."

My hand closed on a knife handle, and I brought it around and shoved it up into him, under his rib cage.

He gurgled and stepped back in shock, just as the lights came back on.

Blood was gushing out of him, and the knife handle. I felt nauseous and sick, and he went down with a gurgle.

I was covered with blood—the robe, my legs, my arms.

I screamed.

The door to the studio opened, and Carlo stared at me first, and then down at Taylor. He crossed the room. "Are you all right?" he asked, starting to take me in his arms, but I pushed him back.

"He—he was trying to—" I gasped out. "Don't touch me—covered...blood...don't..."

"Help...me..." Taylor said in a wheezing croak.

As we stood there watching the light in Taylor's eyes went out, and with a heavy sigh, he died.

I stared at Carlo. "Oh my God, I killed him."

He kissed me. "Are you all right?"

"I killed him."

"I'm going to call my lawyer, and the sheriff," he said. "Go sit on the couch and wrap yourself up in that blanket—you're going into shock."

I did as he instructed, and felt the medal in my pocket.

I was a killer.

CHAPTER SIXTEEN

I don't know how long I sat there in the studio, waiting for Carlo to come back. The storm had passed, and the sun had come back out.

Everything was weird, I felt like I was having an out-of-body experience. Nothing seemed real, nothing seemed right—it was like I was walking around in a strange dreamlike state. Once we were back at Spindrift, Carlo sat me down in his office and sent Juana for coffee. The lawyer—Seth Pennington—showed up in casual clothing and asked me a lot of questions. I answered them as honestly as I could—I had been walking back from the house next door when the storm broke, and I took shelter in the studio. When he was finished with me, all he said was, "When the sheriff questions you, just answer what he asks—don't give him any more information."

I just nodded in response, still numb and in shock.

I've killed someone.

The strong, hot coffee Juana had brought me was taking some of the chill out of my body. I was still naked underneath the bloody robe, but Seth wouldn't allow me to get cleaned up or change. "The sheriff needs to see you just as you are," he'd responded when I asked if I could put some clothes on. Seth took some pictures of me, and the dried blood on my arms, legs, and the robe—and was especially interested in the bruises Taylor had left on my upper arms when he'd grabbed me. There were four of them on each arm, the size of fingertips. When he was finished, he smiled reassuringly at me. "It's clearly a case of self-defense," he said, patting me on the head—which made me feel like a pet of some sort. "But I'll be here with you, and whenever he asks you a question, don't answer until you see me nod, okay?"

"Okay."

Carlo's doctor also showed up at some point before the sheriff—and checked me out thoroughly. I answered his questions while he shone a penlight into my eyes and checked my reflexes. "You seem to be handling this relatively well," he said, leaving a packet of pills on the coffee table. He wrote out a couple of prescriptions, which he handed to Juana with instructions to get them filled.

"What are those for?" I asked, gesturing toward the pills on the table.

"Sleeping pills, and some for anxiety. The white ones are for sleep, the blues one for anxiety. I also wrote out some prescriptions for the same medications—that's what I gave your housekeeper. You're certain you feel okay?"

I nodded. I didn't really feel okay—I certainly didn't feel normal, whatever that was. I just felt numb, and empty, like this was all happening to someone else, not to me. It felt sometimes like I was watching myself, watching these people hover around me and asking me questions before going off into little groups and whispering about me.

At one point I went to the bathroom, and once I'd shut the door behind me I dropped the medal into the tank and put the lid back on. *Better not to have it on me*, I thought, and went back into the office and sat down on the couch.

I sat there in Carlo's office, drinking hot coffee and hoping that I'd eventually get warmed up. I was wrapped in the same blanket I'd used at the studio.

And when Sheriff Tate came in to talk to me, I was ready.

He looked stressed, and I couldn't blame him. I'm sure there was never much crime in the Hamptons, let alone murder—and in the course of one day a murder that was over a year old dropped into his lap, and a few hours later a fresh one came along—both involving the same family. He sat down across from me, and I smiled weakly at him. "Hello, Sheriff Tate," I said in a very small, weak voice. Carlo was standing behind the chair where Seth took a seat, and was smiling at me encouragingly. "I don't suppose you imagined you'd be back up here again today."

Sheriff Tate managed to smile at me. "No, sir, I certainly didn't." He retrieved his notebook and flipped it open with a sigh.

"Show him the bruises," Seth ordered, and I pulled up the sleeves so the sheriff could see them.

"Looks like fingerprints," the sheriff observed, adding that he'd have the crime scene guys take some pictures of me. "We're going to need your robe, too."

"I'm not wearing anything underneath it," I replied with a slight shrug.

"I'll send Olivia to get you some clothes." Carlo walked out of the room.

"Can I wash the blood off me now?" I asked.

Sheriff Tate bit his lip and looked over at Seth. Seth replied, "I did take pictures of him, Sheriff. I'll be happy to sign an affidavit authenticating any you might take with your phone."

So, once again I stood up and the Sheriff took pictures of my arms and legs, and me in the bloodied robe. Carlo came back in while that was going on, and once we were finished, I sat back down again.

"You can go ahead and wash up now if you like," Sheriff Tate said.

"I'll wait until my clean clothes are here," I replied in a monotone. Carlo gave me a worried look and I gave him a faintly reassuring smile back.

"Walk me through what happened," Sheriff Tate said.

So I told the story again. My voice remained in an unemotional monotone. I told him how I went over to see Nell, but not why—and he didn't ask. I told him how I got caught in the storm on my back and took shelter in the studio, stripping off my wet clothes and putting on a robe.

This was when Olivia showed up with some clothes for me, and I excused myself. It seemed like I was in the bathroom a really long time—scrubbing my skin until it turned red, and putting on my new clothes. She'd brought me sweats, and they felt warm and comfortable against my skin.

I flushed the toilet, and the water turned a weird brownish color. I flushed it again, and this time it was clear.

I smiled to myself and walked back into Carlo's office, sitting back down in my original chair and sipping my coffee. I gave the sheriff a weak smile. "Where was I?"

"You were looking for something to eat," Seth prompted me, earning him a frown from the sheriff.

"I found some goldfish—the crackers—and was eating them when he arrived." I replied, frowning a bit, trying to remember exactly how it had happened. "He startled me and I dropped them— no, wait, I dropped them before he got there. I was picking them up when he arrived." I gave the sheriff a sad look. "I'm sorry, Sheriff, everything happened so fast…"

"It's okay, son. Go on," the sheriff said, not unkindly.

"So, anyway, Taylor opened the door and came in. I was startled, and he scared me."

"What was Taylor Hudson doing there?" Sheriff Tate asked.

"He trespassed frequently," Carlo said from behind me. "I had warned him any number of times he wasn't welcome here, for all the good it did me." He gave a slight shrug of his shoulders. "I kept telling him I was going to have him arrested for trespassing, but he didn't care."

"He was looking for something," I said. "A medal of some sort, that meant something to him and Timothy from when they were kids. Every time I saw him he asked me about it. He wanted me to look for it here in the main house—he wouldn't come here."

The sheriff looked at Carlo and back at me. "When you say Timothy, that would be Timothy Burke you're referring to?"

I nodded. "Yes, he told me they grew up together and had been friends…more than friends…almost all of their lives. The medal had sentimental value to him, and he really wanted it. He said that was why he kept showing up at the studio, and he asked me to look for it, since I lived here and could look in places he couldn't. I didn't find it." I sighed. "It clearly meant a lot to him. I felt bad for him, but I never did find it anywhere."

"So he came here in the middle of a storm to look for it?" The sheriff's voice sounded disbelieving. "Come now, that seems a little strange."

"I don't know why he came by today," I said. "He had an umbrella. He—he seemed a little unhinged…" I coughed. "He did accost me last night at the ball in the studio. I'd gone there to get away from the party for a moment and he followed me in there. He tried to kiss me—I didn't want to be kissed."

"You said he seemed unhinged. What did you mean by that?"

"He seemed—*different.*" I took another drink of my coffee. "I think—I think the news about Timothy unhinged him a little bit, I don't know. He never scared me before, not even last night when he tried to force himself on me—I mean, last night when I made it clear I wasn't interested, he backed off. Today, I got the feeling he wasn't going to stop." I bit my lower lip. "And he kept bringing Timothy up—talking about the body being found and he didn't seem—right. He kept talking about how Timothy should still be alive…a lot of it didn't make any sense. I can't remember everything he was saying, but he was scaring me." I shivered again for emphasis. "I kept backing away from him. I tried once to go around him but he moved. He was backing me into a corner—well, he backed me up until I was up against the kitchen counter, with nowhere to go." Saying the words brought back the memory sharply, of how it felt to be backed up, scared, how much bigger than me he was… I started shaking and a tear ran out of my right eye. I took a couple of deep breaths, wiped at my eyes, and said, "Sorry."

"Did you try to call for help?"

"I did yell, once, but the studio is so far away from the house, and even if it wasn't raining so hard I knew no one at the house would hear me…but I was terrified, so terrified, especially after—" I stopped.

"After he what?"

I looked him right in the eye. "After he admitted killing Timothy."

Carlo inhaled in a sharp gasp, but other than that silence fell over the room.

The sheriff cleared his throat. "You're saying he confessed to you that he killed Timothy Burke?"

I nodded and kept my eyes locked on his. "Yes, Sheriff, he did. I was so terrified. He told me he was going to kill me, just like he had killed Timothy. He was unhinged...the look in his eyes—he meant every word of it." And I proceeded to tell the story Carlo had told me about Timothy's death—only as if Taylor had told it to me.

When I worked for her, Valerie had once told me the best way to lie and make it believable was to keep it as close to the truth as possible. She was right, as it turned out. All I had to do was tell the truth—the story Carlo had told me—only tell Sheriff Tate that it had been *Taylor* who'd told me the story.

"And I was scared, I kept backing away as he came closer and closer—and he tried to force himself on me." I held out my arms and showed the bruises on my upper arms where he'd grabbed me. "And I reached for the knife and stabbed him." I covered my face with my hands and let go of the rigid self-control I'd been practicing. I started to cry, and once I gave way, my entire body shook as I sobbed.

The sheriff stood up, and closed his notebook. "Thank you for your time. There will be an inquest, but I really don't see any reason for charges." He stood up. "Mr. Pennington, of course he'll need to come down to the station to make a formal statement, but the evidence seems to back up his story."

"Of course," Seth replied and walked him out of the room.

Once the door closed behind them, Carlo sat down next to me on the sofa. He took my hands. "I love you so much, Mouse," he said wonderingly. "You're unbelievable."

I looked at him. "And now we're free of Timothy, Carlo. We're free at last."

He pulled me into his arms. "You're absolutely amazing."

I closed my eyes and relaxed into his embrace.

The inquest was held a few days later, and I had to get up and tell the story again. I told it plainly and simply, apologizing to the court at the beginning and letting them know I was on anti-anxiety medication. I saw Maureen Drury out in the spectator's gallery as the district attorney asked me questions. I had refused to speak to her, and I knew that Nell never would. She'd have a story for *Street Talk*—and probably a good one. She was a good writer, after all.

I couldn't help but wonder if she believed me.

The grand jury determined that I had acted in self-defense.

The investigation into Timothy's death was also officially closed.

Once the grand jury was dismissed, Carlo and I pushed our way out of the courtroom through the throngs of reporters and cameramen, and got into the back of the town car.

"We're going to go away for a while," Carlo told me as the car pulled away from the curb. "Get away from Spindrift and all the incredibly bad memories here. Would you like that, Mouse?" He put his arm around me.

I rested my head against his chest. "I would like that very much, Carlo."

And the next morning we went into our voluntary exile.

I doubt that we shall ever return.

About the Author

Greg Herren is the award-winning author of fourteen novels, and has edited eight anthologies, including the award-winning *Love Bourbon Street: Reflections On New Orleans*. He currently lives in New Orleans. He has published over fifty short stories, and is a member of the Mystery Writers of America, the International Association of Crime Writers, Private Eye Writers of America, and Sisters in Crime. He has worked as a personal trainer, and published over fifty articles on health and fitness. He began his career as a book reviewer, and has published over a thousand reviews and interviews with authors as varied as Margaret Cho, Dorothy Allison, and Laura Lippman. A long time resident of New Orleans, the flavor and culture of his beloved adopted city colors all of his work.

Books Available From Bold Strokes Books

Timothy by Greg Herren. Timothy is a romantic suspense thriller from award-winning mystery writer Greg Herren set in the fabulous Hamptons. (978-1-60282-760-8)

In Stone by Jeremy Jordan King. A young New Yorker is rescued from a hate crime by a mysterious someone who turns out to be more of a something. (978-1-60282-761-5)

The Secret of Othello by Sam Cameron. Florida teen detectives Steven and Denny risk their lives to search for a sunken NASA satellite—but under the waves, no one can hear you scream... (978-1-60282-742-4)

Andy Squared by Jennifer Lavoie. Andrew never thought anyone could come between him and his twin sister, Andrea... until Ryder rode into town. (978-1-60282-743-1)

Sara by Greg Herren. A mysterious and beautiful new student at Southern Heights High School stirs things up when students start dying. (978-1-60282-674-8)

Boys of Summer, edited by Steve Berman. Stories of young love and adventure, when the sky's ceiling is a bright blue marvel, when another boy's laughter at the beach can distract from dull summer jobs. (978-1-60282-663-2)

Street Dreams by Tama Wise. Tyson Rua has more than his fair share of problems growing up in New Zealand—he's gay, he's falling in love, and he's run afoul of the local hip-hop crew leader just as he's trying to make it as a graffiti artist. (978-1-60282-650-2)

me@you.com by K.E. Payne. Is it possible to fall in love with someone you've never met? Imogen Summers thinks so because it's happened to her. (978-1-60282-592-5)

Swimming to Chicago by David-Matthew Barnes. As the lives of the adults around them unravel, high school students Alex and Robby form an unbreakable bond, vowing to do anything to stay together—even if it means leaving everything behind. (978-1-60282-572-7)

Speaking Out edited by Steve Berman. Inspiring stories written for and about LGBT and Q teens of overcoming adversity (against intolerance and homophobia) and experiencing life after "coming out." (978-1-60282-566-6)

365 Days by K.E. Payne. Life sucks when you're seventeen years old and confused about your sexuality, and the girl of your dreams doesn't even know you exist. Then in walks sexy new emo girl, Hannah Harrison. Clemmie Atkins has exactly 365 days to discover herself, and she's going to have a blast doing it! (978-1-60282-540-6)

Cursebusters! by Julie Smith. Budding psychic Reeno is the most accomplished teenage burglar in California, but one tiny screw-up and poof!—she's sentenced to Bad Girl School. And that isn't even her worst problem. Her sister Haley's dying of an illness no one can diagnose, and now she can't even help. (978-1-60282-559-8)

Who I Am by M.L. Rice. Devin Kelly's senior year is a disaster. She's in a new school in a new town, and the school bully is making her life miserable—but then she meets his sister Melanie and realizes her feelings for her are more than platonic. (978-1-60282-231-3)

Sleeping Angel by Greg Herren. Eric Matthews survives a terrible car accident only to find out everyone in town thinks he's a murderer—and he has to clear his name even though he has no memories of what happened. (978-1-60282-214-6)

Mesmerized by David-Matthew Barnes. Through her close friendship with Brodie and Lance, Serena Albright learns about the many forms of love and finds comfort for the grief and guilt she feels over the brutal death of her older brother, the victim of a hate crime. (978-1-60282-191-0)

The Perfect Family by Kathryn Shay. A mother and her gay son stand hand in hand as the storms of change engulf their perfect family and the life they knew. (978-1-60282-181-1)

Father Knows Best by Lynda Sandoval. High school juniors and best friends Lila Moreno, Meryl Morganstern, and Caressa Thibodoux plan to make the most of the summer before senior year. What they discover that amazing summer about girl power, growing up, and trusting friends and family more than prepares them to tackle that all-important senior year! (978-1-60282-147-7)